BY DONALD HONIG

DONALD HONIG

THE

SWORD

OF

GENERAL ENGLUND

A NOVEL OF MURDER
IN THE DAKOTA TERRITORY, 1876

SCRIBNER

New York   London   Toronto   Sydney   Tokyo   Singapore

SCRIBNER
1230 Avenue of the Americas
New York, NY 10020

Manufactured in the United States of America

1 3 5 7 9 10 8 6 4 2

Library of Congress Cataloging-in-Publication Data
Honig, Donald.
The sword of General Englund / Donald Honig.
p.   cm.
1. Dakota Territory—History—Fiction. 2. Generals—Dakota Territory—
Fiction. 3. Murder—Dakota Territory—Fiction.
I. Title.
PS3558.05S96   1996   95-33279
813'.54—dc20   CIP
ISBN 0-684-80321-6

FOR CATHY AND MICHAEL

CONTENTS

PART THREE: AFTERMATH

FORT LARKIN,
DAKOTA TERRITORY

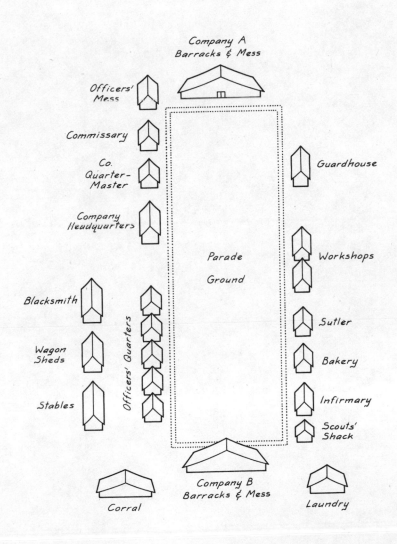

Company A
Barracks & Mess

Officers'
Mess

Commissary

Co.
Quarter-
Master

Company
Headquarters

Guardhouse

Parade

Ground

Workshops

Blacksmith

Officers' Quarters

Sutler

Wagon
Sheds

Bakery

Stables

Infirmary

Scouts'
Shack

Company B
Barracks & Mess

Corral

Laundry

MAY 1876
WASHINGTON, D.C.

When he first heard about it, on a May afternoon that was warm and breathless with the promise of an approaching Washington summer, Captain Thomas Maynard had just returned to his small office at the War Department. He had spent the previous few hours in conversation with several senior officers; under discussion had been the arrangements for July's Centennial celebration in Philadelphia. Maynard had been assigned to the contingent accompanying General Sheridan. The occasion would be a historic one, and memorable, and, aside from being a captain traveling with a battery of generals and colonels, Maynard felt himself fortunate to have been selected. He was about to begin making notes on the meeting when the door opened and Major Overman entered the office.

The major was a tall, dignified, long-bearded man who looked more like a Presbyterian minister than an officer in the United States Army, and indeed at that moment he was facing Maynard—who had risen to his feet at the major's entrance—with a solemnity that seemed to have him on the brink of a sermon.

"The damndest thing, Tom," the major said quietly, after closing the door behind him. "Out at Fort Larkin. You know Fort Larkin, don't you?"

"Yes, sir," Maynard said. "In the Dakota Territory. A small outpost."

"Very small. I don't know why it was ever established. But the damndest thing. The information just came in. I don't think I've ever heard anything like it."

Maynard waited. If this hadn't been a senior officer standing there facing him he would have urged the man to come out with it; but apparently the major was still having trouble absorbing whatever it was he had just heard and come to impart, as if it had yet to be accorded full credibility within himself.

"There's been a tragedy out there," the major said, still with his brink-of-the-sermon solemnity, held fast by it.

Maynard's first thought was for the Fort Larkin garrison, which was, after all, not large and was located in a remote area which had recently reported some Indian activity.

"A tragedy, Major?" he asked.

"The commanding officer has been killed."

"In the field?"

"No. On the post. In his office. Stabbed to death. Details are still sparse, and it's not clear whether there was a breach of fort security or it was something else."

"Something else?" Maynard asked.

"We just don't know yet, Tom. It's still a muddle at the moment, I'm afraid. Apparently a sentry was also killed."

"That would suggest a security breach, wouldn't it, sir?"

"So it would seem," the major said. "But it has an irregular feel to it. The on-site officers are investigating, of course."

"Surely at a post that small they should be able to find the answer."

"Yes," the major said, "they should. But I wonder."

"Who was the officer killed?"

The major studied Maynard for a moment before responding.

"General Englund," he said.

"Englund?" Maynard said, frowning with disbelief. "It hardly seems possible."

"How do you mean? That a commanding officer should die that way, or that it should be General Englund?"

"Well," Maynard said, looking down at his desk for a moment, "both, I guess."

"I'll probably agree with you on both counts," the major said, "after I've thought it through. Anyway, I just wanted to inform you."

"Thank you, sir."

The major went to the door and placed his hand on the knob. He paused, thinking about what he wanted to say, then looked at Maynard. "I always knew," he said, "that man would not have a normal death."

PART ONE

NO
SMALL
MATTER

CHAPTER 1

JULY 1876
MISS ENGLUND

"Yes," Captain Maynard said, "I wish I could have known him."

"He wasn't just a soldier," Miss Englund said, "although of course that was his profession and what he was proudest of being. He said to me once that the calling of professional soldier obligated a man to develop his every intellectual capacity, that a soldier who knew only how to fight was little more than a savage."

In peacetime, Maynard thought. He doubted there had been any such stress on intellect from 1861 to 1865, when armies were colliding like rampant oceans, when a man's every sense could be violated in a split second, when orators proclaimed the nobility of the plain soldier and balladeers competed to celebrate him, and women just like Miss Englund bloodied themselves to the elbows helping bandage and succor the wounded and the dying. But now, with the war a decade past and receding rapidly, what was a soldier there for? What was he all about?

The arbor afforded some slight relief from the blazing sun and the relentless July heat. He was by now familiar with the nation's capital at this time of year, when what felt like the eternal, unforgiving heat got under your clothing and seemed to be enveloping you, making you feel as though you were answering for every sin committed or contemplated. But Miss Englund, sitting on the small bench across the slate path from him, seemed unreached by the insufferable temperatures. In her weeds, from black straw bonnet to the hem of her commodious black skirts, she was in perfect repose. Her black-gloved hands lay folded in her lap. She was a sculpture of poised bereavement; yet, the smooth whiteness of her young face, the prideful blue of her eyes, the wisps of yellow hair curling at the rim of the black bonnet were at odds with her somber appearance. Talking about her father had seemed to instill in her an added measure of pride, squaring her shoulders and stiffening her back. Well, Maynard thought, she's a soldier's daughter. A general's daughter. He himself had worn the uniform now for fifteen years, if anything with always increasing pride and fealty. More than for country he had bled for the army during the war, marching more on behalf of the uniform than because half the country had seceded. But she had army breeding; there was a stillness at the core of her devotion, an innate and impermeable loyalty that bordered on piety. It was as if she, her kind, understood intuitively all of the things he believed but could not articulate. Because she had been bred to it—he had taken notice, in the living room, of the oil painting of her grandfather, the first General Englund—it had been in trust for her before she was born, like an inheritance.

"He graduated second in his class at the Point," Miss Englund said. "One of the most brilliant cadets they ever had."

"His record in the war bespeaks that," Maynard said. "The Peninsula, Fredericksburg, Gettysburg, Cold Harbor."

She smiled primly, a faint light of appreciation entering her china-blue eyes. He had never seen a face so fine and delicate, so clear-eyed and sweet-lipped. He averted his eyes for a moment, embarrassed by his own enthrallment.

"He always put himself at the forefront of the action. He was twice wounded, you know. And the horses he had shot from under him. 'We stopped counting,' his adjutant said to us once."

"It was that kind of courage and leadership that showed us the way," he said.

"President and Mrs. Grant came to this house to pay their respects. And so did General Sherman and General Sheridan."

"You must have been very proud."

"But he was more than a soldier," Miss Englund said, her voice poignant in its pride. "His was a far-reaching mind. He was learned in Greek and Latin, he had set much of the Bible to memory, and wherever he was he tried to find time to study the local flora and fauna. Did you know he published a monograph on developing the frontier? It's a most profound and farsighted treatise."

"I'm sure I would enjoy reading it," he said.

"I've never seen him as excited as when he learned he was being assigned to the Western frontier. It was his conviction that the nation was going to 'Grow West'—that was his phrase—and that he could be at the birth of that growth and development pleased his sense of personal destiny."

"Personal destiny?" Maynard asked.

"Yes," Miss Englund said, narrowing her eyes just a fraction. "It was his credo that only a man who believed in personal destiny could achieve anything significant among the

limitless opportunities facing us. But believe me, Captain
Maynard, though it sounds like a pompous posture, it was
anything but. It was an expression of humility. He used to
say that without a sense of vision no one could lead, and
that without humility vision was clouded. That, he said, was
a lesson of the Bible."

Sitting there in the arbor's latticework shade, surrounded
on one side by the garden's motionless full-bloomed growth
and on the other by the large three-storied house and its
rows of curtained windows, feeling the heat of the white-hot
sky under the collar of his blue jacket, Maynard was aware
as he had never been before of the cross-grained byways
that formed his life's topography, from Adirondack forest
down to the roads of war through Pennsylvania and northern Virginia and then later to the Southern Plains and the
Southwest. Hard and mean and exhilarating all of it, rough-
companioned, rashly beckoning, primitive, with no forgiveness for mistakes. True, he had striven in other directions
too, turning his idle hours to conscious efforts to polish
himself, reading good books, practicing polite speech, working endlessly to give dignity to his handwriting. He had always sought educated companions and listened intently
when they spoke. He believed he had made splendid
progress in elevating himself. But sitting here with Miss Englund returned to him some of the old feelings of awkwardness and incompleteness.

"Faith is the engine," Miss Englund said. "I heard those
words from my father many times. And the kind of faith he
was talking about wasn't spun from gossamer; it wasn't
something for just the prayerful and fainthearted. Faith was a
powerful stimulant. It was guidance and inspiration. It was
the fire of life. Faith was what brought the Pilgrims across a
treacherous ocean to unknown shores. Strong men were
nothing without it. I suppose you saw that during the war."

"Many times," he said.

"It brought you through the gravest of trials."

"Always."

"The story of the sword is true, you know."

He had of course heard the tale; its telling had swept through regiment after regiment of a dispirited Army of the Potomac after the stunning defeat at Chancellorsville. They told how General Englund had ridden to one of his encampments, dismounted, climbed to an earthen mound, and called for a gathering of the men. He began to speak of faith and will and the righteousness of their cause, orating, it was said, initially to an indifferent audience of veterans who already believed in the righteousness of their cause and had been fighting for it with faith and will, with little to show for it except dead comrades, unimaginable suffering, and a series of humiliating defeats. But the general continued to speak, stentorian voice roaring, it was said, like cannon fire, his eyes aflame with passion, his fervor beginning to infect the men like a wild spirit, continuing to exhort them even as masses of black thunderheads swarmed and thickened overhead and rain began falling. Still addressing his men, the general raised his eyes skyward as lightning ripped through the clouds and a deafening concussive thunder exploded and then went bounding through the heavens. It was then that he shouted out, "We are at one with God!" and still with eyes upraised reached his right hand across his body and unsheathed his sword from its gilt-decorated leather scabbard and holding it by its silver grip pointed it heroically to the heavens as the rain began to pour. And then he drew back his arm and like some Olympian of ancient contests hurled the twin-edged length of steel high into the air where it seemed to soar endlessly and at the very moment it attained its apogee a tongue of lightning suddenly sizzled and snapped at it and with a burst of blinding white light the sword tumbled end over end through the air until finally falling to earth scorched and crumpled.

"Men saw it happen," Miss Englund said. "Some immediately knelt and prayed. They said it was an epiphany."

"Yes," Maynard said.

"My father could evoke powers," she said in a mild, understated voice. "Certain men are given that. He didn't think it so remarkable, which of course made it all the more remarkable. He said it derived from faith, deep, deep faith."

"Exactly so," Maynard said.

"And so you have been charged, Captain Maynard, to find out why such a man was deprived of his life in so cruel and cowardly a manner."

"Yes."

"Our prayers and our thoughts will be with you every waking moment of every day."

"The charge is a solemn one," Maynard said, "and believe me when I say it isn't being undertaken lightly."

"I know that," Miss Englund said softly, smiling benignly. She reached out one small, black-gloved hand and brushed it across his fingertips. "I have every confidence," she said.

CHAPTER 2

JULY 1876
GENERAL
NORTHWOOD

"The cold-blooded murder of a general officer is no small matter. The army has a very stiff back about this incident and I assure you that no one is going to sit easy until we know what happened and why."

General Northwood was sitting back in his chair, legs crossed, eyes somberly studying the ash at the end of the burning cigar he held in his fingers. His thinning hair barely covered a large head that gave the impression of great cranial capacity. His eyes were at once shrewd and ironic—the eyes of a man who commanded many but who was still beholden to a few. His most distinguishing facial feature was his gray horseshoe mustache, the ends of which hung below his jawline.

Maynard found a sardonic humor in the fact of a general's murder being of no small matter to the army. More specifically, he knew, it was of no small matter mostly to the generals, which was strikingly evident from the moment he first heard of the death of General Alfred Englund. He had stepped out into the corridor at the War Department after hearing the news when a furiously irate brigadier general, followed by a pair of grim-faced lieutenants, went striding by. "Goddammit," the general said, to no one in particular but as if trying to make some critical adjustment in the universe, "this is not the Mexican army."

They were sitting at a corner table in the bar of Willard's Hotel on Fourteenth Street, post-dinner whiskies in front of them, an inert webbed canopy of gray smoke hanging overhead. A steady hum of conversation flowed from the other tables where employees of government of all ranks were sitting, along with hotel guests. Within the rise of conversation Maynard could detect Spanish and French being spoken. There were cigars and whisky at virtually every table, along with a candle burning in a tall brass holder. The candles were decorative, with more than adequate light coming from wall lamps and chandeliers. The marble floor was stained from tobacco-laden expectorations.

"The President feels this most keenly," General Northwood said, bringing the cigar to his bluish lips and pulling deeply on it, expelling the smoke softly, watching it turn and weave in front of his face. Too many cigars had discolored his teeth. "He knew Englund, of course. He had admiration for the general, less so for the man. Englund was strange, eccentric, not Grant's sort. I've sat with Grant for many an hour, when he was general and even now, when he's top dog. And he's never changed. Takes the direct way, right down the heart of the road. You'll never meet a man who's more to the point. You start talking about your conversations with the Almighty and Grant starts clearing his throat."

"Was General Englund that extreme?" Maynard asked.

Northwood sidled his eyes for a moment, as if contemplating not just the content of his response but the tone in which it would be spoken.

"General Grant—and he was *General* Grant at the time— once said that the man had the temperament of a Southerner. This was said near the end of the war. I don't think Grant was being derogatory but was rather searching to identify a certain characteristic and make sense of it. I believe he was thinking of Jackson when he said that. Old Stonewall. The kind of fervor that comes from excessive piety, from too convinced a relationship with the Almighty." The general fixed Maynard with a piercing glance, as if to stress that a confidence was being imparted.

"I understand, sir," Maynard said. He was bent forward, hands folded at the edge of the table, the cigar General Northwood had given him burning between his fingers. The sedulous attention he had given his dark wavy hair was evident, and there was similar correctness to the careful trimming of his thick mustache. His blue uniform had been pressed that morning, the gold buttons polished. His forage cap was on an empty chair that was pressed flat against the table. His comportment was a study in self-conscious deference; Captain Maynard's face seldom changed expression in the company of a senior officer.

"It's a troublesome business, Tom," Northwood said in a tone of mild annoyance. "But it's come my way and I'm handing it to you. The President received a heartfelt petition from General Englund's widow and daughter and it moved him deeply. The army, he said, must find out what happened and the family is entitled to know."

"I met with Miss Englund this morning, sir."

"She's quite a little lady," Northwood said with an abstract nod, puffing on his cigar. "Quite. I've known her since she was a child. As beautiful and delicate as a flower, but a general's daughter through and through."

"She's very proud of her father."

"Well," Northwood said, furrowing his brow, "he was an unusual man. Outstanding record. Can't take that away from him." He carefully removed cigar ash by sliding the burning tip across the edge of the small brass tray. "Went through the whole four-year match. Told me once his only regret was he wasn't with Sherman on the march through Georgia and South Carolina." Northwood grunted and murmured, "Englund was a vindictive man."

"How did his men feel about him?"

"That's always hard to say. You never *really* know what they're thinking, do you?" Northwood said with a wry smile. "But they followed him. Anyway, Captain, you're not supposed to worry about what they're thinking. You make sound tactical decisions and everything will take care of itself."

"Soldiers being soldiers."

"That's correct."

"That story, sir, about General Englund's sword."

"What about it?"

"Is it true?"

"I don't know. I wasn't there. But Englund believed it," Northwood said, adding, with a brief mischievous glance, "whether it happened or not. Anyway, what I want to know is what happened at Fort Larkin in the Dakota Territory on the night of May 14, 1876. The on-site officers have come to no conclusions and that's not satisfactory."

"Are you satisfied with their efforts, General?"

Northwood heaved his large shoulders. "I don't know," he said. "There are good men out there—I know some of them—but maybe they're too close to it. Anyway, whatever their efforts, I'm sure as hell not satisfied with their results. They've got a goddamned murderer in their midst, in the ranks or among the commissioned officers, and we want to have him. Maybe it's too much to expect to get an answer when men are investigating themselves, their friends. My good friend a murderer?" the general asked rhetorically. "No, can't be. He's a gentleman. We'll look elsewhere. Well, we can't have that. So we're sending you, an outsider, somebody whose objectivity is assured."

"It couldn't have been Sioux renegades, General, breaching fort security?"

"Not the way it happened," Northwood said firmly. "Not when you've examined all the details." Then, lowering his voice for a moment, he added, "It was a senior officer. We're convinced of that."

"How will I be received, sir?" Maynard asked.

"Captain, you're going out there with a mandate from the President of the United States, the Chief of Staff of the United States Army, and the Secretary of War. Besides that, they'll be happy to welcome you and get it cleared up. With the commanding officer having had a Bowie knife stuck through him, I would imagine some of the other senior officers are having restless nights. It's a small station, in a damned lonely place, and after what just happened to George Custer, well . . ."

"Yes, sir," Maynard said.

"The Indians out that way haven't caused too much trouble. There've been a few skirmishes, but nothing serious. But you never know. So, Captain Maynard," the general said, inserting the cigar at the corner of his mouth for a moment, then removing it. "You're a bright, ambitious young officer. You're undertaking a sensitive commission under the direct orders and with the blessings of the chief archangels of your nation. So, Captain Maynard."

CHAPTER 3

JULY 1876
GETTING READY

The boardinghouse where Maynard lodged was a half mile from the War Department, which was just about a proper-sized walk for a man on his way to work and he enjoyed it, even during these brutal summer days, for he was generally on his way early enough, before the sun had taken much height. The way home, of course, was less direct. Department business sometimes kept him at his desk until past six o'clock (particularly since the Custer disaster a few weeks before) and when he finally did get out he would head for the bar at Willard's, followed by dinner, then a game of billiards or a chair in the lobby where he sat and smoked his pipe and watched the variegated crowd come and go, from roughly clothed Westerners to elegantly tailored ministers from London and the Continent. Maynard had spent some small amounts of time in New York and Philadelphia, and while he had been impressed with the cul-

tural superiorities of those cities, Washington remained his
city of preference. Never mind that it lacked, according to a
British visitor's litany, a decent restaurant, an agreeable
club, a permanent theater; what stimulated Maynard's appreciation for it was the city's unabashed lack of subtlety.
Though the inner mechanics of deals and decisions may
have been obliquely constructed, you always knew what
they were talking about: power and influence, who had it,
who might impart it, who might attain it. He could stare at
a pair of conversing men on the other side of a noisy lobby
and conclude if they were talking about it, for it animated a
passion in the body not too dissimilar from that of a lad
watching his first descent of petticoats. He delighted in its
proximity and every evocation: in its gestures, its aura, its
cannonading laughter, and even in its reserve, when two
men who had been talking quietly virtually forehead to forehead slowly leaned away from each other, each with fixed
expressions of position taken, advantage gained.

There were, Maynard believed, two approaches to the ac-
quisition of power—you besieged, attacked, and tried to
wrest it away; or you absorbed it through your senses,
which you accomplished by hard work, good fortune, and
strategic proximity. His chosen approach was the latter, the
quiet, practical, ostensibly untraveled path, whether he was
sitting at his desk at the War Department or walking the
same Washington streets as presidents, cabinet members,
congressmen, or sitting in the same dining or reading rooms
with them, breathing and expelling the same air, watching,
listening, and above all feeling the excitement of power
seeping into him with sinewy permeation, feeling its fit to
the round edges of his fingertips, and knowing that he was a
proper and respectful receptacle for it, because he knew he
had the utmost respect for it, that he would never dishonor
it through misuse, that the honorable use of power was the

finest tribute a man could pay to the nation that had so recognized and entrusted him. He had in his mind so ennobled
the image of success that he considered the possession of
power and its exertion as being virtually one and the same.

Already, on those streets and within those gathering
places, certain solemn and magnificently bewhiskered lions
of government were nodding to him in passing, while a
number of the clever young men of the future greeted him
by name and occasionally invited him to dinner or joined
him in a game of billiards (at which Maynard had labored
to make himself particularly adept). He was not an especially religious man; he would offer integrity and character
and desire, and his reward would be secular: rank, authority, immeasurable personal satisfaction. The sweetness, he
would think, and in a wondering, quizzical way he often did
think in this vein, would derive not from ascendancy over
his fellow men but rather from being triumphant over what
had once seemed an inescapable lifetime of banality and
anonymity.

One thing he would not miss, Maynard thought as he
opened his valise and laid it in two halves on his bed, would
be the Washington summer, and he doubted if the capital
had a place more sweltering than this top floor of the boardinghouse where he had been living since his arrival here two
years ago.

He began packing the valise with the two thick folders of
reports and testimony that had been sent from Fort Larkin,
then covered them with blouses, trousers, underclothes, toi-
let articles. He then carefully laid in the books he had chosen to bring along: Shakespeare, Emerson's *Essays,* Pope's
translation of the *Iliad*, and a collection of Byron. He didn't
know how much time, if any, he would have for these stout
companions, but he wouldn't have dreamed of so long a
journey without them.

"So you're off today."

The voice came from the doorway, where John Harrison, first lieutenant, United States Army, was standing, although in his long johns top, blue trousers, and fallen suspenders he looked decidedly unsoldierly.

"You're up early this morning, John," Maynard said.

"To wish you Godspeed," Harrison said. He was a slender young man, just several years out of West Point. A rather self-indulgent thick black mustache was so ill-suited for his thin face that it looked like a stage prop. Youngest son of a wealthy New England family, he had been ordered into a military career by a bleakly reserved father whose motive seemed to add up to little more than completing his children's accounts. As far as Maynard could see, those years at the institution on the Hudson had been observed by Harrison with minimal dedication and little thought toward service and opportunity.

Harrison folded his arms and leaned in the doorway, watching his housemate tuck and arrange things in the valise with a meticulous touch that finally made Harrison smile.

"Don't forget your overcoat, Thomas," he said. "There's no saying how long you'll be out there. I hear winter comes early in that country and with full-blown suddenness. A chap I knew at the Point said that one day you're admiring the autumn landscape and the next you're wading through knee-high snow."

Mention of snow and overcoats sounded incongruous amid the dead, humid inertia of a Washington summer.

"I don't envy you this assignment, Thomas," Harrison said.

"And why is that, John?" Maynard asked, standing back and contemplating the nearly full valise.

"Because of the possibility of failure."

Maynard shook his head and smiled. Only a man like Harrison, probably doomed forever to be a first lieutenant, would have such an observation to make.

"Of course failure in and of itself," Harrison said, "is no great crime; but when your charge comes directly from President Grant and General Sherman . . ."

"I don't think I'm going to fail, John."

Harrison smiled appreciatively. "Ah," he said, "that self-confidence. I suppose I don't know that feeling, and I further suppose it's what they saw in you in the first place. After all, bypassing a wagonload of senior officers . . ."

"A soldier does what he's asked."

"It's a ripe assignment, if you bring it off. And you will, Thomas. My mind is clear on that. One of the keenest young officers we have."

"Are you quoting someone?" Maynard asked.

"Colonel Becker."

"To whom?"

"To another officer. Within my earshot. Are you flattered?"

"No," Maynard said simply.

"No, not you," Harrison said soberly. "You wouldn't be. You'd be insulted if he hadn't said it. Not that you're given to preening. It's just your damned gift for doing the right thing. Sometimes I wish I had it."

"Sometimes, John?" Maynard asked with a chiding smile.

"There's the rub, Thomas. Expectations. I can't do much wrong because they neither ask nor expect much of me. But you—you never put a foot wrong. So if you do . . . well, what else do they have to occupy themselves with in peacetime? Now in war, that's another story. Look at how some of our noblest generals misreckoned and miscalculated during the war. But in war your blunders are covered up by blood and noise."

"If you're this cynical at your age," Maynard said, "what will you be like as an old man sitting on a veranda?"

"I'll be an amusing old codger. A sage, to some."

"Anyway," Maynard said, "you'll be pleased to know that I see in this mission an obligation higher than the one I have to the President or to General Sherman or General Northwood."

"To Miss Englund."

"Well, John, you do pay attention."

"My God, Thomas, the way you were prattling on about her last night."

"I don't prattle."

"Of course you don't. But I understand perfectly. What you received from the President and the Chief of Staff, via General Northwood, was a cold-blooded military directive, which you accepted with a crisp salute. What you did with Miss Englund was make a promise."

"Sort of," Maynard said. He sat down now on a cushion-seated round-backed wooden chair and folded his arms and crossed his legs.

"So while the lack of success would merely be an ephemeral piece of paper on General Northwood's desk and an inglorious but wholly forgivable pause in your career, to Miss Englund it would have to be a personal, self-abasing, red-faced *mea culpa*. I like that smile, Thomas—you're not even entertaining the slightest possibility of it, are you?"

Harrison entered the room and sat on the edge of the bed. Idly he fingered a neatly folded blue tunic that lay in the valise.

"I daresay she's won your heart, Tom," he said. "And not a bad thing either. It will make your investigations more intense, more determined. What is the army and all its cannons and banners compared to the ache in the heart of a young lady?"

Maynard smiled indulgently.

"Do you know what I object to in this life, Thomas?" Harrison said moodily, staring as if mesmerized by the tunic in the valise.

"What is that, John?"

"How little control we have over it. Soldier or civilian, young or old, rich or poor, quick or dull. Here we have your situation. A few months ago at some damned end-of-the-horn little outpost two thousand miles away some malcontent takes a knife in hand and for some good reason, or maybe for no reason at all, stabs to death somebody named Alfred Englund, and now here in Washington somebody named Thomas Maynard must undertake a long, long trek to find out why. And I have to give up a good friend and housemate."

"We have to find the answer, John. What you say may be very philosophical, worthy of an evening's learned discussion over cigars and brandy . . ."

"Then you don't care how life tosses you about?"

"I live in a framework of my own devising, John. As long as the tossing is done within it, I don't resist nor do I shake my fist at the sky."

"Nor do you ask the key question."

"Which is?"

Harrison smiled self-consciously. The hot morning sunlight was full in his face. "*Why?*" he said.

"No, John," Maynard said, shaking his head slowly. "Because to that there is no reasonable answer. But to the questions I'm going to be asking at Fort Larkin . . ."

"There will be an answer. Suppose it makes no sense?"

"Everything, finally, makes sense."

"A frightening notion," Harrison said abstractedly. "A corporal was also murdered at the outpost, correct?"

"On the same night. That's part of the inquiry."

"Solve one, solve the other."

"I daresay."

"But no one cares about the corporal, do they?"

"I care," Maynard said.

"So do I. A man of flesh and blood and dreams. His name?"

"O'Bannion. Corporal Peter O'Bannion."

"Why do you think he was murdered, Thomas?"

"He may have seen something."

"Or knew something."

"It would be the same," Maynard said.

"I should be careful if I were you, Thomas."

"I've given the matter some thought."

"After all, you're not going out there to pin a decoration on anyone."

"I'll watch my back."

"Yes, you will. You'll be fine. You'll come back to glory and accolades. And Miss Englund."

CHAPTER 4

PRESENT AND PAST

His superiors only saw him listening and acquiescing, gave him orders and then expected them to be fulfilled, as they always were, to the extent that once the orders had been given he was forgotten about and only the orders remembered. He was little more to his superiors than the piece of paper upon which they executed their commands and desires. No one of higher rank ever wondered or cared what he thought, or if he even thought. Maynard knew this, understood it, accepted it, and in his way preferred it. The army owned him body and soul, his allegiance and his morality and his integrity; but because of its own vast and unyielding palisades of codes and systems the army was not interested in the inmost chambers of his thought, where the soldier belonged to himself.

This time he was more than some bloodless functionary carrying out an assigned task that at completion would be nodded at with satisfaction and then filed away forever, with all the afterthought given a relic in a catacomb. This time there was more to it. While he would perform his duties with all the dedication the army expected, this time Tom Maynard was impelled by a more driven fervor to succeed.

It was the miracle of fascination, he thought, that now, days after the fact, and here, sitting on a wicker chair in a Pullman parlor car hundreds of miles from Washington, listening to the iron wheels carry him deeper and deeper into the Western night, he could still feel as though it had been a viselike pressure, the touch of the gloved hand that had been no more than a butterfly's wing against his fingertips. Her grief had given rise to her pride and strength, yet in her eyes had been a waif's appeal. He was the army's special inspector in the matter, a man charged to make sure that generals were not up for the slaughter on the frontier; but for Miss Englund he was more—the avenging arrow who would bring bitter satisfaction to the corner of her heart that was a general's daughter, and a certain sweet surcease to that corner that was simply daughter. Although he had laughed at the summation, he had to agree with John Harrison's depiction of a sorely desired future: "Thomas, you want majors and colonels saluting you by day and Mrs. Maynard, née Englund, kissing you by night." How could he explain it to John Harrison, who hadn't wanted to be there in the first place and was therefore content to go no further? You must make every exertion to continue the ascent. In the peacetime army constancy and dedication were like an aroma. You remained at all times at the service of your ambition (in war it was courage; in peace, ambition), and when the opportunity arose let it serve you. Maynard knew he was right because there had had to be something that made General Northwood reach past more senior officers and select him for this.

He sat in the nearly deserted parlor car, legs crossed, smoking his pipe, his narrowed eyes gazing at but not seeing the wainscot paneling, oscillating with the ceaseless rhythms of travel, listening to the delicate tinkling of the chandelier that was traveling across the night-covered spaces of America like some ornate lateral-flying meteor.

He was a professional, battle-scarred soldier, veteran of some of the most murderous campaigns in history, yet the death he would always most vividly recall had occurred far from the field of honor. War was noise and confusion and the heart-rending suffering of friends and strangers, whose deaths had come during times of such high-pitched terror and passion as to have forfeited any claim to reality. Maynard had always bowed his head and gone forward in battle with such iron determination to survive it was as if he had slipped from his physical being and let it carry on as some independent and insensate thing, unfeeling and unrecording. *Feeling most keenly not feeling.* Devising protection should he survive, weaving a netting to snarl and confound the gathering nightmares.

The memory that had plunged deepest and embedded most eternally dated to that autumn of 1860, that autumn of shining air and blazing leaves, a self-communing world of Adirondack forest, towering trees, shafts of chill sunlight slanting through cathedral stillness. Recurrent memory had polished the day so many times over it had burnished the scene into a vision that passed before his eyes in full dimension, so that he could see his seventeen-year-old self and Ad Marston stalking the forest for deer, rifles in hand, crackling through the crisp, high-veined autumn leaves, pausing now and then to listen for some telltale rustle.

They had always been keen, good-natured rivals, these boys who had grown up together in inseparable bonds of friendship. Though they had always faced the world as one (their world, of course, which existed within a ten-mile radius of the Adirondack village of Maple Creek), rough and fresh and heartily confident, when they regarded each other now it was with an utterly compelling urgency to prove who was the better man. The need for such affirmation had, at that lusty and uninhibited time of life, suddenly transcended the criteria of speed of foot and strength of arm, thanks to the most riotous and upending invasion that could storm the blood of seventeen-year-old boys.

Her name was Sarah Wilman, their age, daughter of the man known like some eleventh-century icon smasher as Wilman the Newcomer because he was just that, new to Maple Creek, where he had arrived the previous winter and established with his wife and five children (Sarah the eldest) a feed and grain emporium. Soon the boys Tom Maynard and Ad Marston discovered the newcomer's eldest with her mischievous eyes, coquette's smile, blooming femininity and leaped with single irretrievable bound from the springtime of adolescence to the hot summer of young manhood.

Enraptured, they contested for her attention, foolishly and noisily at first, wrapping their arms around each other's shoulders and coming to the feed and grain store to gawk and smile and employ all of the guile that passed for teenage sophistication in Maple Creek in 1860. Then they ran footraces along the hard, knotty mountain earth of Main Street, the racecourse passing directly in front of the feed and grain store of Wilman the Newcomer and the amused eye of his eldest.

And then Ad Marston began realizing that the footraces that he was losing by a half step were symbolic; that the half step was always naggingly present be it in a footrace or a turkey shoot or an arm wrestle or in an exercise of mountain wit when they sat on the bench in front of the feed and grain store with Sarah Wilman. If it had been a half mile perhaps he might have seen clear to deal with it; but the half step was maddening. When he said to Tom, *She likes us, she really does*, he received no answer, and his failed attempt at equation left him brooding.

On an early September morning Ad, turning more and more sullen as the symbolic proportions of that half step lengthened in his psyche, went to the large, two-storied, rather ramshackle frame house at the edge of the village where Tom lived with his father and two older brothers (the mother had died years ago), who made their living off the forest timber, who piled into a wagon in the mornings and followed the trail higher into the mountains where the camps were and spent their day whipping ax blades into the hides of the endless maples, birches, and evergreens; a vocation that would soon enough be Tom's as well. When Ad cut from the road and entered the front yard the Maynards' terrier came bounding forward. Ad knelt to accept the dog's excited greeting, cuffed the animal gently a few times, and asked where the boyo was. The answer came in drifting laughter from an upstairs bedroom, though it was not for him, it was private, intimate, and it soon stopped. Then it came again, again like a hiding sound, though this time there were two sounds, mingling but distinct enough that Ad turned and ran from the yard, across the road, and dove into the brush and lay there flat on his belly staring at the house while the terrier, which had run with him as far as the edge of the yard, stood panting, watching him, its tail whipping.

Confused and frustrated by whatever this game was, the terrier began barking, advancing and retreating with each thwarted, toneless shout. Then the faces appeared at the upstairs window, Tom's first, rising tentatively straight up from the sill and then Sarah's, for a moment just the two faces, looking like a pair of sculpted objects balanced ear to ear on the window's edge, surveying the yard, warily, curiously, and then as if manipulated from below turning to look at each other and then laughing and with that same manipulatory simultaneity sinking from view and not reappearing again. Ad lay concealed in the brush until the terrier tired of the game and stopped barking and turned and padded back to the house.

Two nights later, after having drained a half bottle of cheap whisky pulled from his father's stock, Ad sought out his friend, confronted him on Main Street, and, standing on wobbly legs, weaving, barely coherent, challenged Tom to a knife fight. Tom listened with uncomprehending wonder, trying to read his friend's eyes for an explanation, and then soon understood, though certainly not the specifics of it, knowing not what Ad knew but surely what he felt. Several others gathered around, smelled the whisky, laughed at the inebriation which they believed accounted for the confrontation, and led an unresisting, barely ambulatory Ad away.

If the others chalked up the scene to whisky-drenched foolishness, Tom did not. The half step was now a gorge and Ad had fallen through. A wariness now existed between the friends. The days of mindless camaraderie and rambles of little consequence were over, the scenes of artless uncompounded performance for the eye of Sarah Wilman were past. Tom, in his freshly dissolved virginity, had begun behaving with new seriousness, talking about full-time employment in the timber camp, and though no explanation for this new view of life was given, it was tacitly understood. Ad, who had endured the building frustration of losing by half steps, was now faced with the prospect that the race was coming to an end.

Teenagers did not live by traditions; nevertheless, Tom Maynard and Ad Marston, aged seventeen, had been taking to the forest each October since achieving their measures of independence to bring down a deer. The advent of the golden season seemed momentarily to arrest their tension and once more, rifles in hand, they climbed the trails to where the forest still seemed to grow and soar with pristine purity.

As they went higher and deeper into the forest Tom became more and more aware of his friend's silence. While he no longer expected the old banter, neither had he anticipated a brooding shadow who remained a dozen paces behind; nor was he any longer able, he knew, to tease his friend with a quip or expect one in return. The old pattern had gone asunder and none as yet formed in replacement. He knew he was being watched, studied, contemplated; he could feel the presence of rancid emotion. And then he began feeling the weight of another presence: it was not the two of them stalking the forest, but three; and though her physical presence was elsewhere, Sarah Wilman was never more with them than in those tantalizing wordless hours they spent passing in and out of the slanting, spiritual pillars of sunlight that burned through the autumn trees like sacred paths to heaven. Toned yellow by the unfallen leaves of beech and birches and reflected so that it seemed to be coming from all directions, the sunlight gave the impression of a golden interior lighting, casting up from the forest floor and out from the hard white trunks of the birches. If either had been constrained to speak his foremost thought, her name would have been in first utterance. The difference was fatally this: for Tom her presence was reality and comfort; for Ad, a shadow gnawing and embittering.

They heard the sounds before they saw the men. There was a rustling and crashing of leaves and then the rise of voices of men obviously on the move, hurried, agitated. The clash of loud human voices in this place was as alien to it as violins would have been. The boys halted and waited. Soon they could see the men breasting through the brush and filtering among the trees, intermittently struck by the irregular sunlight. Some were wearing coonskin caps with furry tails, others floppy slouch hats. From a distance their hurrying pace made them look like they were galloping as they sprang through the brush and leaped over the fallen timber.

The boys had already recognized the voices and now the familiar faces came toward them. There were eight of them, armed with rifles and some with sheathed knives as well.

What are you boys doing up here? one of the men asked.

Out for deer, Tom said.

Then the warning and the advice and the story came excitedly at them all at once. They had better turn around and get right back to the village and keep a sharp eye while they were at it, too, because there was some unaccountable madman or lunatic loose up here, who'd come roistering into the village, drunk a bottle dry, got into a few scrapes, and finally spun around with a loaded shotgun and killed somebody, then stolen a horse and ridden off. They'd found the horse and then found the trail heading up into the forest and by God they were going to find him. All of this told angrily and impatiently, to get it out of the way so they could go on. They refused the boys' offer to enlist in the search, ordering them out of the area and back to home and safety. Suppose we come across him? Ad asked. How will we know him? What should we do? Already departing, the men shouted out a description distinctive enough and finally the injunction: you shoot him dead.

Then they stood and waited, until the men and the voices and the noises had faded back into the silence from which they had come. Tom looked at Ad, who had been staring at him and who continued to stare as though in the midst of a long meditation, as though mentally taking size and measure, and what had brought them to the forest in the first place—that primal urge to hunt down and kill simply for the letting of blood—suddenly whirled about inside of Tom and fostered an impulse as primal as the original but this time at the antipodal end of the equation: survival.

We had best get back, Tom said, staring hard in the eye at him, as if to say *I know what you're thinking, which gives me total license. So you had better step careful.*

Suppose we see him? Ad asked.

We'll bring him down.

I'll take first shot, Ad said. I've got the keener eye.

Do you? Tom said doubtfully.

And now making the journey back there were four: Tom and Ad and the palpable presence of Sarah Wilman and the multidimensional shadow of whatever murderous lunatic might be afoot in leaf or brush, an already blooded rifle in hand, who was a substantial threat from anywhere nearby and a potential one in the mind of silent Ad Marston who, as before, was following Tom, the latter feeling more and more the aching vulnerability of his own back. When Tom paused with the pretense of listening, ostensibly for the substantial threat who might be anywhere, Ad stopped also, maintaining the twenty or so pace difference between them. Once Tom turned around, saw Ad standing there, rifle held diagonally across himself, still staring at Tom with the same flat meditating eyes, waiting for him to move again.

The sounds behind him were so light Tom began to feel as though he were being tracked by the ghost of some damned Iroquois whose moccasined foot knew every flat and soundless landing point in the forest. And then there were no sounds at all and Tom suddenly whirled about. Crouching, he shouted Ad's name several times, then began running. He stumbled upon an above-ground root and went flying headfirst into a swale and rolled over several times through the moist vegetation, his rifle pitching ahead of him. Getting to his knees, panting, as much from fear as from exertion, he picked up the rifle and gripped it tightly as though it were a spar in the open sea, remaining motionless, listening intently, hearing nothing but a high breeze whirring the needles in the pine.

He remained still for several minutes, feeling encased in the surrounding silence, as if beyond its locked box there were rackets of sound he could not hear. Once more he called out his friend's name, tentatively, in his voice an implicit warning, as if stressing the danger of what was now transpiring. And again he heard nothing, not even the hymn of the pines now, as if it were all menacingly poised, irrevocably tilted so that it could only fall; in the suspended tilt was already the motion; it was happening. *He's going to leave me here dead and blame the madman who himself will be gunned down before being asked if he had shot one or two.* And then take her hand in his and together mourn and regret the barbarous mischances of frail mankind.

He got to his feet and began moving, hunched so low his back was almost parallel with the ground, looking deformed as he went warily through the swale, his rifle pointed ahead of him. Heaps of dead leaves had gathered in the depression and they crackled underfoot. He came up out of the swale, walking straighter now, fear making a weather vane of his neck as he swiveled it this way and that, trying to determine in which direction the danger lay, the utter silence telling him it was there, settling if not settled, somewhere not far off, concealed and observant and waiting.

He pressed on across clumps of moss and chains of partridgeberry, sliding through lifeless brown fern fronds and crowds of wild pink and white asters. He stepped over the gray husk of what once had been a mighty cedar and was now a nest for sour-looking molds and fungi, around them still evident the scorching left by the dagger of lightning that long ago had shocked it to death. When he saw dozens of other dead trees slanted over and caught in the limbs of their neighbors he knew he was in a part of the forest he had never ventured to before, a place that once upon a time had shrieked with a celestial electricity that had snapped and murdered the trees around him. Cedar and ash and yellow birch were dead here, and further along spruce and hemlock, and scattered about like tokens of mourning were last spring's fallen pinecones, gray-tipped with resin. The overhead foliage was almost too dense to allow sunlight and suddenly the temperature seemed to have fallen. He moved deeper into an almost sunless pine forest, and now he was moving without sound across a thick carpet of pine needles, dark green on the surface, a rusted brown where his boots pushed aside the top layer.

He stopped and crouched among breast-high plumage and gathered himself to listen, to sift every minute sound, to separate the fluttering bird wing and the thin piney whisper from the falling footstep. He was listening so intently that he found himself detecting the barely audible ticking of myriad spent leaves wrinkling themselves. He waited, holding his rifle against his chest, for a moment shutting his eyes, as if to allow his ears to gather the power of every sense.

The sound made him open his eyes and he knew Ad Marston was near; and the sounds following were slow and tentative enough to make him know that Ad had lost him, that Ad's sole available tactic was to decipher a sound and guess a direction, and that it would be Ad, the hunter, who was going to have to move, and then it would be the alerted unseen prey who had advantage.

He peered through the leaves, waiting, listening. Ad was moving again. Tom cocked his head, trying to infer direction from sound, with interminable patience and barely breathing intensity transforming himself from prey to hunter. Through the leaves he saw his friend; Ad was fragmented by the brush, parts of him appearing and reappearing, rifle leveled before him, back curved, stalking. Feeling his legs beginning to ache from his crouched position, Tom shifted his rifle forward, jammed the stock against his shoulder, and sighted along the barrel and through the veined leaves, crooking his finger against the trigger. His mind was dead, his body empty of thought and feeling. Only the gathered tension.

At the last he called out the name, his voice running along the barrel of the rifle and through the leaves and reaching Ad like a blow. Ad whirled, swinging the rifle with him, startled into shooting from the waist, shooting not at anything but the sound. The one shot ignited the other; the one was wild, far off the mark; the other went straight home.

Jesus. He had shot him right through the eye. The first erupting gush was out by the time Tom reached him and now the wound was pulsing streams of thick bright blood, rolling it down the blackened face and down to the red leaves of autumn that lay around Ad's head. He was lying on his back, his right arm thrown out, the rifle still gripped in his fingers, his legs spread wide. Jesus, Tom whispered.

He covered the body with pine boughs, stacks of them. And then, chilled and frightened, he went away.

CHAPTER 5

THE OFFICIAL REPORT

Report from Colonel Marcus Bruckner, Acting Commanding Officer, Fort Larkin, Dakota Territory. June 9, 1876.

On the evening of 14 May, 1876, General Englund announced an officer's call and gathered together in his office a group of his senior officers. In addition to myself, there were Lieutenant Colonel Scheffner and Majors Fordyce, Josephson, and Patman. The general stressed that the gathering, which was called for nine o'clock, was to be regarded as informal, open to a free exchange of ideas. We met in the general's anteroom at the appointed hour and were then requested by the general to join him in his office. A semicircle of chairs had been arranged in front of the desk and we were invited to be seated. General Englund then rose from behind the desk and with a box of cigars in hand went to each of us. Each officer partook of this generous hospitality.

General Englund then led a free-ranging discussion upon various matters, including the likelihood of a campaign against a band of Sioux who were believed to be in encampment in the environs of Fort Larkin. The general indicated that the commencement of the campaign awaited only a scout's report on the size and disposition of the hostiles. All present agreed that this was a potentially troublesome assemblage of Indians and heartily endorsed dealing with them. General Englund informed us that the specifics of what he felt would be a brief but conclusive campaign would be forthcoming shortly. Discussion then drifted into reminiscences of the late war, in which the majority of the officers present had participated. General Englund then introduced a bottle of brandy and with his own hand poured us each a modest portion. We all stood and drank a toast to all who had fallen in the late war. Soon after, the evening concluded. It was approximately 11 P.M.

Each officer then returned to his quarters and each has sworn that there he remained until summoned by subsequent events. The exigencies of this report demand, without prejudice, the inclusion of the companionship status of each officer that evening. Though married men, Majors Fordyce and Josephson were alone that night, their wives having gone East to be with family. Colonel Scheffner's wife was present, but this couple are known to have lately occupied separate sleeping quarters because of personal inharmonies. Major Patman is a bachelor. I myself returned to my quarters and retired for the night with my wife. General Englund, whose wife and daughter had recently returned to their home in Washington, remained alone in his office after we left, saying he had to attend to some work before retiring. No one was on duty in the gen-

eral's outer office when we left, a not uncommon occurrence at that hour of the night.

At approximately 11:30 P.M. the lamp in General Englund's office was seen to be still burning. Some few
minutes later a lone horseman rode into the fort, after
having been passed by the sentries. He crossed the parade ground and dismounted outside of General Englund's office. The rider was one Rennay Duchard.
Duchard is a scout who at the time was in the informal
employ of the United States Army and who was given
occasional assignments by General Englund, who
seemed to hold him in high regard. Duchard had been
absent from the fort for three or four days before his
return. It is assumed that he reported to General Englund, and but briefly, for shortly after he was seen at
the stables, attending to his horse. He was then seen by
a sentry at the south end of the fort heading for his
quarters. Although the night was especially dark, the
sentry was certain that the man he saw was Duchard.

For the next several hours the fort was peaceful, with
no untoward comings or goings. At approximately
2:30 A.M. it became known that one of the sentries on
duty in the parade ground area had not reported since
midnight. The officer of the day accepted responsibility
for the delay in reporting this. His explanation was that
he believed that the sentry, Corporal O'Bannion, had
made a sick call to the guardhouse. (The officer has
been duly reprimanded for his remissness.) When it
was realized that the sentry was unaccounted for the
senior officers were notified and a search immediately
instituted. (Desertion was ruled out when it was ascer-
tained that no horses were missing.) Some few minutes
after 4 A.M. the search came to a tragic conclusion
when the body of Corporal O'Bannion was discovered

under a blanket in the stables. Later examination revealed that he had suffered a fatal knife wound in the abdomen. A study of the ground revealed markings that indicated the corporal had been struck down some distance away and the body dragged boot heels down to the place where it was found. It was estimated by the post surgeon, Dr. Gilbert, that this heinous act had transpired sometime between midnight and 1 A.M.

At this point I was notified. Fearing that fort security might have been breached by renegades, I issued an immediate call to arms. I then sent an orderly to notify General Englund. The orderly reported back that the general was not in his quarters. I hastened to the general's headquarters and there, by mine own eye, made the gruesome and lamentable discovery. General Englund was lying dead on the floor, a Bowie knife having been driven nearly to its grip into his upper back between the shoulders.

As the now senior officer, I ordered an immediate inquiry into the circumstances of these two deaths. Everyone—all officers, enlisted men, and all personnel connected with the fort—was asked to give an accounting of his whereabouts between midnight and two o'clock in the morning, the latter hour being Dr. Gilbert's most outside estimate possible for the time of General Englund's death. Our investigation informed us that virtually all of our number were at those hours abed or preparing to retire. Of the six sentries on duty at the time, five heard nothing out of character, while the sixth was the unfortunate Corporal O'Bannion.

It became the conclusion of those deputized by myself as a Committee of Inquiry (myself, Lieutenant Colonel Scheffner, Major Fordyce, Major Josephson, and Major Patman) that Corporal O'Bannion had been slain first and General Englund soon after, the logic being that it would have been extremely difficult and hazardous for anyone to have come and gone without being seen had Corporal O'Bannion been on duty. It was the further opinion of the committee that General Englund had personally known his assailant, to whom he had given entrance at that hour. Struck from behind, the general had evidently been taken by surprise, as there was no evidence of physical struggle. The death weapon, it later developed, was the general's own—a memento said to have been taken from a captured Confederate officer, and which the general had kept with him for years. The knife had been hanging in a sheath on a wall in the general's office and was familiar to all who came and went.

After the first, necessarily cursory questioning of everyone had been done, a disturbing fact was brought to my attention. It developed that the scout Duchard had departed from the fort sometime before dawn on the morning the bodies were found. Since it is firmly assumed that he had been the last person known to have spoken with General Englund, Duchard's behavior calls for some explanation. From that day to this, he has not been seen by anyone affiliated with the United States Army, though he has been reported seen in the hills north and west of the fort and to have occasionally, albeit briefly, appeared in some small towns and mining camps that lie within several days' ride from this fort. Despite what appear to be overtly incriminating actions, it is not my intention to pass judgment on Duchard, though admittedly he remains a most intriguing factor. Why he should have wanted to murder General Englund and Corporal O'Bannion, why he should have calmly gone to his quarters after having done so, and why he should have decamped under such dramatic circumstances leave behind a conflict of questions that await their answers. To this moment it is still believed that Duchard remains in the Territory and it is still our unwavering intention to find him and have him for questioning. Nevertheless, to focus too exclusively on Duchard might, in my opinion, divert inquiry from the one who might truly have committed these awful and cowardly crimes; therefore, all avenues of investigation remain open.

To this day, and despite all good efforts, the question of who murdered General Englund and Corporal O'Bannion remains without answer, though of course the matter stands open and shall so stand until such answer be given. I need not stress that the matter continues to retain within the bosom of all concerned the same urgency for solution which it had on that terrible morning, though I must in candor admit that to this moment our best efforts toward resolution have met with frustration.

Because it might be pertinent to the body of this report, I must append a report of another as yet unaccountable and unresolved occurrence. Two days after the events of the awful morning it was discovered that someone had broken into General Englund's domestic quarters (which I had ordered to be locked). It was obvious that a strenuous search had been made of the general's desk and papers—little else had evidently been disturbed. Whether this event was related to the general's death can at this juncture only be speculated upon, but since nothing of value appeared to have been removed I am of the opinion that the burglary was a coda to the murder. If this be true, it leads to the conclusion that the murder of General Englund was not

some spontaneous strike of wrath or irrationality but
was rather of deeper structure.

Along with Colonel Bruckner's report were many pages of
individual testimony given before the Committee of Inquiry.
Most of the statements were brief and almost unavoidably
similar: I was in bed at that time and I heard nothing. Nevertheless, Maynard felt, within these pages lay a compass direction that would lead to the truth. Why the officers at Fort
Larkin had not yet determined that direction, he could not
say. Nor would he at this moment begin to speculate. The
best thing he could do, he thought as he laid his head back
against his seat and gave himself over to the soothing pulse-
beat of rail travel, was to dismiss it all from his mind until
he arrived at the fort. Instead, with amused self-indulgence,
he allowed his mind a leap ahead, envisioning the accolades
and rewards of a successful investigation. There would be
the envious admiration of his colleagues at the War Department, the gruff congratulations of General Northwood, a ci-
tation from General Sherman, perhaps even a word from
President Grant. And of course the appreciation of Miss Englund, who had promised to think of him every day and to
remember him in her prayers. Good God, Maynard thought
with a roguish smile as he sat alone in the parlor car, watching nighttime America pass darkly through the windows,
here and there an isolated light, eerie in its solitude. Good
God, he thought again. Had any man ever been given so
bountiful an opportunity?

At Chicago a dining car was attached to the train and instead of having to dash out for quick meals at railroad lunch
counters Maynard and his fellow passengers were able to
dine comfortably and in a luxury that seemed incongruous
when they glanced through the window at the rough and
sparsely populated country they were passing through. The

table linen was snow white, the silverware heavy and regal to the touch, and the menu included fresh vegetables and choices of elk, grouse, antelope, beefsteak, and mutton chops.

A tablemate at dinner was a man named Dunston, portly and middle-aged and hopelessly gregarious, and worse, recently back from a grand tour of travel that had taken him through Europe and as far as Egypt. The tour's chief accomplishment, he said, was to make him appreciate America the more. It was because America was so young a country, by all standards still in swaddling. Unlike the lands he had visited across the seas, America was a country that was still pure and simple and aboveboard, a land of clear days and honest nights. Too young to have mysteries, and wasn't that good? Mysteries had a tendency to impose gravity and somberness, be it upon a nation or a house or a face. Wasn't that right? But none of that here. Not in America. With one exception of course, he said with a wink. A woman. A woman ought to have a bit of the mysterious about her, what do you think?

Maynard took the Union Pacific train to Omaha, where he got off. The depot was filled with people: fur trappers, adventurers, fellow soldiers, gold seekers, salesmen, women with small children, pack peddlers with everything for sale from combs and brushes to stock in Black Hills gold mines.

He caught a stern-wheel steamer heading north along the Missouri channels on into the Dakota Territory. Days later he disembarked near Fort Hale. From here he traveled with a paymaster's wagon out to the small, lonely sprawl of buildings known as Fort Larkin.

CHAPTER 6

MAY 14, 1876
FORT LARKIN, D.T.

It was not going to be a casual post-dinner chat among the officers. Major Patman knew that much. The major had been in the army too long not to be cognizant of his commanding officer: there was never anything casual or offhand about General Englund, a man of plans and contingencies, for whom everyday life seemed to bring new extensions of old battlefields, a complex man whose guarded style of command kept your sense of vigilance poised. For Englund everything was always a severely formal affair, with mind and soul at full dress and relentlessly alert. So, despite the solitudinous posting of Fort Larkin, where it was easy for both instinct and intellect to dull, Patman and probably the other officers as well sensed something pending.

Patman could feel the curiosity as the five of them followed the general into his office, nor did the general's reference to the gathering's informality permit any visible ease.

(Patman had become accustomed to the wariness among these officers and their commander, despite the many years they had served together.) They took chairs in front of the desk: Colonels Bruckner and Scheffner, Majors Josephson, Fordyce, and Patman. Being the junior man by age and experience, Patman had resolved to say little, at least until the conversation had developed a direction. The colonels and Major Josephson had served with Englund throughout most of the war, while Fordyce had joined the staff just before Gettysburg. Despite a comradeship forged in the steaming blood of battle, Patman noted that there was never a moment's ebbing in the distance between Englund and the officers with whom he had served, never any of the wistful, mutually affectionate reminiscences that should have been normal between men so bonded. Bruckner was the explicator (or apologist) once. It was the burden, he said to Patman, of having had the command of, and responsibility for, thousands of men who were now dead or maimed or crippled. The general, Bruckner said, accepted his onus and carried it his own way. Major Josephson (on another occasion) had it differently. That's his way, Josephson told Patman. I think he was carved from the underside of an iceberg. He would be no different if he'd spent his life farming or running a dry goods store. While the evaluations made Englund no clearer to him, they helped limn in Patman's mind the gentlemanly Bruckner and the earthier Josephson.

The "free and open discussion" began with Englund sitting at his desk, the others puffing the cigars he had offered, though he himself had not lit one up. Patman was amused by his cigarless general; abstinence in this case was Englund's way of establishing his distinction, his separation from them. Even Fordyce, who abhorred tobacco, was constrained to sit and puff serenely. Five elongated brown chimneys released streams of smoke that commingled over their heads in a gray cloud that barely moved in the lamplight.

"As you know, gentlemen," Englund said, "the Laramie Treaty is now obsolete, and in its obsolescence is a salient lesson. It was an impulsive and misguided act of goodwill executed by a nation not yet fully aware of its growing strength and destiny. Young nations, like young men, should not make promises that maturity will not allow them to honor. The treaty guaranteed the Sioux lands in the western part of the Territory in perpetuity. The discovery of gold in those lands changed all that. The Indians don't understand gold, the significance of it. There's the brutal reality right there: How can you deal with a people who neither understand nor appreciate gold? I'm not talking simply of avarice. That gold is certainly not going to enrich any of us personally. What I *am* doing is pointing out the inevitabilities that accompany the discovery of that precious, indestructible, and irreducible metal. The discovery of gold means that a nation has attained a further elevation of growth and maturity; it is further corroboration of all the dreams and convictions of the Founding Fathers, as well as further justification for the shocking four-year war we fought against our brethren and for the war we are now waging in what today are godforsaken places but which tomorrow will be communities with schools and churches. You only have to remember that it was the hand of God that pressed that gold into the ground and left it there for thousands of years, waiting for the white man to come and unearth it.

"Some people, notably in the Eastern press and in certain corridors of government, are saying that we've broken our word with the Indians. Well, gentlemen, I say that we are keeping our bond with the Lord. I hold no malice against the Indian, but I do recognize and must obey a higher obligation, which we have been deputized to carry out. The In-

dian lives only to hunt and to commit warfare. He has no
mind for anything else. How do you reckon with someone
who has no idea that history has already begun washing
over him with tidal fury? How do you reckon with someone
who has no idea that history even exists? Do the railroad
and the telegraph line forever end where the Indian begins? I
think not. The Indian has been deluded by the fact that the
plains and the mountains and the rivers never change, by the
belief that what he is doing today he will be doing five thousand years from now. He cannot conceive that he is already
sharing the continent with cities and factories and universi-
ties, that the world of ideas has crossed the seas to him. So
he stubbornly persists in pursuing a static, unevolving way
of life that is as primitive today as it was for his furthest an-
cestor. Is it too late for the Indian? Gentlemen, it was too
late for him the moment the first ships of discovery sighted
the North American continent. Those masts were the handwriting against the sky.

"It has become the responsibility of the frontier army to
put an end to the predatory, rapacious, and murderous ways
of the savage Indian. If he will not change his behavior and
turn himself over to the reservation agencies then our duty is
clear. The Indian Bureau has admitted loss of control of the
situation; though how a bureau some thousands of miles
away in Washington thought it could administer and induce
a policy in the Dakota Territory represents naïveté at its
greatest extremity. As you gentlemen know only too well,
the final implementation of policy—what I have been
known to describe as the judicial bayonet tip—is left up to
us. The government proposes and we dispose. I remember a
superior of mine during the war with Mexico, when I was
still a lieutenant all fresh and pink from the Point, telling
me—this was a fellow ripe with every villainy necessary for
survival front and back—telling me, 'Give them victory and

you'll never be asked a question, and the dead will never get inside of your dreams.'

"So when a bureau of government admits that it has lost control of the exercise of its policy it becomes time for the soldier to begin reaching for his rifle. There becomes only one way to stop the panic among the men of goodwill who write impossible treaties, only one way to end the chaos and return tranquillity to the management of government, and that is to apply without compromise the anointed power of government. We will seek out the pagan foe and twist his purpose and terrorize his terror a thousand times over, and where he creates darkness we will bring light, where he makes storms we will create idylls, what he has defiled we will make sacred."

Fascinating, Patman thought, and frightening. So lucid, yet with a certain gripping madness. A full rainbow of passion contained in an iron grip. His eyes had not left Englund's face for a moment. The general had been speaking to them and through them, as if addressing some ghostly tribunal only he could see. His lacquered black hair was angled and combed flat across a head that was a trifle too narrow for his trim body, so that it looked as if it had been squeezed up through the collar of his jacket. Those cosmically gazing eyes burned black with resolve under stormy black eyebrows. Deep groovelike seams ran the length of either cheek so that his face looked as though divided into quarters. He had the short, spadelike beard of an Elizabethan courtier, and from his thin-lipped mouth issued a rich, carefully modulated baritone that a thespian would have envied. Now and then the general would fix his eyes on one of his listeners and for ten or fifteen seconds make a direct address as if to nail every word upon the man's memory.

"Well, gentlemen," Englund said at the conclusion of his statement, "how to the ready are we?"

"We are always at the ready, General," Colonel Bruckner said.

"Exactly what is on the horizon, General?" Colonel Scheffner asked. "A patrol, a campaign?"

"The days of poking and jabbing at the Sioux are over," Englund said.

"Hear. Hear," Colonel Bruckner murmured.

"For too long," Englund said, "it has been the opinion of certain thinkers in Washington and among the Eastern press that if we kill a few Indians it would intimidate and pacify the many, whereas such action only serves to enflame the many. So it will be the object of this campaign—and I don't put this cynically—to kill the many and pacify the few. Lest this sound too bloodthirsty, let me elucidate for you the long view: if we strike with conviction now it will bring an end to these wars and ultimately preserve many more lives than are consumed, both for the Indian and the white man. If the Indian continues to kill he will eventually be exterminated. There is no doubt of that. It is virtually arithmetical in its inevitability. But that isn't up to us, gentlemen. We can only respond; the essential decision is to be made by the Indian."

"In my opinion, General," Colonel Bruckner said, "it's past time this was done. God knows we're going to be facing a better-armed foe than we would have several years ago."

True enough, Patman thought. For the past half-dozen summers rough-hewn entrepreneurs had been heading up the Missouri to appointed rendezvous with the Indians and engaging in barter—robes, hides, and furs for Henry or Winchester magazine rifles and cartridges, which the Indians maintained were for hunting purposes, which didn't entirely convince their trading partners nor did it especially concern them either. Patman had heard of a skirmish last summer after which the soldiers were dismayed to find the Indian dead better armed than themselves, with Henrys and Winchesters, Colt's Navy revolvers, and drawstring bags stuffed with copper cartridges.

"Will we be coordinating with other units, General?" Major Fordyce asked.

General Englund considered the question for several moments, his eyes moving from face to face.

"Not precisely," he said. "General Terry will be moving with infantry and guns from Fort Lincoln, abetted by General Custer and the Seventh Cavalry. General Gibbon will be marching east from the Montana stations with the Seventh Infantry and a few squadrons of the Second Horse. And General Crook will be marching north with a most formidable contingent of infantry and cavalry."

"And our role, sir?" Colonel Bruckner asked.

"Our role is not to unite with the main body but to secure our area and to use discretionary force if necessary. It has become necessary."

"Sir?" Colonel Scheffner said.

"Two prospectors rode in some days ago and told of a rather large Sioux encampment a few days' march north of here. Those men didn't have any more than that to say because, not being in the employ of the United States Army, they decided to give the site a wide swerve."

"I'd say they were prudent, General," Major Josephson said.

"You would say that, wouldn't you, Major?" Englund said with a rare, slow smile that revealed a row of large upper teeth, none of which hung close to the other, the gaps tiny but apparent.

Patman glanced at Josephson; if there could be a smile at once servile and contemptuous, Patman saw it on the lips of his fellow major. The smile on the face of Josephson, who was nearly bald, with large gray muttonchops like a sagging halo around his face, impressed Patman as being as intimate a communication as it seemed possible to have with the general.

"We're all anxious to play our part, General," Colonel Bruckner said. "I think I can speak for all ranks."

"A decisive blow struck here," Colonel Scheffner said, "can get the campaign off on a speedy foot."

"Which I'm sure General Sheridan will take note of," Englund said. "His feelings about the Indians approximate those of the rest of us."

"It's been pointing to this for years," Colonel Bruckner said. "There's no reason why Sioux raiding parties should any longer be tolerated."

"They should never have been tolerated," Major Josephson said.

"It will be a hard campaign," Colonel Scheffner said. "You know how the Sioux regard the Black Hills. That ground is sacred to them."

"Then it is only appropriate," Englund said, "that they should be buried there."

As close to an expression of wit as he'll ever get, Patman thought, noting the taut, mirthless, self-satisfied expansion of the general's lips. Picked out by Englund's riveting gaze (which didn't seem to know that his lips were smiling), Patman responded with a serene smile of his own.

"Do we have any idea, General," Colonel Bruckner asked, "of the size and disposition of the Sioux encampment?"

"For that information," Englund said, "I am awaiting the return of Mr. Duchard, whom I so charged when I dispatched him last week. With his report in hand—and I expect it shortly—we can begin our tactical planning, though I must say I have not been idle these past days. Troop strength and individual assignments have been drawn up, approaches and deployments have been considered; but until Mr. Duchard's return it all remains tentative. The overall campaign is the largest ever undertaken against the Indian;

this may well be our sole opportunity to strike a blow in it. Gentlemen, I intend to be heard from."

"Yes, sir," said Major Fordyce, upon whom Englund's eyes had alit.

"To that end I'll be working here late again tonight," Englund said.

"We'll be at the ready, General," Colonel Bruckner said.

"You'll not be taking the field with us, Colonel Bruckner," Englund said.

The colonel stirred uncomfortably in his chair for a moment. He wet his lips, then bit softly into his underlip. Tall, impeccable of carriage, with a face almost aristocratically distinguished—privately his men referred to him as "senator"—Bruckner appeared visibly to be working to maintain his poise.

"Why is that, sir?" he asked quietly, as if Englund's simple declarative statement had contained an element of the abstruse.

The feigned innocence in Englund's face seemed close to mockery.

"By decision of the commanding officer," Englund said.

"Is that decision open to appeal, General?"

"How long have you been in the army, Colonel?"

Well, shit, Bruckner, Patman thought, you've left yourself wide open for this.

"More than fifteen years, General," Bruckner said. "Much of that time serving on your staff."

At least, Patman thought, he didn't say *loyally* serving.

"Then you know my decisions are not lightly made," Englund said, "nor are they subject to interrogation."

The uneasy silence that followed was broken by a self-conscious clearing of the throat by Colonel Scheffner, followed by an audible expulsion of breath by Colonel Bruckner.

Patman was keenly aware of not being surprised by Englund's brusqueness toward the man who was not only the fort's second in command but also an old friend with whom the general had shared the unspeakable years of blood. Patman found himself mildly amused, like a child witnessing a spat between a pair of formidable elders each of whom strode about with the aura of having a private compact with sunrise and sunset. Nor was he embarrassed by Bruckner's discomfiture, poor Bruckner, who was given to beginning sentences with a quiet and confidential *The general and I . . .* Bruckner could be particularly irritating because he was not just a pompous man but one with some foundation for his pomposity, the courage he had displayed time and again during the war being described as "inspirational," "nerveless," "resolute." These accolades, compounded by a natural self-regard, had served to give the colonel the look of a man waiting to be fitted for his pedestal. So Patman was not surprised by what he deemed Englund's arbitrary decision, for it was not unlike the general to humiliate an officer that way, with a quiet thrust from the shadows that was reasonless and unexpected.

Patman was grateful when the brandy appeared on the table, for he knew that here was the signal that the meeting was nearly over. The general smiled to himself as he poured the drinks, as if the service he was performing made him feel satisfyingly democratic. When the glasses were ready and each man had one in hand, they all rose to their feet as Englund raised his glass to offer a toast. Patman was expecting the upcoming campaign to be observed and solemnized, but the general's thoughts were on the past.

"To the war, gentlemen," he said, the corners of his eyes narrowing with sentiment. "To the long crucible so nobly endured. To the beloved and blessed dead."

Last to bring his glass to his lips was Major Josephson, who, before drinking, muttered, "At Fredericksburg."

General Englund turned around and contrived to stare at the several maps tacked to the wall.

"Thank you, gentlemen," he said, voice stiff with formality. "And good evening."

The officers left. Outside, the night was dark, cloud layers covering the sky and its dazzling fullness of prairie stars. The last curling edges of ebbing winter could be felt pawing in the soft wind. Two months before, in mid-March, a mammoth blizzard had come roaring at them, plunging the world of Fort Larkin to thirty degrees below zero while winds that seemed capable of rending asunder the very heavens whipped and lashed the blinding snow into vortical furies. Winter's maniacal benediction, Patman had thought at the time. Winter's way of making you thankful for fire, for warmth, for blankets, for walls; winter's way of making sure you will greet cousin Springtime with proper gratitude.

The good nights were perfunctory. Colonel Scheffner and Majors Josephson and Fordyce went off, heading for their quarters along officers' row.

Colonel Bruckner had said good night, then made no move. He seemed abstracted, standing as ever with that tall, cool dignity, as if eternally on parade. Maybe he wasn't really pompous, Patman thought, standing behind the colonel and watching him. Pomposity was, after all, an acquired characteristic. Maybe Bruckner had just been born that way, with that panoply of airs and postures, and we settle with our envy by dismissing him as a creature of vainglory. A man second in command to an officer like General Englund was never going to be fully known anyway, particularly if he possessed the self-esteem of a Bruckner.

"Colonel?" Patman said, stepping forward.

Bruckner was clearly startled as he turned around.

"Major," he said. "I thought you'd turned in."

"Just about to, sir. Unless . . ."

"Unless?"

"I thought you might want to talk, sir."

Bruckner's face never changed expression—that expression of a man waiting for coronation. He didn't say, "What about?" He didn't say, "Talk?" He didn't say, "Thank you, Major, but no." He didn't say anything; he merely stared at Patman with mild indignation, as if displeased at having been caught with a thought out of place.

"Good night, sir," Patman said. They exchanged salutes.

CHAPTER 7

MAY 14, 1876
FORT LARKIN, D.T.

As he watched the tall, patrician Colonel Bruckner of
pride impermeable stride into the night, right arm swinging,
like an apparition on ghostly parade, Patman couldn't help
wishing that he'd been a keener student of this maddeningly
fallible and endlessly fascinating condition of blood and
breath called humankind, that he could pierce the shields
and the shadows with wisdom. *I wish I knew so much
more*, he thought; *but considering that I don't, it would do
just as nicely to know a hell of a lot less.* Nor did he want to
know merely facts—he knew enough of those—but reasons,
and why certain consequences and not others evolved from
out of them.

As he walked alone to his quarters, Patman thought
about Josephson's toast—it had been almost grimly muttered. The reference to Fredericksburg had brought a sudden, telling change to the atmosphere. Soldiers who had

shared combat together sometimes spoke cryptically, or so it sounded to outsiders. He had not, of course, been at Fredericksburg, but that whole magnificently mismanaged battle, like all the rest of them, was so vivid to Patman that he occasionally thought he had. But really, all he knew about the Battle of Fredericksburg was its terrain, its weather, the strategy, the horror. He knew enough to know that if you hadn't smelled the smoke and heard the noise and the nuances within the noise, then you didn't know the battle. What he had was unearned knowledge, and therefore meaningless. Josephson's toast was further evidence of this. Something had happened on that field that the chroniclers had missed, something that left behind evident, unresolved tension. They had all been there, Englund, Bruckner, the others. Well, Patman thought, let them judge themselves and each other. Differences that had grown out of battlefield experience were blood-soaked knots to those involved, veritable barbed thickets to the outsider. Whatever it was, leave it to them. After all, Englund had once thrown his sword into the air and seen it struck by lightning, or so the tale went. That whole lurid story smacked of severe Old Testament admonition; a lost page of Scripture, Englund's apocrypha, enough to shock only God knew what into the mind of a man who was already susceptible to such things. (Bruckner's self-esteem was at least confined to this world.) So who could say what had happened at Fredericksburg?

No, Patman thought, I wasn't there, nor would I have wanted to have been, not even in retrospect, which seemed to be the most desirable time in the life of a soldier; the time when things were boldest and a man stood to his most critical height, when the things he did (or did not do) established forever his relationship with himself; not even that wistful, subtly reconfiguring concatenation of yesterdays could give Fredericksburg the least appeal. If there was a nightmare on the scroll of Civil War battles, a testament to war's most tragic conjunctions—battlefield heroism and command post obtuseness—it was Fredericksburg. Patman would rather have taken his chances at Gettysburg or the Wilderness or Cold Harbor; but as it was, he had taken his chances nowhere, not having graduated from West Point until 1867, by when the guns were two years cold and memories were beginning to ripen.

So Patman was the outsider, because they had all gone through it, to one degree or another: Englund, Scheffner, Bruckner, Fordyce, Josephson. Patman was in his oblique way a cohesive influence, for when he was among them around a table they seemed to fall naturally into fraternity, because they had all done the one thing and he had not. Since each man had trod more or less even ground during the war, what were they to each other? Nothing—until the man who had not been there joined them and unwittingly molded them into a shape, despite whatever resentments and enmities might lie suppressed among them. No one consciously worked at making Patman feel the outsider, with Patman being the first to admit that his caste was self-conferred. But the feeling was unavoidable. Be it in the most numbing perplexities or with the slyest nuances, when they spoke of the war, Patman stood outside of the ring. He understood perfectly.

In fact, what Englund had spoken of tonight, the campaign shortly to begin, would be Patman's first blooding, an opportunity to move closer to his brother officers. There was no truer way of achieving this than shared danger, and for a young, untried officer the danger lay not just forward of him but all about. In the eyes of his men as well as in those of his fellow officers, he would become his conduct and his behavior; if anything went wrong, he would become that wrong. Patman, however, had every confidence in himself, a confidence that began with a resolve not to underestimate the Sioux.

He understood very well the importance of having battle citations on his record, that merely being a bright and efficient leader of men was not enough. So Patman had requested the transfer from St. Louis to a frontier posting, even if it did mean separation from his beloved fiancée, onto whose finger he had slipped a ring the night before departing. He wondered how she would adapt to this life. Officers' wives—everyone's wives—seemed to age poorly on the frontier. Even Scheffner's young wife, the belle of Fort Larkin, some thirty or so years younger than the colonel, was beginning to look older than her twenty-five. Of course Annabelle Scheffner had problems other than the hard weather and grainy life of the frontier to contend with. General Englund fancied her.

General Englund more than fancied Annabelle Scheffner, that enchanting two-year bride of Colonel Joshua Scheffner, who more than doubled her in years and who compounded the disparity by what seemed a natural lack in vigor. It was as if the lifelong bachelor had made up his mind early in life to marry and then had allowed the decision to petrify, only to see it thaw itself out and carry forward as if time had not passed.

Not every man was a candidate for cuckoldry (and in that truism lay a deception it could be fatal to disregard, Patman thought), but if ever one was it was Scheffner, brave in war, befuddled in peace, who, like his brother officers, followed Alfred Englund with a fidelity that was itself a study in men not so much loyal or devoted as dominated and bewitched. A man so unquestioningly in thrall had already compromised so much of himself that all the rest was vulnerable. It had been a different Scheffner who led his columns of infantry at Antietam and Cemetery Hill and through the tangled nightmare of the Wilderness, a man unafraid to come within sparking distance of enemy bayonets. Not a man to trifle with? His commander knew better. His commander seemed to feel (and this was Patman's guesswork) that a man who was the epitome of physical courage had to have flaws elsewhere, one of them perhaps an overcooked regard for authority that was actually intimidation, more specifically the authority which he had followed in war and peace for more than a dozen years.

Scheffner had simply let it happen, step by step, as if waiting for an official order that he needed before interceding on his own behalf. In the beginning he didn't see it, then wouldn't see it, then saw it but refused to believe it, while blindness, rationale, doubt, and finally bewildered acceptance simply piled up and crisscrossed and left him with no avenue of escape or action. That Englund was suave and skilled at this there was no doubt; after all, the affair had begun while the general's own wife and daughter were still in residence at the fort. But Mrs. Englund was frail and vague and hopelessly Bible-driven, and Patman wondered if she was even capable of noticing her husband's increasingly overt demonstrations of attention to Mrs. Scheffner at the dances and parties organized for the officers and their wives, or if she noticed whether she fully understood what was happening. And the daughter was so dazzled by the father that Patman believed that Miss Englund would have fired a bullet even into any dream that dared insinuate against her father.

The affair began not long after Patman's arrival at Fort Larkin the previous summer, and the bemused newcomer wondered what the other officers thought. But it was never referred to, not even obliquely, which Patman soon learned was not necessarily discretion but part of the circumspection with which they regarded their commanding officer. Patman believed that the illicit couplings took place in the general's office late at night, when the commander made it known he would be there with orders not to be disturbed, and that Mrs. Scheffner simply went there as bidden, after only God knew what kind of conversation with her husband. Patman believed that he had read enough books and listened to enough tales to know that a man who could galvanize and lead brave men through shot and shell wasn't necessarily able to command the will of a single woman, especially one who had spotted just that flaw in him. So Scheffner knifed his own pride and sealed his lips over the matter rather than engage in a battle he could not win and indeed had already lost. A man whose mind naturally turned to tactics, he seemed to feel that in this campaign a muted defensive position was wisest, that he would dig in and wait for attrition to do its work.

When the ferocious Plains winter came and shut down life on the surrounding prairie and sealed the fort in upon itself, it seemed that Scheffner's strategy had worked, at least as far as Patman could tell. General Englund and his family took their evenings alone together (with endless discussions about the Bible, according to an orderly), while the other officers and their wives sat together, the men smoking cigars and sipping whisky and weaving through amiable conversations, the women sitting nearby with knitting or books, Annabelle Scheffner most frequently in amicable conversation with Miss Englund, nearest to her in age.

It was during these evenings that Patman was most able to gauge the character and personality of Mrs. Scheffner. His conclusion was that this was no wallflower the colonel had plucked on a visit East and brought back with him to Fort Larkin. Annabelle was a strikingly handsome woman, with lustrous brown hair that she wore pulled severely back, setting off a strong-featured face highlighted by a pair of dark eyes that always appeared to be in wry appraisal when they alit upon you. She referred occasionally to a hard life on an eastern Pennsylvania farm, implying that Scheffner—who had family in that area—had rescued her from an unappealing future. Whimsically, Patman equated her presence here with that of many of the enlisted men in the barracks: joining the army to escape from some disagreeable alternative, in the case of the men a variety of causes ranging from woman trouble, problems with the law, unemployment, boredom, a calendar of bleak tomorrows, a search for adventure. Whatever spirit she had brought with her to Fort Larkin, Scheffner had not been able to rouse or anyway to sustain. But Alfred Englund had done both. Compared to Englund and his vigorously self-ordained missions, Scheffner was a monotonous man, ominously irrelevant. No doubt Scheffner had somewhere along the way painted a portrait of his commander, replete with the tale of the sword that had been invested by the heavens, and by the time she arrived Annabelle was already beguiled and halfway to Englund's bed, whetted by tales of the general's indestructibility, with the further impression that that which was indestructible had also to be irresistible.

The will of Englund had in one way or another broken them all: Bruckner, Scheffner, Fordyce, Josephson; Scheffner to the extent that the wife, too, had been engulfed. And yourself? Patman asked. No, not yet. But he'll try. I only hope I know it when he does.

The winter passed and the affair began again. Patman knew it from Scheffner's face. And knew it further when it was announced the general was returning wife and daughter to Washington for a prolonged stay.

PART TWO

AT
FORT
LARKIN

CHAPTER 8

ARRIVAL

They've been watching us for miles now, Maynard thought as he and his small party approached the fort. The modest dust cloud kicked up by the paymaster's wagon, the three supply wagons, the eight-trooper escort, and Maynard himself upon the horse lent to him at Fort Hale would have been seen by now by any keen-eyed officer of the day scanning with field glasses. The dust rose and hung over their back trail as if too inert to dissipate or resettle, becoming a sort of midair foliage that seemed appropriate for this blazing heat and this long trail through nowhere. The relentlessly unchanging landscape no doubt made a few puffs of dust in the distance an event of compelling interest for the men of Fort Larkin. A fort manned by just two companies of infantry and a small squadron of cavalry was almost by definition a place generally bypassed by history's greater imprints.

"You can just begin to see her now, Captain," the lieutenant in command of the escort said, riding abreast of Maynard and pointing his finger out into the shimmering heat.

Rocking monotonously in his saddle, Maynard could as

yet see nothing resembling a fort. The trail dipped and rolled its way through a wide tract of short, tufted buffalo grass, some of it permanently crushed by the impact of innumerable passages.

"You must have really ground your heel on the wrong toe to be sent out here," the lieutenant said. He was wearing a yellow campaign hat with the brim pinned up, and had a blue bandanna knotted around his throat. He sat his horse comfortably, reins loose in his fingers.

"Why?" Maynard asked incuriously. "What's wrong with this post?"

"Have a look about," the lieutenant said, extending his arm upon the air, as if this gesture were making the landscape appear. "Nearest settlement is maybe fifty miles and that's not much more than a few groggeries, a brothel, and a lot of prospectors in log cabins who have more faith than is good for them. Summer feels like the bad side of hell and winter freezes your asshole shut."

"It's that way in a lot of places," Maynard said. He could afford to be cavalier about it, he thought, since he knew he wasn't going to be there for very long.

"All they do out there," the lieutenant went on, "is drill and go on misery details. The sutler has the worst-stocked shelves you ever saw and the laundresses are ugly as sin."

"I suppose it's got its function."

"Less and less, now that they're driving the Indians up north. The 'hostiles,' " the lieutenant said, mocking the government euphemism. "It was established a few years ago," he said, "when the gold craze started. The government tried to keep the prospectors out because of the treaties, but how in hell are you going to keep people out of a country where gold is being dug? So in came the army. The Good Old Army. Right, Captain?"

"Underpaid, underappreciated, and overworked," Maynard said, winking at the lieutenant.

"So the next thing you know we're out here building forts and protecting the prospectors and the settlers and the drunks and the whores, which only meant more and more of them coming out . . ."

As the trail rose with a slight swelling of the ground the lieutenant pointed ahead.

"Now you can see it, can't you?" he said.

Yes, now Maynard could, though it was a fort only because he knew there was one out there. Gradually, however, he began to be able to distinguish the small buildings, for the moment little more than smudges in the distance. Depending on your perspective, they looked either broodingly mad or nobly heroic out there on the Dakota prairie, with no visible reason for their existence in this empty land that didn't even look abandoned but rather never discovered, a piece of Creation-day labor that had been forgotten.

"Some of the boys have been stationed there for two, three years," the lieutenant said. "Larkin has its share of deserters. Between being sick of the station and dreaming about all that gold in the Black Hills, they light out now and then. Probably a lot of them end up reenlisting in the Montana Territory. You know how it is, Captain," the lieutenant said with a sly laugh. "A pea-green recruit walks in knowing the manual of arms and close-order drills. Now, I don't hold with deserters, but to look at it honestly, you can just about read the mind of a man who wants to get away from Larkin."

"I've seen worse places," Maynard said.

"If that's so, then I'm glad this is the first time we've traveled together," the lieutenant said with a laugh. "And on top of all that, this post has got its own special story. I presume you've heard of the murder?"

"What murder is that, Lieutenant?"

The paymaster's wagon began moving just a bit more quickly now, the double span of horses sensing journey's end and anxious to get on with it. The array of small, low buildings was no longer so distant, the structures beginning to stand out from each other. Maynard could see the flagpole rising from the parade ground, or at least he knew it was there because he could see the colors hanging limply in the hot windless air as if they had nodded off.

"The commanding officer was murdered a few months ago," the lieutenant said. "It was in May, just before our last trip out. General Englund. Very well-known officer. Somebody put a knife in him. Dirty business."

"Why was he killed?"

"Well, they won't know that until they make an arrest. It's a case of *who* coming before *why*."

"So they haven't caught him yet."

"Not so far as I know," the lieutenant said. "Hell of a thing, with all the Sioux and Cheyenne in the Territory, to be killed by one of your own."

"It couldn't have been renegades, then?"

"Unlikely. There were sentries posted. I understand the drill is very correct at Larkin. You can't let it get slack in a place like that, otherwise the whole thing goes to hell. So maybe it was an enlisted man gone lunatic from the boredom. But I don't think so. I think it was an officer. Probably a senior officer."

"Why do you think that?" Maynard asked.

"Well," the lieutenant said, "the army's a great place for nursing grudges, isn't it?"

They reached Fort Larkin just before sunset, riding in leisurely, giving Maynard time to form deliberate first impressions. Larkin was not a regimental headquarters and thus not a major station; with its two companies of infantry and modest-sized squadron of cavalry, the fort accommodated around two hundred men, not including the civilians in the sutler's store, the laundresses, and the for-hire scouts that came and went.

"Fort" was a misnomer now for the outposts that were like signets of invasion and occupation throughout the Territories, for they were neither walled nor fortified, bearing no resemblance to what had truly been forts during the colonial wars and the Revolutionary War and throughout the early decades of westward expansion. Typical of Western outposts built after the Civil War, Fort Larkin had no outer wall, no log stockade, and no sentry platform as defense against direct assault. Maynard had once heard a general at the War Department say that protection based on vigilance rather than reliance upon a wall made a man a better soldier. And so they were enclaves, clusters of crude, functional, minimal-standard buildings raised (by the hands of the soldiers themselves) on the prairies, with as much open ground around as was necessary to remove the threat of surprise attack, and yet not too far from timber and near water; built to protect railroad tracks and telegraph lines and emigrant trails and to defend and reassure the settlements that were beginning to populate the vastness of half a continent, a population that ironically would soon doom the forts to obsolescence.

"Sounds like they're expecting you, Captain," the lieutenant said facetiously as drums and bugles began announcing the half-hour signal for dress parade. The martial music sounded incongruous in this lonely place, under this endless sky that was reddening and empurpling with end of day. Men had gone fervently to war under the throb of that music, when the bugles seemed to pounce and the drums to roar; but out here, upon an unwanted and uninvaded prairie, it echoed empty and intrusive, almost satiric.

As the lieutenant and the escorts moved on with the wagons, Maynard paused at the north end of the parade ground and stared at Fort Larkin. The parade ground was a long, rectangular tract formed by two rows of rather indifferently constructed buildings that had almost a professional look of the temporal to them: built not to last by men who were themselves in transitory service. On one side was a lineup of half a dozen detached buildings with raised front porches and curtained windows that showed a bit more care and concern taken with their log construction than the rest. In every fort Maynard had ever seen, the officers' quarters were immediately evident. A gap of about thirty feet separated the last officers' residence from the commanding officer's headquarters, a flat-roofed building constructed of logs chinked with a mix of mud, lime, and sand. Adjacent were the rough-hewn buildings of the company quartermaster and the commissary. Facing these on the other side of the parade ground were the guardhouse, workshops, sutler's store (where outstanding bills would be settled now the paymaster's wagon had arrived), bakery, and infirmary. At either end were company barracks and mess hall, while further off were the corral, laundry, and blacksmith. The stables and wagon sheds were located some distance behind officers' row.

Several fatigue details were being marched back to their barracks as Maynard dismounted in front of the headquarters building. He handed the reins of his horse to one of the men of the escort that had accompanied him, who then led the horse off to the stables. Maynard looked down at himself, then beat the dust from his uniform with the palms of his hands, standing for a moment amid the puffing clouds of prairie dust. The burning heat was fading with the setting sun, and the first shy coolness of approaching evening could be felt.

He mounted the steps of the headquarters building and entered. A corporal sitting at a desk in the outer office immediately rose and snapped to attention. Maynard identified himself and asked if Colonel Bruckner was available.

The corporal turned on his heels and knocked on the door behind him, then entered and announced the arrival. Maynard heard a voice asking that he be sent through.

Colonel Bruckner was just rising to his feet and extending a hand of welcome as Maynard entered. Maynard saluted, then removed his forage cap and came forward and accepted the handshake. Bruckner motioned him to a round-backed, wide-seated black chair, then resumed his own seat behind the desk.

A plain, unpatterned carpet covered the office floor, its fringe not quite reaching the wall in any direction. The regimental colors hung on the wall, along with several maps of diminishing scale: the United States, the Montana and Dakota Territories, and the Dakota Territory. There was also a framed portrait of an officer Maynard recognized as General Englund. Probably taken in Mathew Brady's Washington studio, it showed a stern-faced Englund in full dress, replete with epaulets, sash, and sword, with a Napoleonic hat grandly on his head. It was a costume Maynard could easily imagine being worn by the man sitting before him. Bruckner was tall and splendidly proportioned. His beardless, aristocratically handsome and studiously serious face was crowned by a full head of wavy gray hair that appeared to have been minutely fussed at with comb and brush.

Bruckner's war record (which Maynard had familiarized himself with, as he had done with all of the senior officers at Fort Larkin) was impeccable. He had formed a volunteer regiment in his native Massachusetts soon after Sumter, been given a captaincy, and later served under Englund throughout most of the Army of the Potomac's major engagements, being several times cited for bravery and resourcefulness. Though not a professional soldier (he had been a schoolteacher before the war), Bruckner had opted to remain in the army. When Maynard had been studying the regimental records before leaving Washington, someone in the War Department had said of Bruckner, "He looks better in a uniform than anybody in the army." And General

Northwood, in a rare moment of candor, had remarked of Bruckner, "He stayed in because he likes to command. When you see him you'll know what I mean." And now Maynard saw him and now he understood: Bruckner, the uniform, and its authority seemed one of nature's trinities.

"Tedious journey," Bruckner said.

"Quite," Maynard said. Though he was bone weary from the trip, his mind had put itself to work the moment he stepped into the office and saw the picture of General Englund and stood where the general had been murdered last May during the silent hours of the night. There was but the single entrance to the building, with a row of rather small windows high on one wall. There was only one way in and out of this office, and Maynard had just taken it.

Maynard felt himself undergoing a rather frank and undisguised scrutiny, which he understood perfectly. Bruckner knew that whatever opinions and judgment the army had of the matter and of his own conduct regarding it would be somewhere reflected in Maynard's attitude. Unquestionably the army was not without some criticism of his management of the affair—Maynard would not be there otherwise—but to what depth that dissatisfaction went Bruckner was not sure. (Maynard could detect shades of resentment in the colonel's consummately maintained poise.) Finally, confronted by Maynard's blandly unchanging and unrevealing face, the colonel felt constrained to say, "We welcome you, of course, Captain Maynard. But I hope your presence is not too harsh an indictment of the efforts we put into trying to resolve the matter."

"I was merely sent out to be of some assistance, Colonel."

"A fresh perspective."

"Approximately that."

"I assure you we made every effort humanly possible to discover the identity of the assassin."

"There has never been any question of that, sir."

"Remember, Captain," Bruckner said, raising a lecturing finger, "along with the tragedy of General Englund's loss, this is a stain on the entire regiment. And remember, too, what happened puts every man at this post under a cloud. In the name of fairness, it is imperative that that cloud be lifted."

"I understand the general's death was a great personal loss for you," Maynard said.

Maynard thought he saw just the slightest fissure in Bruckner's flawless comportment as the colonel stirred uneasily in his chair for a moment.

"Yes," he said. "It was. We had served together for nearly fifteen years, through good times and bad. We had a friendship that was based on mutual respect."

Maynard reached into his pocket and produced the letter he had been instructed by General Northwood to deliver. Bruckner opened it and read it, his eyebrows rising slightly and his underlip thrusting for a moment as he did. He put the letter down.

"A most impressive letter of deputation," he said. " 'With the authority of President Grant and General Sherman,' etcetera, and signed by General Northwood. We are to cooperate with you completely, and of course we shall."

"I'll try to be as inconspicuous and unintrusive as possible," Maynard said.

"You'll do what you must, conspicuously or otherwise. And of course you know that this letter dissolves any obstacles of rank for you as you go about exercising your commission. I'll see to it that my officers understand that. We all want this settled as quickly as possible."

"All but one," Maynard said with a smile.

"Ah yes, all but one."

"In your report, Colonel, which I read with great care, you stressed the activities on the night of the murders only

of yourself and the officers named Scheffner, Josephson, Patman, and Fordyce. What am I to conclude from that?"

Bruckner sighed. "Yes," he said. "It's very delicate. But it's
what our Committee of Inquiry finally pared it down to."

"Committee of Inquiry?"

"It consisted of the four officers you mentioned and myself.
It got very uncomfortable at times, but I saw to it that we
forged ahead as conscientiously and objectively as possible.
We were able to eliminate from suspicion all enlisted men and
noncommissioned officers because of bed checks taken at
just about the estimated time of the murders. Everyone else
was accounted for: the sutler and his family were abed, as
were the laundresses, while the surgeon and his steward
were in the infirmary seeing to the sick. As far as our other
commissioned officers are concerned—four lieutenants—
one was in the infirmary, two had retired early with their
wives, and the other was conducting a two-day patrol some
miles south of the fort, with horse. Also, two captains had
been reassigned to Fort Lincoln before the tragedy."

"And your senior officers?"

"Well, as you know from my report, we had all gathered
with General Englund right here in this office. When we departed we all heard the general say he was going to remain
here for a while—and there was no adjutant on duty, which
was apparent to all. Thus we all left together, ostensibly to
quarters, but outside of myself, none can positively establish
that that is exactly what he did."

"Yes," Maynard said, "I understand that from the report."

"Mrs. Bruckner was there when I returned."

"Asleep?"

"Yes. But she swore at the inquiry that she heard me
come in."

"Did she note the time?"

"She had no reason to."

"Did you have any conversation with her?"

"No."

"Excuse me for asking these questions, Colonel."

"Captain, this is why you're here," Bruckner said evenly, a subtle reprimand in his tone. "If you're not decisive in your posture you'll get nowhere. Just remember by what authority you're here."

"Thank you, sir, I will," Maynard said. "Now, the wives of Majors Fordyce and Josephson were back East?"

"Correct."

"And Major Patman is a bachelor?"

"Yes."

"And Colonel Scheffner and his wife, as I understand it, were occupying separate rooms in their quarters as a result of some domestic unhappiness."

"That is correct."

"So there was no corroboration of arrival at or remaining in quarters for any of them, united with the fact that they all knew the general would be working late and that there was no adjutant on duty."

"Ergo the shadow of suspicion. But I must emphasize, Captain, that each man participated in the inquiry with complete thoroughness and diligence, and any information that we compiled was cross-checked by us all. What was most impressively done was the elimination of possible suspects."

"But according to your conclusions, one of your committee members had something to hide."

"Not entirely," Bruckner said, raising one finger. "There is one other, and, if I might add, the most likely of all."

"Duchard."

"If flight is an indication of guilt, then he is our man. Not only was he the last person known to have seen General Englund alive, but he flew out of here soon after the discovery of the body."

"Did anyone speak to him?"

"No. He left at the height of the commotion."

"Where is he now?"

Bruckner allowed himself an indulgent chuckle.

"If we only knew," he said. "I've had parties searching for him all summer, but he's a wily one. I've heard that he's still somewhere in the Territory. There are towns and settlements scattered around and he was last reported seen in one of them about three weeks ago. We still intend to have him."

"If he was guilty," Maynard said, "why would he remain in the Territory?"

"One report we had indicated he's suffered some sort of injury and may not be able to travel great distances. In any event, his actions militate strongly against him. We've made it plain that he's been accused of nothing, that we simply want to talk to him."

"What sort of man is he?"

"Something of a scoundrel. A product of the frontier. Some years ago he was known to be trading rifles to the Indians for pelts and hides and so on. Then he prospected for gold and came up empty-handed or else lost it all to the gentlemen with the high hats and silk vests. Last year he came in and offered his services as a scout. General Englund took him on on a per diem basis for, say what you will about him, the man knows every rock and gully in this country."

"His work was satisfactory then?"

"I hate to be complimentary about his sort, but it was. General Englund once referred to him as 'the eyes of Fort Larkin.' Duchard is a mix of daring, courage, and villainy."

"His kind are often shrewd," Maynard said thoughtfully. "Why, then, I wonder, would he fly out of here under such circumstances?"

"Answer that question, Captain," Bruckner said, "and I suspect you'll be heading home, back to commendations from . . ." and he finished his sentence by tapping Maynard's letter with the tips of his fingers.

CHAPTER 9

SERGEANT BARRIE

Maynard was assigned a house in officers' row that had been occupied by a young lieutenant, who suddenly found himself "ranked" out of quarters and doubling with another lieutenant. The house was the last in the row and smallest of the officers' quarters. It had two rooms, the bare minimum of battered-around utilitarian furniture, illumination by candlelight, and just the one attempt at providing some comfort—a crude carpet had been made of tied-together corn sacks.

He put his strapped-around straw valise on a bed that was larger than a barracks cot but which didn't appear any more inviting to sleep in, though in his weariness it had a welcoming look. He had no sooner sat down on the edge of it than he heard the crisp arrival of someone, boot heels me-thodically striking each plank step and then two sharp raps on the door. Maynard sighed.

"Come in," he said.

The door swung open and from out of the evening twi-light a sergeant appeared, shut the door behind him, and with ramrod posture saluted. Maynard returned a weary salute and stared cynically at him.

"Sergeant Billy Barrie, sir. Reporting as per ordered."

"Billy?"

"That's what my sweet mum always called me. Sir."

"What does it say on your enlistment sheet?"

"William."

"So how shall I call you, Sergeant?"

"However you please, sir." Standing rigidly at attention, Barrie had still not made eye contact with Maynard, gazing fixedly into the gloomy candlelit interior of the quarters. He stood several inches under six feet, lean and hard as a rail, his generously freckled, fair-complected face burned red from the sun. The earnest expression seemed a bit stagey on a face that nature had designed for whimsy.

"All right, Barrie," Maynard said. "Stand at ease. Better still, have a seat. Under the circumstances, we're going to have a relaxation of military etiquette, but only in private. If there's any breach of it in front of the other men you'll be chin-deep in mule shit. Understand?"

With a quirky smile and nod of the head Barrie indicated he understood, though he was still reluctant to sit and in fact didn't until Maynard again asked him to.

"This looks most irregular, Captain," Barrie said, sitting on the edge of a wooden chair, hands folded at his beltline.

"It is most irregular, Sergeant."

"Suppose somebody walks in?"

"Nobody's going to walk in; not without knocking, anyway. Not even Colonel Bruckner. And if they do, you just sit right there. You don't move your ass unless I tell you to. Do you understand?"

"Oh, you speak very clearly, Captain."

"You're a long-service man, aren't you?"

"Sixteen years, Captain."

"And you were in the war."

"It got to where it seemed they couldn't have a battle without me being in it. But it's all right, Captain, because once you go through that it makes the rest of life seem like the paradise gardens."

"Even in the Dakota Territory?"

"Anywhere, sir."

"And you keep reenlisting."

"That's right, Captain. Always into this regiment. The officers all know me and that always gives you a bit of margin. I'm duty sergeant of Company B," Barrie said with evident pride. "The first sergeant runs the company, of course, but I run the first sergeant."

"Does he know that?" Maynard asked, concealing his amusement.

Barrie made a face. "Never," he said, shaking his head.

"So you know this garrison as well as anyone. Am I correct?"

"I know my own company, Captain."

"Come on, Barrie. I've walked every road you have, so don't give me any horseshit. If a sergeant of your experience and wit doesn't know something then it's not worth knowing. You're curious and inquisitive but discreet, a man who knows when to seal up and listen, who knows what to say to whom and what not to say to whom. I think you're a man who knows how to get a thousand words back for the expenditure of a half dozen. You're very good at seeing what you're not supposed to, and you see things the way the eagle does as well as the worm. You know how to keep a confidence. You're the repository of every secret, sin, and shame in the garrison. I'll wager that at one time or another you've covered up the infraction of just about every rule in the army book of regulations. I'm being complimentary, Sergeant, not critical."

"I hope so, sir," Barrie said.

"You're the man I want assigned to me."

"But, pardon me, Captain, but how can you know all this on ten minutes' acquaintance?"

Not quite, Maynard thought. But he wasn't going to tell how after receiving this assignment he had requested and studied the service histories of every man at Fort Larkin and finally gleaned from the roster of Company B Sergeant William Patrick Barrie. Sergeant, not first sergeant, after sixteen years, which meant—by Maynard's reckoning—that this was in all likelihood a man who shunned serious responsibilities (always a sign of the gentle rogue), who liked to slide a bit, though never seriously (there were no derelictions on his record; awarded his stripes eleven years ago, he had thus far never lost them, not even for a short time). Maynard knew the type, and was now convinced he had found an exemplar: experienced veteran, efficient though not particularly ambitious, shrewd, dependable, trimming none but the careful corner, a likable scoundrel, trusted and accepted from above and below, a private cynic, and no doubt sentimental.

"You know everything that goes on at this fort, don't you?" Maynard said.

"I do my best to stand aside from things that are outside my concern, sir," Barrie said, staring at Maynard with an expression of unconvincing innocence.

"Then you're telling me that I'm wrong, that I've made a misjudgment."

"Not exactly, sir."

"Are you my man or are you not?"

Barrie hesitated, looking uncomfortable, as if the seat of his chair was turning warm. Maynard could sense the man's thoughts flying, about to settle in decision.

"Well, sir," Barrie said, "it *is* a noncom's obligation to be informed."

Maynard smiled tightly, running a finger across his black hedge of mustache.

"But I'm not a tattle," Barrie said.

"Sergeant, I'm not interested in who's a drunkard, who's a slacker, who's a whoremaster. I don't give a damn who cheats at cards or which laundress has the clap. The company misfits are none of my concern. I'm here on one charge only. Do you know what that is?"

"Yes, sir."

"I thought you would."

"Well," Barrie said, "I'm with you on that, Captain. Don't think there hasn't been a lot of unease among the enlisted men about this. The men don't like the idea of knowing there's a knifer on the grounds. I'm sure that when they sent you out here they said, 'We want the murderer of General Englund.' Well, don't think that we don't as seriously want the man that killed Corporal O'Bannion."

"Well, I want him as seriously as you do. And so do the people who sent me out here."

"Yes, sir."

"How well did you know O'Bannion?"

"I knew him all right. He was a Company B man. He was a good fellow, working through his first enlistment. He was just twenty-three years old, Captain."

"Was he well liked?"

"I never heard a word said against him."

"Was he content?"

"Like the rest of us, sir. He took what came along. He did his share and let it go at that."

"Are you and the men in the ranks satisfied with the investigation that was made?"

"Well," Barrie said, "it didn't come up with answers, did it?"

"Do you believe it was handled as vigorously and impartially as possible?"

"That's not for me to answer, Captain. But I should think it was, considering that a general was murdered."

"Informally, Barrie, what is the thinking in the barracks?"

"We know it wasn't an enlisted man, since bed checks were made at about the time the murders were done."

"And everybody was accounted for."

"To a man."

"What about the noncoms?"

"All accounted for. That should be in the report."

"It was. So what you're saying is that the feeling in the ranks is that it was an officer."

"That's the feeling, Captain," Barrie said, staring at Maynard as if to say, *You want honesty, here's honesty.*

"How did the men feel about General Englund?"

Barrie smiled self-consciously. Then he cleared his throat.

"You know how that goes, Captain," he said. "He didn't take much notice of us, nor we of him. A general is there, and he's not there. There was no particular feelings against him. He seemed fair enough, though if the captain will permit, a bit full of himself."

"Barrie, I want you to speak your mind on this matter at all times. Anything you tell me will be held in confidence. I give you my word."

"As an officer and a gentleman, sir?" Barrie said with a sly look, but the moment he said it he knew he had misspoken, for the assertion of amity that had been evident in Maynard's eyes was replaced instantly by a harder, less redeemable expression.

"Look, Barrie," Maynard said, "don't get *too* clever about this. I may be an officer, but as far as you're concerned, no gentleman. It's none of your business, but I'm not West Point, I'm up from the ranks. I don't believe in a caste system, but that doesn't mean I can't be pretty goddamned miserable to be around. So just remember: I came up from the same hole in the ground that you did."

"Only further."

"Slightly," Maynard said icily.

"You're an ambitious man, Captain."

"Do you find fault with that?"

"No, sir. I think it's commendable. Ambition is always commendable. Except—if I may say so, sir—in the army it can sometimes be a ticklish business."

"Really?"

"An ambitious man sometimes manufactures his opportunities. In the army that can be troublesome."

"Haven't you ever served under an ambitious officer?"

"Probably, sir. Couldn't always tell."

"But with me you can."

Barrie remained still.

"You have to trust your officers, Barrie," Maynard said.

"So we must, Captain. Always."

"And have you always?"

"Sir?"

"Trusted your officers."

"It's part of the faith, sir. If we can't trust our officers, then the water will always be over our heads."

"Is there any officer at this post that you have doubts about?"

"No, sir."

"You trust them all."

"Some more than others," Barrie said quietly.

"That's fair enough."

"I wouldn't want to say more than that, sir."

"Do you trust me, Barrie?"

Barrie seemed to have been holding his breath, and now he expelled it audibly. He took a long, detached moment to make a candid study of Maynard which under other circumstances would have been impertinent.

"I think I do, sir," he said.

"Sergeant, I can't order you to tell me things that you don't want to, that I don't know you know. I can only appeal to your sense of what's right."

"I'll be your man, Captain."

"Then I take you at your word."

"But I assure you, Captain, none of them are magic. My words, I mean. They haven't helped so far."

"How deeply were you interrogated?"

Barrie shrugged. "All they wanted to know was where I was at the time."

"Which was?"

"Heading for my blankets after the bed check. The first vouched for me, and I for him."

"I guess there was no need for them to ask you more," Maynard said.

"Just so, Captain. Can I ask you this, sir: How come they made you pack mule for this job?"

"General Sherman thought I could get it done."

Barrie's eyebrows rose. "General Sherman? Well. Well, Captain. General Sherman. Well."

CHAPTER 10

DINING WITH
A MURDERER

Maynard never thought of himself as being given to melo-
dramatic contemplation. Nevertheless, as he walked
through the mild evening air toward the officers' mess, there
the thought was, sudden and unsummoned, more of an
amusement in his mind than a caution: *You'll probably be
dining with a murderer tonight.* If Duchard was not his
man, then it in all likelihood was someone he was going to
meet and soon be at table with, someone who had thus far
evaded detection, someone very clever and prudent, who
had participated in the inquiry into his own crime and
emerged with good name intact. And this, too: someone
who knew exactly why he, Maynard, was there. Someone
who would be breaking bread with him, being cordial, amiable, while all the time taking the emissary's measure and
calculating every nuance.

The officers' mess was in a small log building next to the
commissary. The dining room was oblong, with a long,

cloth-covered table in the middle. The chairs were high-backed, suggesting an incongruous formality. Two small serving tables stood against one wall, on either side of the kitchen door. The meals were prepared, Maynard was informed, by a soldier of French birth who true to his heritage possessed unusual culinary skills. His venison pâté, made especially this evening for the visitor from Washington, was, Maynard admitted, worthy of the best Eastern restaurants. The rest of the meal, however, consisting of antelope steak and vegetables from the soldiers' garden, was less impressive, as was the overly sweet pudding dessert. The coffee was standard army lung-scraper, though the post-dinner brandy—again in honor of Captain Maynard—was smooth enough to make Maynard long for his evenings in Willard's. The meal was served by a pair of soldier-servants, selected for decorum and discretion, and paid, out of the commanding officer's pocket, five dollars per month apiece for their extra service.

Taking note of the thick linen tablecloth and the sterling silver utensils, Maynard gave high marks to the Bruckners for trying to bring the amenities of civilization to a place where these touches were in short supply, Fort Larkin being a noticeable example of such a place. It was usually the wives who insisted upon and provided the tangible niceties of happier stations. They would follow their husbands from posting to posting, each time packing their belongings in barrels and chests and boxes, rolling the bedding into wrappings of waterproof canvas and moving on, sometimes to a veritable metropolis of a place like Fort Lincoln, other times to Fort Larkin, over which hovered the remoteness of an ocean island.

It was not the most congenial of tables, and Maynard wondered how much of this was due to his own disquieting presence. It was no secret to anyone why he was there. He was both a reminder of what had happened as well as fresh notice that it wasn't over. Generally, new assignees were made to feel welcome, particularly at out-of-the-way posts, but Maynard hardly qualified as an assignee. He was received cordially enough, but during dinner very little of the conversation, superficial at best, was directed toward him. He didn't regard it as a case of incivility so much as a studied attempt to appear insouciant about him. It was as if, under the circumstances, a few innocent gestures might be mistakenly taken up, that no one wanted to be thought unduly ingratiating themselves with him, as though it might somehow be construed as incriminating. Not once were the murders at Fort Larkin alluded to, not once did the name of General Englund cross the table, not once was the purpose of Maynard's presence referred to. It was understandable, he supposed, but given his single-minded concern with the subject its avoidance seemed to create an artificial atmosphere.

Colonel Bruckner presided at the head of the table, where he seemed completely at home. A man of stately bearing, born to lead, officiate, be uniformed, and occupy the head of table. Mrs. Bruckner sat on his right. They appeared an ideally suited couple. She was as aristocratic-looking as he, haughtily attractive, exuding the cool self-discipline and restraint of an officer's wife. If she was punctiliously aware of her station at Fort Larkin, she was also not without warmth and a gentle humor, and it didn't take one long to appreciate that she was her husband's superior in mind and thought (though a superiority most tactfully worn). She had greeted Maynard graciously, asked him about his journey, about friends back in Washington that he might have seen (and was too canny an officer's wife to lift even an eyebrow of disparagement about the crudities of Fort Larkin).

Maynard was content to keep his own conversation at a minimum, for it gave him a chance to study and appraise the others, to allow impressions to form.

The voice least heard was that of Major Philip Fordyce.

While Maynard was aware of being gauged and measured (however furtively) by them all, Fordyce barely took notice of him. Fordyce, who had gone through many of the grand amphitheaters of carnage with Englund, was a stocky, dark-haired man whose large eyes and prominent nose united to form a face vivid with antic character but who struck Maynard as a man filled with the tension of unresolved conflicts. At times he seemed to spiritually vanish from the company, chewing his food abstractedly, eyes staring dully at nothing. When Colonel Bruckner said grace before the meal, those eyes had shut and that head had dropped and with clasped hands Fordyce appeared to become suffused with piety.

On Maynard's right sat Major Edward Josephson, another of Englund's 1861–1865 comrades who had gone on serving with him, who had been breveted a brigadier toward the end of the war. Josephson wore his battles in his tough, shrewd-eyed face, which a broken nose had turned slightly askew. He was bald on top, with patches of gray clinging like ruffled wings to the sides of his oval-shaped head, his cheeks decorated with gray muttonchops. Maynard had a sense of an impatient, choleric, disgruntled man, one who had indeed been aggressive and successful during the war. Maynard recalled reading in the man's file at the War Department that Josephson had been fanatically devoted to his men and in the fiercest engagement could always be found at the head of his columns of infantry. Josephson's interest in him had seemed limited to knowing what service Maynard had seen since the end of the war. When Maynard mentioned the Southern Plains and the Kiowas, Josephson nodded and granted the Kiowas their fighting capabilities. The Sioux, however, he maintained, were more formidable in combat, responding better to leadership, with that leadership being extremely sound tactically. "You ought to know that," Josephson said. "Just in case."

The most cheerless man at the table was Lieutenant Colonel Joshua Scheffner. He was a thin, sunken-chested, melancholic-looking man with piercing dark eyes, whose drooping black mustache seemed to accentuate his sallow cheeks. A black forelock hung over his forehead. Sitting across the table from him, Maynard occasionally looked up to find himself being appraised by Scheffner's wryly amused eyes. *This bastard is trying to guess what I'm thinking*, Maynard thought as he tried to deflect Scheffner with a polite smile. Maynard knew all about Joshua Scheffner. A true hero of the republic. Wounded four times, at Malvern Hill, Chancellorsville, twice at Gettysburg, where he had stormed about rallying his men, leg torn open by a minié ball, using a rifle as a crutch. Probably still carrying a bit of rebel shot in that boneless body. An unlikely survivor.

On Maynard's left sat Annabelle Scheffner, a most implausible wife for the colonel. Scheffner had watched Maynard's face carefully when introducing her, as if waiting for some trace of reaction (Maynard hoped he had shown none when what might normally have been expected to be the word *daughter* was pronounced as *wife*). Mrs. Scheffner was, by Maynard's reckoning, a good twenty-five years younger than her husband, and where the colonel was physically withered, she was at womanhood's full bloom, and Maynard felt he was halfway toward understanding their separate bedrooms. Her dark brown hair was combed back from a strong, handsome face that was highlighted by smooth-planed cheeks, sensually lit brown eyes, and a bright, mischievously suggestive smile. She wore a black dress buttoned to the throat and around her shoulders a red shawl that hung down and draped a full, swelling bosom. Maynard had never seen a senior officer's wife quite like this one. She resembled in sensuality the second wives of certain eminent Washingtonians, or, less gallantly (he admitted guiltily), the proprietress of one of the tonier Washington brothels he occasionally visited. Maynard felt involuntary curiosity about the domestic disharmony Colonel Bruckner had alluded to. No doubt a casual question to Sergeant Barrie would satisfy it.

If there was one member of the dining party with whom Maynard felt some slight kinship it was Major Bryan Patman. Closest to Maynard in age, Patman had a pleasant, clean-shaven, roundish, almost cherubic face that seemed designed for almost anything other than commanding men in battle, particularly such unfixed and unorthodox battle as must be waged with Plains Indians. By his record, Patman had, in fact, not yet commanded in battle. He seemed a likable character, amiable, intelligent, alert to the foibles and vagaries of personality around him. He absorbed the conversation, put in his word—usually a lighthearted contribution—and then resumed what Maynard felt was a comfortably self-possessed, slightly condescending posture. The new breed of officer, Maynard thought; unscorched, untortured by the great war, heart fresh, soul still intact. A new wisdom perhaps; a man more inclined to parley and strive for agreement than to rush to arms.

As the evening wore on, however, Maynard began inexorably to feel less kinship with Patman and more with the others. Not the man's fault, Maynard reasoned, but Patman had a face healthy with serenely lived years, with none of the carven ruins and bruises inflicted by exposure to battlefield butchery. In the faces around the table were pomposity, brooding abstraction, hardness, grimness. The faces of men who had been to the weather. And my own? Maynard asked himself. What did others see in it? Certainly not the lines nor the pronouncements originally intended by nature. On the one hand, Patman was to be envied; and yet, Maynard thought, would I give up what I know for the sake of looking as I was meant?

At the conclusion of dinner another of civilization's rituals was observed: the ladies retired and the men remained at the table for the lighting of cigars and the pouring of brandy. It was then, finally, that Maynard became the focal point. What, Colonel Bruckner wanted to know, was the reaction back East to the Custer disaster?

Maynard threw back his head and exhaled a stream of cigar smoke up toward the log ceiling.

"Disbelief, initially," he said. "Naturally, no one believed such a calamity was possible, particularly to a command led by George Custer."

Josephson laughed sardonically.

"If there was one command in the United States Cavalry vulnerable to being annihilated by a band of Indians," he said, "it was Custer's. No other officer displayed a greater distance between common sense and foolhardy courage. And that's not hindsight," he added, scowling at Bruckner, as if expecting some interjection.

"We all knew Custer, Edward," Bruckner said placatingly.

"What happened to the disbelief when the news came in?" Scheffner asked. He had a low, insinuating voice, one that implied it already knew the answer to whatever question it was asking.

"It remained disbelief for a while," Maynard said, "but of a different character. It wasn't any longer 'It can't be true,' but became 'I can't see how it could have happened.' Then it became a matter of not wanting to believe it. That's when it was still just a newspaper story; but then some confidential reports from General Terry came in. It was true all right. I was at the Continental Hotel in Philadelphia at the time, with General Northwood and General Sheridan and a large contingent of officers to attend the Centennial celebration. The reports were forwarded to General Sheridan there."

"That must have put a damper on things," Scheffner said.

"It certainly did," Maynard said.

"We had worse tragedies during the war," Bruckner said, "but none so incomprehensible."

"Absolutely, Colonel," Maynard said. "That's what made it so shocking."

"Who are they scapegoating for it?" Josephson asked.

Maynard smiled cynically around his clenched cigar, saying nothing.

"I'm serious," Josephson said.

"I know you are, Major," Maynard said.

"It won't be Custer," Scheffner said. "I assure you."

"Since he's already been canonized," Fordyce said tonelessly, "it would be blasphemy."

"General Custer," Bruckner said from his place at the head of the table, "was a most able officer."

"He was that," Josephson said, adding after a meaningful pause, "in the Shenandoah Valley. In 1864. Against a traditional foe. But he didn't know how to fight Indians."

"How *do* you fight Indians, Edward?" Scheffner asked.

"I'll tell you how not to," Josephson said. "By not regarding them as mindless savages. I don't give one drop of spit for the Indian as a human being; but as an opponent in the field, he's got my total respect."

"Never underestimate a foe," Fordyce said to no one in particular, as if talking to himself. "Goliath was the first to learn that."

"I understand that enlistments multiplied after news of the Little Big Horn spread through the country," Maynard said.

"Dead heroes are potent symbols," Bruckner said. "Much more so than the living."

"Yes," Patman said, making one of his few utterances. "There's nothing like a massacre to make the army seem a desirable place to be."

Bruckner, apparently not unaccustomed to irreverencies from Patman, smiled indulgently.

"Captain Maynard," Bruckner said, "based on what you

heard in the corridors of the War Department, would you not agree that their mighty victory over Custer and the Seventh Cavalry was actually a fatally self-inflicted wound for the Sioux and their allies?"

"I can assure you, Colonel," Maynard said, "that the determination to settle with the Sioux once and for all is now irrevocable."

"All well and good," Josephson said. "But while the campaign is going on we're sitting here. They're kicking Sitting Bull all the way up to Canada. And we're sitting here."

"Where nothing ever happens," Scheffner said.

An odd thing to say, Maynard thought.

He saw them all again in his thoughts later that night, while lying in bed. The vast stillness outside was broken only by the on-the-hour voices of the sentries reporting as they called out their post numbers and the time, voices that sounded lone and remote, as if they had come floating in with a wind that had eddied its way through the Black Hills and brushed low over the buffalo grass.

Find out what happened, General Northwood had ordered. *Something that heinous cannot be covered. It must finally show itself.* But what in God's name was he supposed to be looking for? These were honorable, hard-service officers in the United States Army. Those faces had seen too much of life's every extreme aspect to betray by glance or gesture; too much for him to be able to discern a line of guilt in any of them (Patman excepted, whose amiable face had thus far recorded nothing). Any manifestation of guilt would by now have worn into the stolid remorse common to any commander with years of warfare behind him.

And then he curled the fingers of one hand very softly into his palm. He could still feel the touch of her small black-gloved hand against his; like some wondrous and ethereal brush stroke it had marked him. Her gesture of trust and hope. He tried to imagine Miss Englund in this place, this Fort Larkin. He tried to see her sitting at that table with that collection of leather-souled officers. Unquestionably, as the daughter of General Englund, she had borne herself with grace. No doubt she had helped organize entertainments during the long, numbing months of prairie winter, poured tea at the ladies' socials, led the way to picnics during the better weather, and by kerosene lamps in the evenings read books and written letters. Always poised and uncomplaining.

No woman since the young and untamed Sarah Wilman had made it through the barriers of his heart as this one had. Was he idealizing her? Perhaps. But nothing wrong in that. Every man's woman should be unique to him, a special pearl cast upon a singular shore.

Dear Miss Englund. He began the letter in his mind, seeing her holding it in her hand, his imagination painting a gentle portrait. *I have arrived at Fort Larkin and begun my inquiry. It is a vexing matter, but as I promised, I shall do my utmost to bring to satisfactory conclusion that which has been so troubling to you.* His mind began fading in and out of sleep, of slowly encroaching dream, the measured words beginning to float in fragments. *As I promised Trust Your faith in me . . .*

CHAPTER 11

TURNING BACK
THE CLOCK

"Pardon the question, Captain, but just how does a man go about finding a murderer?"

Sergeant Barrie had been waiting outside the officers' mess hall for Maynard to emerge after breakfast. Maynard squinted at him in the bright morning sunlight. The captain's blue shirt was open at the throat and his trousers were tucked into his boots. He was wearing a gray slouch hat, the floppy brim shading his face.

"If it's not an impertinent question," Barrie added.

It was 7:30 A.M. and small squads were being lined up on the parade ground for fatigue duty. One detail was assigned to repair work on the guardhouse, another to begin construction of a new commissary. Maynard smiled as he watched the first sergeant reading the orders. The faces of the men were impassive, but Maynard well knew the grumbling thoughts going on behind them: *I've gotten more damned familiar with the pick and shovel than I have with the rifle*. And: *This isn't the army, it's a damned government workhouse.*

He watched them turn and march off, little puffs of dust rising from under their feet. Then he turned back to Barrie.

"It's very simple, Sergeant," he said. "You ask a lot of questions. You let an intelligent man think you're a fool, and you make a fool think you know a hell of a lot more than you really do."

"And how do you separate 'em—the fools and the others?"

"Well, that's when you start operating at a completely different level. Intelligent people can sometimes be very foolish, and fools can sometimes be extremely cunning. You just have to be ready to catch them at it."

"That sounds complicated, Captain."

"And then you get to another level: you want them to get to the point where they think they know what you're thinking."

"If it comes to that," Barrie said as they began walking across the parade ground, "then *you* know what *they're* thinking."

"Correct."

"It sounds like a big fandango to me. What happens if you come up against somebody who's more intelligent than you when you're being intelligent and a bigger fool than you're trying to be?"

"Then I've been foxed. But I don't intend to be. I didn't come all the way out here for that."

"No, sir. It sounds very interesting, all this about what you're thinking and what the other fellow is thinking. Have you put it to work before? Have you ever tried it?"

Maynard smiled and glanced at Barrie.

"Never," he said.

"I see, sir," Barrie said, his voice flat and noncommittal.

"What we're going to do today, Sergeant," Maynard said, "is turn back the clock."

"To that night."

"Yes."

"Isn't it all in the report?"

"Maybe yes and maybe no."

At the south end of the fort, past the bakery and the infirmary, was the shack where the scouts lived, most recently occupied by Rennay Duchard (he had Anglicized the spelling of his first name) and now empty. Even among the crudely erected buildings of Fort Larkin, this one stood out. Put together with logs and planks of unsawed lumber, the place looked possessed of a despairing longing to collapse. One small window was built in next to a door, which, without a sill, scraped along the ground as it was dragged open.

"There's no scout in service now?" Maynard asked as Barrie pulled back the door.

"Not since Duchard took his leave, Captain."

The shack—it was closer to a shed—was built so low that Maynard had to bow his head slightly when he walked in. The inside was little more than eight feet by ten. The floorboards were irregular in length, some not quite making it from wall to wall. An army cot with a straw-filled bedsack and a large yellow footlocker were the only pieces of furniture in the single room. The footlocker was empty. The air in the place was stale.

"Dismal," Maynard said, looking around.

"Better than sleeping under the stars," Barrie said, "which is what they do most of the time."

"I think I'd rather take my chances with the stars."

"Duchard was never here that much. If he was working for us, then he'd be out in the open someplace. Otherwise, he wasn't one of those scouts that like to hang around a fort."

"Where would he go?" Maynard asked, sitting down on the cot.

"You know how those birds are, Captain," Barrie said.

"God knows where he went and what he did when he wasn't taking army pay. If I knew old Rennay though, he was probably poking around the Black Hills looking for gold."

"That was kind of hazardous, wasn't it, given the way the Sioux regard those mountains?"

"He knew his way about. Anyway, Duchard wasn't a man who scared easy. You've known scouts, Captain. They either expect to die any second or to live forever. That's what makes them take their chances."

"When General Englund needed him, how did he make contact?"

"We'd send out word to the towns and settlements around and with whoever passed through. Next thing you knew, here's Duchard riding into the post."

"Where do you think he is now?"

"No idea, Captain."

"He must know we want to question him. So he's probably lit out of the Territory. Wouldn't you say?"

Barrie screwed up the corner of one eye for a moment.

"Not necessarily," he said. "I'm sure he's still got gold on his brain. You know how that sort gets. And anyway, I heard he was in a brawl of some makings and got himself shot or something and isn't up to heavy travel."

"How long ago did you hear that?"

"A few months maybe. People stop by the fort and they talk. We hear things."

"You know him well?"

"Duchard? How well do you ever get to know them, Captain? Men who prefer to live like prairie dogs."

"Try harder, Sergeant."

Barrie sighed, then shifted his weight from one leg to the other.

"We got on," he said. "I did him a favor once. It was the dead of winter and he was here, sleeping in this place, and I got the first to let him bunk in the barracks for a while. Duchard appreciated it."

"That was good of you."

Barrie shrugged. "I told the first, either we let him into the barracks or else we'll be using him as a table for the rest of the winter."

"So you had something of a relationship with him."

"We talked now and then."

The morning sunshine showed as a rectangle of light through the doorway. A wagon carrying several barrels of water rolled past outside, heading for the Company B barracks.

"What kind of man is he?" Maynard asked.

Barrie hesitated. The entering sunlight reached halfway up his chest, leaving the rest of him in shadow. Maynard, sitting on the cot, the sun on his face, was looking up at him.

"Sergeant," Maynard said, "make up your mind. Either I get your complete, truthful cooperation or else you can go and join one of those fatigue details."

"Yes, sir. Well, a hard man to know. Captain, you're familiar with scouts. Was there ever one you could say you really knew? They tend to keep everything inside. I've never known one that didn't, even those who were regular army. The ones that are for hire are even worse. We've all got our secrets, right, Captain? But scouts are alone too much, and I say it isn't the life that seals them up, it's what drove them to it. Nobody starts off in life wanting to be a scout."

"Get to it, Sergeant."

"Yes, sir. That was Duchard. That's how he was. Never said much, but that wasn't it—it was how he kept silent. Think of quiet men, Captain. Some are bashful, some just don't have anything to say, and some just let it seep out of them like a warning. They're giving you a signal, like a lighthouse telling you there's peril nearby. You get a feeling about a man, and it was my feeling about Duchard—al-

though we got on fine enough—that you didn't trifle with
him. If he didn't feel like talking, you gave him distance. It
was the way he was set, Captain."

"He was a hard man."

"Very."

"Dangerous?"

Barrie sighed. He hesitated again. This time Maynard
waited.

Barrie said, "Dangerous the way gunpowder is if you
light a match too close to it."

"Anybody ever light that match?"

"Not to my knowing."

"He'd traded guns to the Indians some years ago."

"We heard that. I don't say he was popular with some of
the men, but that wouldn't bother him."

"Was he a killer?"

"Ah, Captain, now that's unfair."

"You've described a man who might well have such a history."

"I can only give you an opinion, Captain, and I think
what you need are facts."

"Then the fact is you liked him."

"He gave me no cause for otherwise."

"That's fair enough."

"Can I give you another opinion, Captain?"

"Keep right on talking, Sergeant."

"Duchard would never have killed Corporal O'Bannion.
You see, if he had anything resembling a friend in this garrison it was O'Bannion. I told you, Captain, that Duchard
stayed some time in our barracks and O'Bannion was the
only one he ever really exchanged any talk with."

"Why was that?"

"Because of gold. O'Bannion had the fever, same as
Duchard. O'Bannion's father had joined the wagons going
West in the fifties and done some prospecting in the Califor-

nia fields. He'd come up empty, which I guess most of them did, but the fact was he'd been there, and when Duchard heard that, I guess it gave them some common ground. They'd sit and talk about it."

"Did they ever talk about lighting out?"

"Deserting? Obie? Never. He was a good soldier, Captain. He'd made corporal and he was looking ahead."

"All right," Maynard said quietly. He got up and left the shack, head down and shoulders forward until he was back outside in the sunshine. Barrie followed, pushing the door shut behind them. Hands on hips, Maynard gazed thoughtfully across the parade ground at the commanding officer's headquarters.

"What we're going to do now, Sergeant," he said, "is turn back the clock."

"As you say, Captain," Barrie said, watching him.

"According to the report, Duchard rode in at around 11:30 P.M. and went straight to General Englund's office, where a light was still burning. And whose sentry post was nearest to that office?"

"Corporal O'Bannion's."

"All right. He passes O'Bannion, dismounts, enters the office, and reports. He stays for about fifteen minutes. We know that because at near midnight he's seen by a sentry at the south end of the fort—where we are now—leading his horse toward the stables. It's assumed that after seeing to his horse he comes to this rattrap and goes to sleep. At about two-thirty in the morning it's taken under notice that Corporal O'Bannion has failed to report. But an explanation for this wasn't immediately undertaken."

"That's correct, Captain."

"Why was that?"

"The officer of the day thought that maybe Obie—Corporal O'Bannion—had dozed off somewhere."

"Leaving his post uncovered?"

"I'm afraid so, Captain. You know how it is sometimes. A bit lax."

"That wasn't quite in the report."

"I'm not surprised."

"Was O'Bannion in the habit of doing that?"

"Never, sir."

"When did they start looking for him?"

"As I understand it, sometime after two-thirty or so."

"The officer felt that O'Bannion had had enough nap."

"Perhaps the other sentries didn't report to him, sir. You know how it is."

"Do I?" Maynard asked, gazing into the sunlight.

"I would like to state, Captain, that laxness is not the norm here."

"We'll reserve judgment on that, Sergeant. All right. So the search begins. Halfheartedly at first, I'm sure. But when nothing turns up it becomes a bit more frantic."

"They pulled a platoon of men out of Company B for it. The first sergeant was in charge, cussin' like a mule skinner. Then the rest of the garrison was ordered up and told to be at the ready. Just in case."

"What about the senior officers?"

"They were all notified, of course. Except General Englund. They figured they'd wait on that, in case Corporal O'Bannion was after all turned up on the snooze. They didn't go to the general until the body was found, which was sometime between four-fifteen and four-thirty, as I remember it."

"What the hell took so long, in a post of this size?"

"It was under a horse blanket in the stables. They'd passed it a few times until Major Patman thought to turn it back. And there was poor Obie, lying on his back, dead as a Sunday goose."

"And so they then went to inform General Englund."

"Major Patman sent word to Colonel Bruckner and the

colonel sent a man to the general's quarters. At that point we still didn't know if there were Sioux around or not. There was a call to arms and a big ruckus."

"But the general wasn't in his quarters."

"No, sir. The lamp was still burning in his office, so they headed over there and made the lamentable discovery."

"Who found him?" Maynard asked.

"Colonel Bruckner himself, as I understand it."

They had by now walked half the length of the parade ground and were standing outside of the headquarters building, above which a flag blew lazily in the breeze. Maynard pulled forward on his hat brim, trying to keep the sun out of his eyes.

"I'll never forget it," Barrie said somberly. "I've had commanding officers shot away from me during the war, but that was different. Act of God, you might say. Under shot and shell. But this was something once again. Sacrilege, you might say."

"Worse than O'Bannion?" a curious Maynard asked.

"Different, Captain. O'Bannion was my friend, and he was a good boy. But we've seen things on these outposts, Captain. A drunken brawl, the settling of a grudge, and some poor lad is sung away by 'Taps.' A soldier should die in the field, right, Captain? I cried for O'Bannion, I'm not ashamed to say it. But when a commanding officer is given the heave-ho like that . . . well, it just makes you feel haunted. Especially an officer like General Englund."

"He was different?"

"You might say he was. Altogether. He had a look in his eye. Talked to God. 'Englund talks to God,' I heard some of the boys say."

"You don't mean that literally, do you, Barrie?"

"Excuse me, sir?"

"He didn't *really* do that, did he?"

"I don't know, sir," Barrie said. Sidling a look at Maynard, he ventured and added dryly, "We weren't really that close."

"Anyway—"

"You heard the story of his sword, sir?"

"I've heard it," Maynard said curtly.

"And what do you make of it?"

"Sergeant Barrie, right now I'm concerned with Duchard."

"Yes, sir. Sorry, sir."

"Duchard," Maynard said softly, as if to himself, and then under his breath murmured it several more times, as if trying to fix it in memory. Then, staring south along the parade ground at the scout's shack, in a normal voice, he said, "Why does he ride out of here in the middle of the night?"

"I'm afraid you've already suggested the answer to that, Captain."

"No, no," Maynard said, shaking his head. "I don't want to suggest anything. Not yet. And I don't want you to either. So just keep your mouth shut." He ran his hand along the point of his chin. "I wish to hell I knew what time he lit out of here."

Barrie cleared his throat, then repeated the sound. Maynard looked at him.

"Sergeant?"

"Sir."

"You have something to say?"

"The captain ordered my mouth shut. Sir."

Maynard compressed his lips for a moment.

"Barrie," he said evenly, "I'm far from home and friends, in a place I don't want to be, doing a job I don't want to do, and the goddamned sun is getting hotter and hotter. So the last thing I need is some goddamned lazy son of a bitching sergeant tweaking my mustache."

"Duchard was seen galloping on the prairie at five-thirty A.M.," Barrie said quickly.

"On that morning?"

"Yes, sir."

"By whom was he seen?"

"By four travelers on their way to Roseridge, which is a town about eighty miles north of here."

Maynard stared at his sergeant for fully half a minute.

"All right," he said quietly, patiently. "I want this carefully. How do these men know it was five-thirty A.M.?"

"They were camped overnight at a place called Indian Rock, which is not a place at all but a commonly used campsite because there's timber there. It's near a wagon road. Well, they hadn't stirred yet, but the sound of somebody galloping along the road roused them. One of them took note of the time. Then they saw Duchard."

"They knew him?"

"Yes, sir. He's well known in these parts and these gents have been out here for several years. It was first light and they could see him clear."

"Did they acknowledge one another?"

"No, sir. They said he was looking neither this way nor that; that he was riding hell-bent for fury."

"How do you know this story?"

"These gentlemen are in and out of the fort from time to time. They do some trading at the sutler's. One of them asked me what was happening about the tragedies and this and that, and then told me about Duchard. He seemed pretty dead certain about the time."

"And that Duchard was galloping?"

"Like the wind. That's just how he said it, Captain: like the wind."

"This information wasn't in the report."

"No, sir."

"You never told anyone."

"No, sir. Does that matter? Is it important?"

"How long does it take to ride to Indian Rock? At a gallop."

Barrie squeezed one eye shut for a moment. "A good hour, sir."

"How do you know?"

"Because we send woodcutting details out there. One's going out tomorrow, as a matter of fact. Well, now and then somebody has to ride out there with a message, and so we know. An hour, allowing for what wind your horse has got."

Maynard stared at the ground for several moments.

"O'Bannion was killed where, do you think?"

"Probably within a circle of fifty or so feet of here," Barrie said. "It's believed he was then dragged off between command headquarters and officers' quarters to the stables, where he was covered over with a blanket and left. I heard there were drag marks to that effect, though with all the running here and there that night some of them were rubbed out."

"Show me," Maynard said.

With the captain behind him, the sergeant began following the supposed track of Corporal O'Bannion and his murderer. They walked through the narrow shade afforded by the headquarters building, then back into the sunlight, heading for the stables, straight into the warm, settled, unstirring odors of straw and manure. Several cavalry troopers, hatless, yellow suspenders collapsed around them, were working the horses with currycombs. Barrie stopped.

"There," he said, pointing at a spot a few feet from where one of the troopers was standing. "That's where they found Obie."

"Dead as a Sunday goose."

"Just so, Captain."

"Had to drag him—what?—a hundred fifty feet?"

"Near enough."

"Tricky work, under the circumstances. Was there anyone on duty at the stables?"

"No, sir. As a matter of fact, it was very quiet back here that night, as most of the sore-asses were on a two-day patrol at the time."

" 'Sore-asses'?"

"Excuse me, sir. I assumed the captain was familiar with the phrase."

Maynard's face assumed a sternness he did not entirely feel.

"I'm familiar with a hell of a lot of phrases, Sergeant," he said, "but that doesn't necessarily mean they're available to you when we're in conversation."

"No, sir," Barrie said contritely.

"All right," Maynard said, returning to his contemplation of the stables. "Then, whoever left the body here had to get away without being seen, and if he was seen, then he had to have an explanation for being out at that hour."

"If he needed one."

"What do you mean?"

"If he's an officer, nobody is going to ask him why he's skunkin' around at that time of night."

"Yes, but more important than that, he doesn't want to be seen. He *can't* be seen."

"Well, I'd say he knew he was pretty safe, Captain, since it was Corporal O'Bannion's post he was skunkin' through and he knew that poor Obie wasn't going to be talking to anyone about it."

Maynard rubbed his face for a moment.

"Anyone in your barracks now?" he asked.

"No, sir. Shouldn't be, anyway."

"Come on then. Let's light our pipes and have a sit-down."

The Company B barracks were constructed of wood framing and sided with sawed lumber. Like most barracks Maynard had ever seen, they were cramped and poorly ventilated, and he paused for a moment after entering, staring like an old schoolboy returned to the rudimentary rooms of his beginnings, memories loosening and floating free of old moorings. The recollections were immediately ambivalent: not for a moment would he have wished a return to the past; yet the memories came at him with vague wistfulness and no harshness at all, for it was in a barracks not dissimilar to this one that he had begun his adherence to a life and a profession that he had grown to regard with pride and honor and gratitude (there was a time when he could sit interminably blacking his boots and polishing his gilt-edged buttons not because he had been bidden to but out of his compulsive desire to look like a soldier and glitter like one). It was a calling that gathered together all sorts of men and blurred all distinctions as it honed and cohered them into a single unified body of purpose, so that now he was even in service with men who not long ago had charged at him under rebellious banners but who now were one with him under the single allegiance.

"They all look alike, don't they, Captain?" Barrie said, as if reading his mind.

The two long rows of cots, each with its mattress folded back over the springs (Maynard never quite understood the reasoning for that procedure), were three or four feet apart, wooden footlockers in front of each. The aisle running down the center of the long rectangle of a room was some eight feet wide. Cast-iron woodstoves at either end provided heat, though the chief beneficiaries were those who slept closest to the stoves, with proximity being determined by seniority, experience, and after that whatever else it was that elevated one man above another. Kerosene lamps hanging from the ceiling at apportioned intervals provided light. Privates and corporals bunked together, while the sergeants had small individual cubicles adjoining.

They went to Barrie's quarters, which were small and sparely furnished, with cot, footlocker, two chairs, several wall shelves, and a table not much larger than a checkerboard. A well-worn Bible, its black leather cover torn, lay on the cot. Maynard stared at it as he reached for his pipe.

"It's been with me right along," Barrie said, noting the captain's gaze. "Since Gettysburg. It was lying on the ground next to a dead cavalry boy. So I picked it up and kept it."

Maynard loaded his pipe, pushing the tobacco firmly in place with his forefinger. Then he put a match to the rim of the bowl and began puffing, watching Barrie through the rising gray cloud.

"They say," Barrie said, tapping his palm with his corncob, "that a dead soldier goes straight to the arms of the Lord. So I figured if a fellow was so securely placed it wouldn't be a bad idea to carry his Good Book."

"Do you read it?"

"I read it," Barrie said simply.

"Were you brought up on it?"

"No, sir. We weren't religious folk. I've got eleven brothers and sisters. I guess there wasn't time for everything."

"Where are you from, Barrie?"

"New York City."

"Why did you enlist?"

"Just to get out of the way, I suppose. Nobody was going to miss me. And you, sir?"

"Me?"

"Why did you sign up?"

"I don't remember," Maynard said.

All right, Barrie thought. So it was one of those reasons.

They smoked silently for several minutes. Occasionally a soldier came and went, passing the open door without glancing in.

"Am I expected to think," Maynard said, "that Duchard rode in after a reconnaissance, murdered two men, then stabled his horse and went to sleep? Knowing that his arrival was no secret, since he'd been seen by other sentries before getting to O'Bannion? Does that make sense to you?"

"None at all," Barrie said. He was sitting upright in his chair, arms crossed, feet flat on the floor, pipe clenched in teeth.

"It would have been the action of a lunatic."

"Duchard is no lunatic, Captain."

"Is he a murderer?"

"I don't think so."

"So why did he—after being awakened by the commotion that was going on—get out of bed, get back on a horse, and gallop out of here? If he passed Indian Rock at the time those men say he did, then he ripped out of here as soon as he heard that O'Bannion's body had been found."

"But why would O'Bannion's death send him galloping? Why should he think anybody would connect him with it? Forgetting the fact that if he had a friend in the fort it was Obie. And if I follow you correctly, Captain, you're saying that he left the fort before he heard about what happened to General Englund."

"I'm saying it's possible."

"You don't want to let go of him, do you, Captain?"

"I can't. He's still the principal suspect, in everybody's mind."

"It would make everything simple, wouldn't it, sir, if it was Duchard?"

"It would. But that isn't the point."

"Well, you may be right, Captain. But it could be that sometimes a man will go on the run not because of what he

did today but because of what he might have done yesterday. A man with a shadowy history is always wide open to
accusation."

"You're saying that a conscience riddled with old guilts
was what put him on the run. Well, that's always possible,
but not in this case, I don't think."

"Then what?"

"Fear. I think Duchard rode out of here as fast as he could
because he was afraid of something, so afraid that an hour
later he was still galloping."

"He's not a man who scares easily, Captain," Barrie said,
lowering his head for a moment, then raising his eyes, as if trying to present his contrary opinion as prudently as possible.

"I believe that, and that's why I find the idea of fear so intriguing. If I'm right, then what could have frightened such a
man to panic and run?"

"Not the old guilt?"

"No, not the old guilt, and maybe not even any fresh guilt
either."

Barrie held the stem of his pipe against his underlip, staring at Maynard with the most candid uncertainty.

Maynard smiled. "If it helps, Sergeant," he said, "I'm as
bedeviled by all this as you are."

CHAPTER 12

MAJOR PATMAN
PRAIRIE BLOOD

Gusts of morning wind were swirling over the open plain, lifting the fine alkaline dust into the air. A few gently sculpted clouds were shifting themselves across the endless blue sky. The sun was comfortably warm, the heat of the past few days in submission. The wagon road wound among an outcropping of gray boulders still occupying the ground upon which they had been flung eons ago, before the shadow of man and the flight of spirits.

Now some miles from the fort, Maynard and Barrie were mounted upon a pair of cavalry horses, moving slowly, rocking to and fro in their saddles, reins loosely in hand. From the muted discomfort in Barrie's face, Maynard doubted if there would be any more japes about "sore-asses."

They were following a woodcutting detail out to one of the area's few timber supplies, a cottonwood grove that stood between the fort and the nearest settlement, which wasn't more than a few buildings and a groggery for bored soldiers and thirsty travelers. Under the command of Major Patman, the party consisted of eight cavalry troopers, a duty sergeant, and four civilian woodcutters, who had contracted themselves out for the job and each of whom was up on the driver's seat of an empty wagon drawn by a pair of mules. Built to haul freight, the wagons had four-foot-deep beds and were covered by canvas tops stretched over bowed arches.

Maynard and Barrie were along in an unofficial capacity; in fact, while the party was due to be out for several days, they would be riding back that evening. Maynard not only had his list of whom he wanted to talk to but also in what sequence, with Patman, the most recent addition to and relative outsider on the long-serving staff of General Englund, heading the list. When he spoke to the others he wanted to have the advantage (if advantage it be) of Patman's fresher, less jaundiced perceptions of them. And so not wanting to wait for the party to return, he decided to join them and talk to Patman out here.

Maynard felt that his inquiry had taken a significant forward step last night when, after dinner, he had gone to the infirmary and spoken to the post surgeon, Dr. Gilbert. On the night of the murders, Gilbert related, he had been summoned from his quarters to the body of Corporal O'Bannion and later to the post headquarters. The second summons had come from an enlisted man via Colonel Bruckner. When he got to headquarters, the doctor said, he found the colonel alone with Englund's body. They were soon joined by Fordyce, Scheffner, Josephson, and Patman. Maynard, however, was most interested in the enlisted man. When the soldier was sent to him, Maynard asked, did the man know that Englund was dead? No, Gilbert said. Bruckner had discovered the body, then gone outside, stopped the first man he saw, and ordered him to bring the post surgeon.

The soldier then waited outside until dismissed. And how long was this? Maynard asked. By his best calculations, the doctor said, about twenty minutes or so, or around 5 A.M.

By this account, Maynard reasoned, Duchard, who had passed Indian Rock at 5:30 A.M., after approximately an hour's ride, could not have known of the death of General Englund when he left the fort. It was of course still possible, though to Maynard highly unlikely, that Duchard could have committed both murders, then gone to sleep, then risen and galloped out. Maynard realized that by this logic he was placing at the bottom of the suspect list the man who by the fact of his precipitous departure had heretofore been at the top (though it was still possible that the enigmatic Duchard had been responsible for O'Bannion's death). Maynard felt that some obstructive undergrowth had been swept away, opening the ground to a clearer view. It made things not easier but at least somewhat less difficult. Although he knew that his companion, Sergeant Barrie, did not agree with the hypothesis, he still chose to believe that it was not guilt but panic that had impelled Duchard's sudden departure, and that panic, which he had seen seize the souls of brave men on more than one battlefield, was not an irrational act.

The expression of sullen discontent on his companion's face soon drew Maynard's attention.

"Yes, Sergeant?" he asked.

"It's not my place, Captain," Barrie said, sounding like a man sore with displeasure.

"What isn't your place?"

"To comment negatively about the deployment of this detail."

"You're saying that there should be a point and one or two outriders."

"Yes, sir. There's a stand of trees not far ahead, tall grass on either side, not to mention those rocks. This is not picnic country, Captain."

"Are you saying Major Patman doesn't know his business?"

Barrie, his face shaded by the broad brim of his campaign hat, passed Maynard a sour look.

"You wouldn't say that, would you, Sergeant?" Maynard asked, a light chiding in his tone.

"I would," Barrie said, "if asked."

"Do you think there might be some Sioux on the ramble?"

"The army has been chasing and running them down all over the Territory, Captain. They break up into small parties when that happens. You never can tell."

"Well, Major Patman's in command out here. I can't give him any orders."

"What about advice? Sir."

Maynard laughed. "Are you one of these prairie rats that can smell an Indian?"

"I *always* smell 'em, Captain," Barrie said emphatically. "Whether they're there or not. That's how you keep alive out here."

"All right, Barrie," Maynard murmured, "Keep inhaling."

They reached the cottonwood grove in early afternoon. The woodcutters dismounted, stripped to the waist, and with axes borne on bare shoulders marched off into the trees. Four dismounted troopers accompanied them, rifles in hand, while two others rode picket outside of the grove. The duty sergeant and the other two troopers were deployed around the general area, which was open prairie on all sides except for the trees and, about a half mile away, a stark rising of white-rocked ridges, so intensely white in this pouring sunlight it seemed the merest shadow might leave a stain. Without the softening of the slightest touch of vegetation, the rocks looked like some primitive fortress turned jagged through endless, battering besiegement.

Barrie, relieved to finally be out of the saddle, requested permission to turn the wagons around into a four-sided defensive position, which he did after unhitching and tethering the mules. He then climbed up onto one of the wagons and took a seat. He laid his Springfield across his knees. They claimed it was accurate at one thousand yards, to which he always said, Yes, the rifle maybe. But what about the man on the trigger?

He fixed his eyes upon the ridges, which looked malign enough to draw a man's suspicion, and then allowed his mind to satisfy itself with thoughts of untried and damned ignorant officers. They looked splendid on parade, he thought, all polished leather and white gloves, eyes eagle-fierce with authority, chests up and bellies tucked, posturing under fluttering regimental banners, all of it designed to moisten the eyes of old men and send skinny duff-headed boys running hell-bent to enlistment depots. Hell, Barrie thought, sending a streak of saliva over the sideboard and into the dust. Give me some old broken-boned son of a bitch whose trousers sag in the crotch but who was there in the mud and the blood and the dysentery when it was all bought and paid for, who wears it all inside and who is not above giving you a kick in the ass when it's called for. Like Englund had been, despite all the me-and-God thunderation in his face and the arrogance of his step. Englund could stop your heart with a side glance, of course, but he also made you feel tough and bold. Made you feel army. Back in 1861–1865, when the smoke was thick as a dust storm and the drummer boys began humming you on, you never felt like you'd come back hauling Englund's mistakes. In some regiments all that the new recruits got was drilling in close-order movements and the manual of arms. But with Englund you got that and more, relentless training in skirmish drills and marksmanship. With the parade ground strutters you got a lot of *Be prepared to die for your country*. Not with Englund; there was the better, more dynamic credo: *Be prepared to fight for your country*. When last Christmas he came to the enlisted men's party in the company mess hall to pay his respects he had completed his brief remarks with, *I am the sum total of you all*, which earned him three rousing huzzahs. Bullshit, maybe. But Barrie knew that to his final twilight, years after he had stripped the uniform for the last time, he would never forget the man.

Maybe this fellow Maynard had some of those soldierly building bricks in him. Barrie wasn't sure. Genial as a salesman though he might seem, Barrie was careful about where he accorded respect. Loyalty and obedience were always there to be seen, but respect was a man's private business, an invisible decoration you awarded. But there was no doubt the fellow was sharp and that he saw things and that he probably knew a hell of a lot more than he let on, and by the look Barrie sometimes caught in his eye he knew the man had bought and paid for it the hard way. And anyway, Barrie thought, coming to the definitive conclusion, if the man was good enough for General William T. Sherman then he was good enough for Sergeant William P. Barrie.

Maynard and Patman walked off a little way together and took seats on a pair of warm, smooth-worn boulders. Maynard took out his pipe and offered Patman his pouch. The major shook his head.

"I don't have the habit," he said. "Except when General Englund offered a cigar."

"Didn't turn it down, did you?" Maynard asked, filling his pipe. Patman smiled benevolently.

"Courage has its limits," he said.

"Were his officers afraid of him?"

"In a manner of speaking," Patman said, clasping his hands between his knees. "It was more complicated than fear as fear is generally understood. There was a wariness. You could scent it. He was something they didn't quite understand."

"Even after serving with him for so many years?"

"That was probably part of it. They'd gone through it all together, shared experiences that should—usually do—bind men into a special fraternity. But not this group. There was a wedge between Englund and his staff, and because of Englund there will always be a wedge between them individually. I've found soldiers to be basically simple men—I don't mean that pejoratively, Captain."

"I understand," Maynard said, lighting his pipe.

"And considering the sharply defined latitudes of their lives, I think it's a good thing. But when they come across something, or someone, they can't understand it makes them uneasy."

"And Englund made them uneasy."

"Oh yes, quite."

"By design, do you think?"

"No. He was too internally obsessed for that."

"What did you think of him?"

"I thought of General Englund with the same consideration as I do of Fort Larkin and of the army itself: an experience not to be missed, to be endured, and then be done with." To Maynard's curious stare, Patman added, "I've decided against a career in uniform, Captain. This is confidential, of course, but I expect to be resigning my commission in a year or two."

"Disillusionment?" Maynard asked, drawing on his pipe and releasing a thin trail of smoke upon the warm sunlit air.

"I don't think I ever had an illusion; or maybe looking back, perhaps a slightly misplaced romantic one. Some interior regrets for having missed the war. The stories enthralled me, I must admit. I had uncles and cousins who went through it and I never tired of listening to their tales of adventure, which meant they never tired of relating them. It's always different in the telling, isn't it?"

"Quite."

"But I knew almost from the day I received my commission that the army wasn't going to be my life's calling. One of the reasons I asked for a transfer up here was to be able to say that I served on the frontier, although, frankly, I think I would have preferred Fort Lincoln rather than Larkin. But so be it. Anyway, I am now affianced to the prettiest girl in St. Louis and intend to be married as soon as I am out of uniform."

"Do your fellow officers know of this?"

"No," Patman said. "And they wouldn't care one way or the other if they did. I'm the outsider, you see. Oh, they're cordial enough, but I understand. They've been through it all together; the war, Indian campaigns, Englund."

Maynard smiled tightly at that last.

"I'm not being facetious about that," Patman said.

"I know you're not. But outsider or not, you got on with them."

"Absolutely. They're a decent group of men, and splendid officers; though like any men—soldier or civilian—they have their trials and their idiosyncrasies. Of course I know why you're here, Captain, and I wish you well, particularly since until this matter is resolved we're all under suspicion. So my advice to you is not to regard these men simply as soldiers and remember that there's another life, one that has been otherwise conditioned, under the uniform. That might be difficult for you to grapple with, being yourself a career man."

"What you're saying, Major, is that you think one of them did it."

"Oh, I stand under the same cloud, Captain. Five good officers and one scout of dubious virtue. Yes, I do think that among us stands the guilty party. The innocent are waiting for you to absolve us . . . if you can."

"Do you think the inquiry was scrupulous?"

"With each watching the other? I don't think it could have been done more scrupulously."

"You had all met in Englund's office that night," Maynard said.

"It was after dinner," Patman said, reaching down and picking up a handful of dirt. He rubbed at it with his fingertips as if sifting it, then let it slide back down to the ground. "The general gave us a little lecture about the foredoomed condition of the Indians, employing what I thought was some rather tortured logic, and then informed us we would soon be marching out to destroy a band of Sioux who were reputed to be in the area. Then he broke out some brandy to observe the moment and drank a toast."

"And then you all left."

"Yes," Patman said, but then shook a finger in the air for a moment. "But there was one disquieting touch before we did. The general toasted the Civil War dead, and Major Josephson added something about 'especially at Fredericksburg.' That seemed to create a bit of tension, particularly within the general. Then we left."

"Did that allusion have any particular meaning for you?"

"None at all. You'll have to ask Josephson about it."

"You never have?"

Patman shook his head. "No," he said. "I don't feel especially comfortable discussing the war with them. My own sense of inadequacy probably. And Josephson is probably the toughest one of them all. Grimly the fighting officer. Very much frustrated at the moment, with the bulk of the army being on the march elsewhere. I'm sure you understand."

"You got the sense that Fredericksburg had some private meaning for Josephson and the general?"

"Most distinctly."

"Fredericksburg was fourteen years ago."

"I don't think time means anything in the life of a man

who is trained to order and to obey. And without a sense of time's passage things have a tendency to stand still in your mind. They fester."

"What did you do at the conclusion of the meeting?" Maynard asked. His pipe had gone out and he was holding it in his hand. In the quiet, the sounds of the woodcutters attacking the trees could be clearly heard, the chopping coming and going in a rhythmic beat.

"We all left," Patman said. "I exchanged a few words outside with Colonel Bruckner and then went to my quarters. As far as I knew, we all went to quarters."

"But there was this slight delay, while you conversed with Colonel Bruckner, and the others went off."

"It wasn't more than several minutes. As I recall, he seemed preoccupied and we hardly exchanged any words at all. Then he went to quarters, and I followed."

"And the others?"

"Gone by then. It was a rather dark night, I couldn't see anything and I assumed they were all gone."

"You sound like you weren't ready for bed, that you were looking for someone to talk to."

"Frankly, Captain," Patman said, "I was. I guess I was excited by the impending campaign—it was going to be my first—and wanted to talk about it. But there was no one about, so I went in."

"Did you hear Duchard ride in?"

"I may have; I don't remember."

"Did you know him well?"

"Not well. We had a few conversations from time to time."

"I understand he was rather a taciturn man."

"I would say reticent. There's a difference. If you spoke to him of something that interested him, he'd respond. I found him a rather intelligent man—on his own ground, of course—though the other officers, I'm afraid, rated him just one pace ahead of an Indian and generally ignored him. Englund held him in high regard, I know that."

"What did you talk to Duchard about?"

"The Sioux. Since we were out here to master the poor devils I felt I wanted to know something about them. Duchard had been out among them—he even had a somewhat rudimentary understanding of their tongue—and he knew an awful lot about their habits and customs, the way they lived and worshiped. He said they'd been treated unfairly. Not that he had any sympathy for them, but I think he respected them. As one wild man to another," Patman added with a light laugh. "He's put himself in a poor light, hasn't he, running off like that?"

"Why do you think he did that?"

"I'm afraid you'll have to ask him that question, if he ever turns up."

"So you went to your quarters . . ."

"And to sleep, only to be wakened in the middle of the night with word that a sentry was missing."

"Corporal O'Bannion."

"That was his name."

"You were the one who found him."

"Yes, finally. He was at the stables, under a blanket. Then shortly after, we heard about General Englund."

"All of the senior officers were up?"

"The whole packet of us. Bruckner found him. I think he was in shock. I remember him muttering over and over, 'General Englund is dead. General Englund is dead.' Like one of the planets had dropped out of the sky. Frankly, Captain, it stunned me as well. I hadn't known Englund that long, but there was something indelible about him. I think a person's most telling characteristic is his perception of himself, and Englund's was compelling. Larger than life. Sometimes I'd try to tell myself that he was something of a lunatic, just to dilute his presence inside of me. And maybe he was. But the man was absolutely sure of himself, as if every action he performed, every word he uttered, every breath he drew was marked with preordination. I think he knew the Testaments by heart, and quoted them almost with the pride of authorship. Can you imagine what it must have been like to have killed a man like that? Almost an act of deicide. I wonder what Fordyce thinks."

"Why Fordyce especially?"

Patman laughed uncomfortably.

"This *is* confidential, isn't it?" he asked.

"To a reasonable extent," Maynard said.

"Well, Fordyce is a bit around the bend, in my opinion. I'm offering this in compassion, not mockery. You'll talk to him and I think you'll see my meaning. He's still a good soldier, mind you; he can cover my back at any time. But as I understand it, a few years ago, he took a knock on the head in some campaign or other against the Cheyenne, or maybe it was the Sioux, and he hasn't been the same since. Scheffner told me about it."

"How does this manifest itself?"

"In religious zealotry. He's taken to interpreting the Bible literally, which, as you know, Captain, can make things very perplexing. I'm not a blasphemer, Maynard; my faith is as stout as the next man's, but if God gave us souls he also gave us brains to reason with."

"And Fordyce . . ."

"Among other things cannot reconcile 'Thou Shalt Not Kill' with doing what a soldier must sometimes do. And those are just the bubbles on the boiling water."

"Was this of concern to Englund?"

"Scheffner said that Englund was very understanding. Even compassionate. Referring to Fordyce, he said, 'There is the man that was and the man that he has become. As long as there is not interference with his official duties and obligations, I shall choose to deal with the man that was.' Scheffner told me that. And Fordyce has indeed comported himself to the letter. He'd go out tomorrow and kill, if ordered, but then come back and sit and torment himself."

"Is Colonel Bruckner as tolerant of this as Englund was?"

"I've seen no indication of him being otherwise. It enables him to appear noble. And anyway, it was Englund's preference, and I think even in death they're afraid to contradict him."

"You approve of Colonel Bruckner?"

"I don't disapprove," Patman said. "You've seen him. He is what he is. A man of great self-esteem. Too much, perhaps. Englund enjoyed pricking his bubble now and then."

"Did Bruckner resent it?"

"There would be no demonstration of it if he did. A statue has more facial animation than that man." Patman laughed self-consciously. "I was ordered to cooperate, but perhaps I've gone a bit over the mark."

"Colonel Scheffner impressed me as being less than amiable," Maynard said. "Am I correct in that?"

The levity left Patman's face. He contemplated the ground for several moments, wetting his lips.

"Outside of saying I have high personal regard for Colonel Scheffner," he said, "I would rather not comment in detail about him. Nor about Mrs. Scheffner. Let it come from someone else."

"So be it, Major," Maynard said amicably.

"I don't envy you your assignment, Maynard. I don't know how you can make up or down out of any of it. I wouldn't know how to find the answer."

"Oh, I suspect the answer will be given to me," Maynard said with a wry smile. "It's just a matter of recognizing it when it is."

At that moment Barrie's voice bridged the quiet and

reached them; there was tension in it and a pause and an alert, all in the single word: "Captain."

As if the utterance also had a guiding sound, Maynard and Patman got to their feet and looked in the same direction and saw what Barrie was seeing, what both of the cavalry pickets had just seen. The Indians had begun appearing over the crest of the ridge two and three at a time, each mounted on a horse, each being brought to great height by the rise of the crest, pausing for a moment as if to have their portraits captured, and then beginning the slow descent, filing one after the other along the severely twisting trails, their horses surefooted on the hard, abruptly jutting ground. By the time their last had risen over the crest's rocky shoulders there were about twenty of them, each following a leisurely step-by-step pace down the trail, which at points followed a sharp, almost vertical drop through the rocks.

By this time the woodcutters and their troopers had been alerted and were running from the woods to the wagons, covered by the pickets, who were trailing in after them. Maynard and Patman were running toward the wagons, canteens flapping and flying around their waists, Patman's hand on the butt of his Colt revolver.

"We won't panic," he said, turning to Maynard for a moment, the brim of his campaign hat flipping up in the breeze of his forward motion. "We'll find out what it's all about."

Yes, you will, Maynard thought as he ran; but his chief concern was how many Indians might still be behind that ridge. As the odds stood at the moment it would be a reasonably fair fight, if fight there was to be.

The pickets brought the mules and horses into the square created by the drawn-around wagons, while Barrie and the duty sergeant hauled down several ammunition boxes.

By the time the party and their animals were all inside of the wagon formation, the Indians had completed their de-

scent of the rocks and were moving quite slowly, quite casually across the prairie, perhaps a thousand yards distant.
They were riding in from a northerly direction and Patman
ordered most of his troopers into the wagons facing that
way. A few others took up positions in the six- or eight-foot
spaces between the wagons, crouching behind hastily contrived breastworks of unraised tents, kegs, and bedrolls.
One of the woodcutters was handed the unenviable job of
trying to keep the animals from stampeding should a fight
break out. The other three were given rifles and told to be
ready to use them. Then Patman ordered the duty sergeant
to break open the ammunition boxes.

Barrie climbed into one of the wagons with his Springfield.

"Nothing like some easy duty with the woodcutters, eh?"
he said to one of the troopers.

"You think they've come for a fight?" the trooper asked.

"I'll let you know," Barrie said. He squeezed one eye shut
for a moment, then said, "In about fifteen minutes or so."

"They've been surrendering in passels around Fort Lincoln."

"The man who lives longest," Barrie said, "is the one
who believes it last."

Three-inch augur holes had been bored in some of the
side boards about a foot from the top of the beds, providing
protected firing positions, one of which Barrie knelt down
and took up.

The Indians continued forward at a walk, almost imper-
ceptibly closing the distance between themselves and the
wagons, moving without formation, some abreast of each
other, others trailing behind.

Maynard and Patman watched from behind one of the
wagons. Maynard was holding a rifle diagonally across his
chest; Patman's revolver was still holstered.

"What do you think?" Patman asked.

"War party," Maynard said.

"We can't be sure. They may be surrendering."

"They'd more likely go to the fort for that."

"Maybe they just want to talk or bargain for food."

"They'd send one man up alone for that."

"Don't you think that if they meant trouble they'd be bearing down on us already?"

"Major, they *are* bearing down. Slowly."

"I don't want to start a fight unnecessarily."

Maynard made a full 360-degree scan of the landscape. No other warriors were in sight, the prairie quiet in the bright sunlight, the ridge empty. He could not be certain about the cottonwood grove. He suspected that if a larger force was present they would already have appeared. The most frequently employed tactic, particularly in a situation like this, was to send in an initial smaller wave and then, while the defenders were reloading, back it up with the main force. There appeared to be no main force.

"They've been surrendering in small groups all over the Territory," Patman said.

"If they're surrendering," Maynard said, "I don't think they'd take a chance riding up like that, without some indication."

"What indication?"

"One of them comes forward and makes a big speech while the others throw down their weapons." As he spoke, Maynard's eyes remained riveted upon the approaching Indians.

"It might still happen," Patman said. He wet his lips. Small beads of perspiration had formed across his upper lip. He glanced at Maynard's face for a moment, as if hoping to derive there a deeper reading of the situation.

Barrie's voice came from inside the wagon.

"Captain," he said, "they're getting goddamned close."

"No one fire until I give the order," Patman shouted. Then to Maynard he muttered, "They look an unwholesome lot, don't they?" He blinked his eyes rapidly several times, as if to clear his vision.

Still moving at a maddeningly slow walk, the Indians were closing. Patman ran a finger back and forth under the slight, somewhat poutish bulge of his underlip, his eyes not just fixed upon the Sioux but searching, too, as if trying to penetrate to an understanding.

"Get a few men out of the wagons," Maynard said quietly. "If there's a charge there's going to be an encirclement. The men are going to have to swing around in a hurry."

Patman nodded. He passed the order to the duty sergeant, who pulled three troopers out of the wagons and told them to take up positions behind the large, high-spoked wheels. Two of the woodcutters were lying shoulder to shoulder on the shaded ground under one of the wagons. Nobody had asked them what their experience was with rifles.

"Major," Maynard said, "they've given no indication of any peaceful intentions. I'd open up on them now."

Patman drew a deep breath and as he expelled it, said, "We'll wait."

Moving ever closer, the Indians began becoming distinctive. Save for breechclouts and moccasins they were unclad. Some had red, blue, or brown smearings across their breasts and faces. One wore a magnificently feathered warbonnet that seemed to be preening around his head, while another had in place a fierce-looking piece of headgear with horns jutting from either side. Others had eagle feathers in their hair, while several were wearing yellow cavalry campaign hats, leading Maynard to wonder in what gully the previous owners were lying. If it had been quiet before, it was more so now, as if the methodically advancing party were drawing forward with it a more heavily laden atmosphere.

Maynard could feel his nerve ends coiling in the tightening grip of old, familiar tension, a hard unalloyed raptness that didn't seem to know, or care, the difference between Lee's massed divisions and the muted advance of a handful of Indians who seemed guided by a stolid carven pride. The evocation of death had but the single emotional caliber, without degree.

"They've got rifles, Captain," Barrie said, his voice a singsong of warning.

"And cavalry blankets under some of those saddles," Maynard said quietly to Patman.

"Awfully close now, Captain," Barrie called out.

"Major—" Maynard said.

"Not until I'm . . ."

The lead warriors seemed to lunge ahead in their saddles as their legs began beating at the flanks of their mounts and under whoops and shouts the horses sprang forward.

Patman's shouted order to fire was drowned out by a fusillade of rifle fire around him. The opening burst unhorsed several of the riders, the others rushing on, raised rifles blazing. Horses went down, skidding in explosions of dust, their riders tumbling.

Maynard went down to one knee, the tip of his rifle moving with one of the attackers who had broken to a side. His first shot missed, but his second knocked the rider sideways from the saddle and as the empty horse galloped on Maynard watched the Indian strike the ground with back-breaking impact and lie still.

The wearer of the warbonnet surged in close, came within several hundred yards, legs beating in and out upon the sides of his horse, rifle raised high in one hand. With the mass of feathers raging around his head he for a moment looked unstoppable, a figure of nightmare mythology; but then several well-aimed shots struck him almost simultaneously and for several moments he seemed to be wrestling against some invisible grip, writhing this way and that, and then his face flew upward and he pitched backward as his horse rode straight out from under him.

An incoming shot splintered a wagon spoke inches above Maynard's head, making him duck and bury his face against his shoulder for an instant's intuitive protection. Glancing up before returning fire, he saw the grimly earnest face of Bryan Patman, lips rigidly together as he aimed out upon the prairie a Colt's revolver that Maynard doubted he could hit anything with. It still wasn't an officer's face, even in the act of killing, or of trying to; it was the face of a pleasant, responsibly involved man prepared to die on behalf of the right thing, though just what that thing was would no doubt require an elaborate disquisition.

A group of riders broke away into a wide arc, preparing to circle the wagons, and Maynard warned the troopers to defend in all directions. As the Indians came closer a concentrated burst of their fire poured in, cutting through the canvas wagon covers, shattering side boards, perforating a water barrel, killing one of the horses the woodcutter was trying valiantly to hold in place. Silent just moments ago, the prairie now was alive with gunfire and the yipping, barklike cries of the attackers. Through it all the Springfields crackled with a blunt and dogmatic perseverance that bizarrely seemed the only sane and rational notes in the swirling mix of sound, a chorus of would-be restorers to peace and harmony.

Some of the riders presented reduced targets as they swung low in their saddles and fired around their horses' necks. One of these horses was knocked down in full flight, went skidding through a screen of flying dust, and landed flush upon its hapless rider. A chestnut mare in its wake had to leap to avoid the downed animal and for a moment it soared against the sky, hooves galloping on thin air, mane fluttering, stretched-back rider gripping taut reins with one hand, unbound hair flying. It landed with terrific momentum, coming straight on toward the wagons. The Indian raised his rifle in both hands and brought it to his face, right elbow jutting. Maynard felt it aimed directly at him and he quickly shouldered his Springfield, but before either could fire, a shot from the wagon ripped into the rider and spun him around so hard both legs disappeared with the weight of sudden death over the saddle of the empty horse.

The Indians' direct charge now broke into a chaotic encircling, some riding in one direction, others in another, crisscrossing one another. Pausing to reload, Maynard saw at a barely registering glance one of the woodcutters lying aside motionless in his patch of wagon shade, mouth half open and lifeless face oddly tranquil.

From out of the rapidly diminishing band of riders, one veered and broke straight for the wagons, covering the ground so fast he seemed to grow in size with stunning rapidity. Holding his rifle high in one jolting hand, he seemed for a moment to embody the furious pride and anger of a people ruined and displaced by pell-mell invasion of ground maintained sacred by them for centuries. His moment of symbolic grandeur was brief as a shot swept him from his horse and he hit the prairie earth and spun through the dust so fast it looked like a thousand times around, and hard upon the kill came a shrill triumphant yell from one of the wagons, a sound Maynard had heard before in rising unison from masses of charging gray uniforms, but now the single echo from the mouth of some Carolina mountain boy or Mississippi farmer celebrating his marksmanship.

One unhorsed rider rose from the prairie, staggered forward, rifle in hand, fell, then rose again and came stumbling on, the weight of his pain, his rage, his impending doom hunching him over. He came on even as the rifle fell from his hands, shoulders wrenching from side to side as if to shake free of some contact or sensation. A shot missed him, but close enough to rip a feather from his tightly braided hair. The next shot drove him back on his heels, straightening him to full height as he reared back and dropped into the dust.

The remaining riders, five or six of them, now cut and ran, heading for the cottonwood grove, outrunning the few shots that chased after them.

Patman leaned with one hand on a wagon wheel, closed his eyes, and took several deep breaths, a vague, rather inane smile on his lips for a moment. Maynard watched one of the woodcutters cover his dead companion's face with a handkerchief. One of the troopers lay dead between the wagons. Another was sitting back on his hands in the midst of the square, face contorted as his shattered leg was being looked at by the duty sergeant.

"Barrie!" Maynard shouted.

"Still with you, Captain," the voice answered from within the wagon.

The duty sergeant turned from his ministering for a moment.

"Two dead, two wounded, Captain," he said. "Counting the civilian."

"Who else is wounded?" Maynard asked, looking around. Then he noticed the duty sergeant's blood-soaked sleeve. The sergeant, with the tried-and-true face of a thirty-year man, smiled sadly.

Patman was now at Maynard's side, sweaty face shining with excitement.

"Well, we've come through," Patman said. He was smiling and panting. "By God, we've come through!"

Maynard patted him several times on the shoulder, very gently.

CHAPTER 13

PRESENT AND PAST

The army would report it as a skirmish, if the encounter got reported at all, if it ever received any official entry. Maynard had seen similar reports cross his desk at the War Department, the colorless and dispassionate descriptions of men killing and dying. This company of that regiment, this lieutenant, that sergeant, this trumpeter, that private. He had read them without envisioning or wondering a thing, then passed them on. In effect, nothing had happened.

He'd been back in the fort two days now and as he lay in bed hearing the sentries calling out the midnight hour, he was trying to forget the encounter on the prairie and bring his mind back to purpose. But it wasn't as easy as closing one door and opening another. They had buried the trooper that morning and later Sergeant Barrie said to Maynard, "Captain, I really don't know who the hell it was we just put under." "His name wasn't Brown?" Maynard asked. "The boys told me," Barrie said, "that he'd enlisted three different times under three different names. The last one just happened to be Brown. Nobody ever knew his honest name." Nor would they now, Maynard thought moodily. Nor would anyone ever know he was gone now, what family he had, if any.

They had buried Brown, or whoever he was, in the small post cemetery which lay on the north side of the stables. Corporal O'Bannion's grave was there, and in a small fenced-around plot off by itself General Englund's. They would have taken the general's body up to Fort Lincoln for a full regimental send-off with flags and bands, Barrie said, but a few years ago a distinguished officer had died at Larkin (of natural causes) and they had laid his plank box in a wagon bed and begun a solemn procession to Lincoln. By the end of the third day the smell emanating from the box was so strong nobody could ride near the wagon, and by the time the party reached Fort Lincoln the honor guard with black armbands on their sleeves was awash with the crudest imaginable humor about the officer and his odor. So here Englund lay, five feet deep into the sacred earth he had come out to conquer and pacify and civilize. One day, Barrie told Maynard, they'll ship him back East. Miss Englund will see to that, you can be sure.

All right, Maynard thought. It wasn't me who mentioned her first.

What was she like, Captain? Barrie asked in response to the question Maynard hoped sounded offhanded, as if it had just entered his mind. Well, she made you know you were in the army because it was only the army that could bring a young lady like that to a place like this. The politicians say that we are civilizing this land with the stringing of telegraph wire and the laying of railroad track; but I can tell you that the arrival of just one Miss Englund, even for a short time, does more civilizing for a place than all the inventions you can think of. Tripped about with a little blue parasol when the sun was high, always with a smile and a good

morning—not afraid to speak to an enlisted man, which I supposed embarrassed the officer she was walking with. Which
one? Oh, none special. She didn't have a beau out here, if
that's what you mean. But the general didn't like her to go
about by herself, so if she had some doin' to do, like at the
commissary or at the stable where she kept her sorrel, she'd
have an escort, one of the commissioned officers, who for that
little time was considered the luckiest man in the Territory.
Sometimes they'd go out to where there's a stand of trees
about a mile off and have a picnic, Miss Englund and her
mother and some of the officers and their wives. But there was
never any barracks talk about Miss Englund, and you know
how easy barracks talk will float.

She organized things in the winter. Dances, minstrel
shows, tea parties, evenings of bridge. Delicate and fine, but a
general's daughter right through. You could see that. A
showing of royal blood, you might say, but just enough so
that you never minded stepping aside for her. And not just any
general's daughter of course, but his. Born with a bit of his
steel, if you know what I mean. Once, early last winter, a patrol came in with a few wounded after a minor to-do with
some Sioux and Miss Englund went straight to the infirmary
to offer her help. From what I heard, she held apart the
wound on a man's thigh with her fingers while the surgeon ap-
plied disinfectant. And every so often she'd come into the infirmary and read to the sick or help them write a letter if they
were, you know, less than perfectly educated. I am General
Englund's daughter, she'd tell them, which they already
knew of course. But it wasn't as if she was trying to be important so much as she was letting them know how proud she
was of the fact. And he felt the same toward her; you could
see it in the way he'd strut when they were together; prouder
of her than he could have been over any son.

So he'd had it right, Maynard thought. In just a formal

thirty-minute meeting he had seen and felt everything Barrie had described. He had discerned the depths of character in those china-blue eyes, the girlishness and the womanliness all at once, the ethereal belle of any ball and the woman who was unafraid to lay her fingers on an open wound; who could show the most heartrending grief and yet retain her poise, sitting in uncomely black in that maddening heat of a Washington summer. Again he felt on his hand the brush of her fingertips which had closed a circle around his heart. He felt stalwart and invested, lying in his bed in the farness of the Dakota prairie, under a billion cold stars, knowing that he was in her thoughts, and with his strange lonely ache he was able to induce those thoughts through the night and across a continent and re-create them here, making him feel wistfully accompanied.

Not since the sweet untamed Sarah Wilman had any woman drawn the circle around his heart. More than fifteen years of abeyance, and so what his heart was releasing were long-mellowed harmonies and confections, along with a meditation that he had allowed to wander in thought because confrontation might prove too unsettling. Like "Brown's," his own family might still—probably just occasionally now—be wondering whatever became of him. He had written them once, before enlisting, to tell them he had decided to try "the open road" and asking for their blessings and their forgiveness. Even as he was writing it he imagined his father sitting at the kitchen table holding the letter in his thick woodsman's fingers and staring at it with a physically powerful man's sullen impotence, and could imagine his brothers announcing at the saloon that Tommy'd gone off and maybe somebody saying *Probably with Ad Marston*, because Ad's gone too I hear and those boys always were two of a kind and inseparable.

Well, Ad Marston's body could still be lying under pine

boughs in the mountain forest, or somebody could have stumbled upon it, either the next day or the next year or ten years later. If it was a long time after, then somebody would have remembered, one of those old buzzards probably who had nothing to do but sit on a barrel and smoke a pipe and remember. *Disappeared 'bout the same time that lunatic was on the rip up here, remember? The one who murdered somebody in the village.* And lunatic there had been (two, if you want to count me, Tom thought, considering what I did that day). Because late that night he had finally come down the trails, trying to assimilate what he had done, what it meant, what would come of it. Two boys up in the forest alone with rifles and at opposite poles of the same love. That had a certain mad symmetry, didn't it? Wasn't that the sure foundation of an inevitability, something so unpreventable it came virtually with built-in absolution? You didn't have to be a philosopher to know what stormed in the hearts of such boys with such boy-sized emotions (not man-sized, but the other, smaller in scope, more dense, more compact, more abrupt and direct and infinitely more deadly), nor an oracle to know what was going to happen.

He thought he might have ultimately made some accommodation with the principal fact: not that he had shot and killed (all right, murdered) his best friend, but that after Ad had emptied his rifle Tom had him square from here to sundown, was suddenly by virtue of his own loaded weapon not only unthreatened but in command. It wasn't hatred that urged that final unforgiving and irredeemable tension on the trigger: it was love, pure-in-the-heart love for Sarah Wilman, love placed beyond the shadow and menace of Ad Marston, love placed stratospheres over friendship or morality or reason or anything else that might compromise it for even an instant. If there was one ameliorating seed in the whole thing, that was it: in the name of love. Not greed, not hatred, not revenge. Love. That was the stout self-justification and self-forgiveness he brought with him back down the mountain trail.

He arrived home well after midnight, climbing the porch steps and entering the large house with what he assumed was unerring stealth. Even without light he knew where the nails were on the living room wall and laid his rifle across them. As he turned he heard first the crackle in the straw-bottomed chair and then from within the darkness his brother Henry's voice, slow and slurred with a drowsiness Tom recognized. Henry once described his post-tavern routine as "Walkin' it home, nappin' it off, then goin' to sleep just fine."

Where you been? Henry asked. At twenty-six he was the oldest of the three brothers and as such occasionally took a responsible interest in the youngest.

Hunting, Tom said, talking simply to a voice.

You missed all the goin' on, Henry said.

Yes, I heard there was some trouble.

Trouble? I'd say it was a sight more than trouble. We had a real son of a bitch here all right. Crazy or burned up with whisky, they don't know. But with a rifle. Swingin' it around and darin' everybody and finally he shot it off for no special reason and with no special aim and the bullet flew through the open doorway and killed her dead. Shot right through the heart. So quick they said she was probably dead even before she struck the floor. Then he took off up into the mountains and they've been trackin' him ever since.

Shot who? he asked.

The new girl. The pretty one. Wilman's girl. Sarah.

He slipped away at dawn, carrying with him a modest share of belongings in a small burlap sack. He left no note, but paused to tell a neighbor that he was off on the road for a while and to please convey the message to his father. Walking through the cool moist morning, he passed Wilman the Newcomer's store on Main Street and stared moodily at it, feeling swelling inside of him an emptiness that he was unequipped to cope with, knowing only that whatever it was it was driving him off. She was dead and he could not remain.

So it was anguish more than guilt that drove him off. He understood the passion that had urged his finger on the trigger, understood why Ad Marston was lying under the needled boughs high in the awakening pine forest, but the fate or deviltry that had twisted it into unrecognizable shape was beyond understanding. It was that mystery and that irony that carried him out.

He followed the rock-bedded stream from where sprang the waters that gradually widened and expanded into the Hudson River, sleeping nights on the banks of currents heading home to the sea, cadging food where he could or day-laboring for it when he couldn't. He reached Albany and fell in with several other adventuring youths who were living in riverside shanties. He found porter's work in a hotel, but winter was beginning to move quickly and he awoke each morning on his cardboard-covered straw in the shanty with his feet frozen and the fear in his heart that he might be wanted by the law in Maple Creek. Some of the youths around him talked vaguely of heading west, others of going to New Bedford and shipping out on a whaler. Each grandly painted notion sounded plausible to him, but he waited.

It was by chance that he encountered the roving recruiting detail outside of the hotel and he stood and listened as a sergeant explained reasons and procedures to several well-dressed young men. He had heard with uninterest about trouble brewing with the South and the sergeant was talking earnestly about the need to strengthen the army. But as he listened to the recruiting sergeant delivering what amounted to a sermon on the sanctity of Union and the evils of Secession, his mind was considering the onset of something much more immediate—months of dark stolid winter—and his eyes moodily contemplated the sergeant's natty little blue forage cap with its brass bugle insignia and the man's operatic-looking long blue overcoat with cape. Tom had never seen a soldier before, until coming to Albany, and now here he was standing so close to several, the aura of those blue uniforms positively radiating with enchantment. He stared at them contemplatively, with the indecision of someone trying to decide how to spend his last dime. And then he thought again of winter and of the secret under the pine boughs, and he heard himself blurting out, I'll go.

The sergeant narrowed one eye. How old are you, boy?

Tom paused.

Are you eighteen? the sergeant asked.

Tom's face brightened. Yes, sir. Just eighteen.

Well, bless you. We need strapping lads like yourself.

And suddenly emboldened, Tom asked, Is there pay?

The sergeant threw back his head and laughed, so raucous and infectious a boomer it made everyone smile.

By God, he said, you don't think we'd ask a man to defend his country for just a uniform and a handshake, do you? Why, we pay thirteen American dollars every month.

He and the other area enlistees went by train to a recruit depot north of New York City for training. Here he was outfitted with his own blue forage cap and his own blue overcoat with cape, in addition to a single-breasted dark blue wool sack dress coat with a single row of brass-eagle buttons, dark blue jacket which they called a blouse, light blue kersey trousers with dark blue stripes up the sides that identified him as infantry, a pair of dark blue flannel shirts, several pairs of cotton flannel drawers, a leather belt, and a pair of black shoes (which disintegrated in the first heavy rain). Some of it actually fit, and he spent several hours of his first day trading garments with men of appropriate sizes. After that he could hardly pass a mirror without pausing for a moment's stern self-inspection.

So he was regular army when it started the following April. His regiment missed First Bull Run but not much after that. They fought through the Peninsula Campaign, where a Confederate bullet caught him in the shoulder at Mechanicsville, which kept him out of the bloody cornfields at Antietam ("You missed the worst of it," a friend told him when he rejoined the regiment, "which means you didn't miss anything"), but he was back for Chancellorsville and then the prodigious collision of Gettysburg.

By the spring of 1864 he was a sergeant, a survivor in a company that had by now lost some seventy percent of its original rank and file. Not yet twenty-one years old, he had already experienced a dozen lifetimes of death and running blood. There was still more ahead but now he was moving into it with a sense of history and context gained from a winter's lying in his wedge tent reading books borrowed from a schoolteacher tentmate. With spare understanding he read Herodotus and Tacitus, Macaulay and Carlyle, and biographies of Alexander and Napoleon, reading over and over with moving lips the passages that most puzzled him. Through his reading he came to believe that the carnage he was living through was not total lunacy, that the shattered bones and bleeding breasts contained more meaning and less folly than he imagined, that the great flow of history had among its mighty leaps and sonorous plunges whirlpools and tidal furies, all in the bruised and battered name of peace and justice.

His life and fortunes took a pivotal turn in the nightmare Battle of the Wilderness in early May 1864, just west of the old Chancellorsville field, with soldiers going to battle seeing the macabre and ominous relics of unburied skulls and rib cages. The Wilderness was the last place that huge armies should have fought. A tangle of second growth, it was filled with sapling masses and stunted pine and dry intractable thickets, with intertwining vines and creepers that tied it together with savage lacework. There were abrupt starts and thrusts of hillocks and knolls. Sluggish streams moved through gloomy shadows. Swampy bogs yielded soggily underfoot. Woodland roads squirmed through here and there, used by subsistence farmers now chased off by the pall of war, while sudden paths began with no apparent purpose and then ended as meaninglessly, as if their blazers had come this far and perished.

It was here that Lee resolved to fight, under the belief that in these dense, matted, impassable woods formations would go asunder and communications be lost and his two-to-one disadvantage in numbers be neutralized. Grant accepted the challenge and plunged in, pouring his bluecoats into this place that looked like nature's tossed bone to a designing Satan.

Until it had actually begun, Tom could not believe that generals would make war in so sinister a place. It would be impossible to deploy and fight. But then it began, as it always did, with the sound of muskets riding down the wind. And then the chaos, men rushing through the woods, battalions immediately broken apart and separated. They ran through clawing thickets, stumbling over unseen vines and roots, trying under crisscrossing gunfire to make some sense of it. Men appeared, disappeared, took hold of one another and demanded answers.

Whose division are you?

Crawford.

You're in it too. By God, then this is big.

Why? Who are you?

Wadsworth.

I just ran across somebody from Griffin.

Griffin too? Lord a'mighty, this is going to be big.

Officers were hacking their way through the growth with swords, urging their men to stay in rank, but it was impossible to defile in this place; the lessons of the parade ground and of previous battlegrounds were meaningless here. In some areas the rifle fire was so heavily concentrated trees were being cut in two by it. Soon the smoke, unable to rise above the dense, low branches, rolled like a fog, weaving in trapped and aimless clouds, brought alive here and there by red spurts of musket fire, with no one having the least idea of who was shooting at whom.

By late afternoon wisps of smoke were escaping from the thickets as though from pipelike chimneys. Thin red flames were starting to run along the ground like streamers. The shouted cries of Fire! Fire! Fire! were not calls to urge a trigger but were panicky warnings. The tangled woods were beginning to blaze and the wounded were soon confronting roaring furnaces, calling for help, salvation, or the mercy of a final bullet.

Tom, as confused and disoriented as any, long separated from his men, unable in the thickening smoke to distinguish a blue target from a gray and anyway no longer thinking about attacking or defending but only finding some sane passage out—Tom had suddenly resolved to follow one direction and one only: away from the fires that seemed to be growing like lusty red vegetation all around him. Everything around him had become a terrifying confluence of panicky men, of gunfire, of crackling flames.

A plaintive wailing drew him into a thicket where he found a young soldier sprawled amid the thorns, hatless, face milk white and riven with pain and terror, blood running from a chest wound. Throwing aside his rifle, Tom bent and lifted the soldier under the shoulders and began dragging him off, the barbed thorns tearing strips of cloth from the soldier's uniform.

Tom dragged him as far as a marshy swale and there eased him down.

There's others in there, the soldier said, one hand covering the bleeding chest wound like a man pledging allegiance.

Tom returned to the thicket, feeling the fiery heat leap and swarm against his face. He gulped a lungful of acrid smoke and for a moment gagged on it, whirling his face aside and expectorating. Then he saw another crumpled, gasping figure lying amid the crushed bramble. Pushing his way through, he crouched and reached out, taking no notice of the eagle on the man's shoulder straps. He turned the man around, brushed a gleaming red spark from the man's beard, then began trying to get a grip on him.

Never mind me, the colonel said. Help the men.

With some effort—the man was tall and well proportioned—Tom lifted him, the man's bullet-shattered leg splashing him with blood as Tom raised him and slung him unceremoniously over his back, tottering under the burden.

I'm ordering you—the colonel said, his voice weak but irascible.

Be quiet, Tom said, swinging around and staggering through the brush.

Get the men! the colonel said angrily.

Shut your damned mouth, Tom muttered, moving slowly, taking care not to stumble.

He hauled his burden several hundred feet, swerving this way and that to avoid the enclosing fires, the colonel protesting all the way, sometimes coherently, sometimes not. Finally Tom knelt and let him slide to the ground.

Damn you, the colonel muttered, then winced, his beard trembling.

Tom looked back. There would be no returning; the

flames had already consumed where he had just come from and were snatching at twigs and branches and leaping voraciously forward, filled with a voluminous crackling and a dense airy roar. Trees were coming down, trunks eaten bare by seething red fires. A sudden wind acted as a bellows, throwing the flames yet higher and further and carrying with it the sickening stench of burning flesh. Through the smoke he caught glimpses of men limping, running, vanishing almost as quickly as they appeared.

Once again he bent and raised the colonel, whose suffering seemed to make him more leaden.

Save yourself, the colonel murmured.

With the colonel once again on his back, Tom continued on, away from the fires, away from the thick poisonous white clouds. Like ghosts men began appearing around them, floating out of the woods as silent as the pursuing smoke, processions of saints and martyrs, bleeding, broken, confused, while from somewhere around the sounds of gunfire reported that madmen were still fighting within the deadly crucible of the Wilderness.

The colonel became momentarily delirious, asking to be set down near cool water among the wildflowers. Tom stumbled on, once kicking against a pile of smoldering duff that flashed up like a silent shellburst, threw an incendiary glare, and then receded.

Finally he struck a wagon road and fell in with a gathering of the lost and the dumbstruck. Here he laid the colonel into an ambulance wagon. Abruptly the colonel sat up and confronted his savior with a pair of red angry eyes.

What is your name? he demanded.

Sergeant Thomas Maynard was the weary answer. And then, noticing for the first time the eagled shoulder straps, he added, Sir.

● ● ●

It was months later, with the army huddled down in winter quarters near Petersburg, when Tom was summoned to the regimental commander's log cabin. There he was awaited by a tall, severe-looking colonel who was standing erect but evidently needed the support of the cane he held in his right hand.

Sergeant Thomas Maynard? he asked.

Yes, sir.

Do you remember me?

No, sir.

You carried me on your back out of the Wilderness fires. Did you carry so many that you don't remember?

No, sir. Not that many. I do remember you now, sir.

Do you also remember that I ordered you to put me down and that you told me to shut my mouth?

No, sir. But if I did, I apologize.

I didn't ask for an apology, Sergeant. What with one thing and another, it's taken me this long to track you down. And now I want your stripes.

Sir?

To replace them with a lieutenant's bar. If that is suitable to you.

Yes, sir, Tom said.

My name is Northwood. Colonel Northwood. You've been assigned to my staff. How does that sit with you?

Just fine, sir.

Good man, Northwood said, with a slow, approving smile.

I'll tell you why Northwood likes you, another staff member, a major, said to Tom after the war. Not just because you saved his life, but because he thinks you've got brains. That's why he was so delighted that you stayed in after so many others mustered out. If you didn't have brains he would have let you go after the war. But he respects you. And Northwood's got the ears of Grant and Sherman, don't forget. You've landed yourself a soft cushion, Tom boy.

The cushion became a cactus in 1870, when Northwood was assigned to Fort Supply on the Southern Plains Frontier to help the army contend with Kiowas and Comanches. Tom saw some bloody engagements with these fiercely skilled warriors, further distinguishing himself in Northwood's eyes. After a few years Northwood was recalled to Washington, promoted to brigadier general, and assigned to the War Department. With him went the young man whom Northwood would occasionally jocularly refer to as the only man ever to disobey one of his orders and live to tell the tale.

The last time he had written to his family in Maple Creek was in 1865, two months after the end of the war. He told them he'd served through it and come out all right. But even after all of that, after all of those colossal battles and unspeakable experiences, after the cordwood dead of Gettysburg and Cold Harbor, he remained haunted by a single figure lying under a cover of pine boughs whose needles had long since browned, and he told his family he was once more a civilian and was heading for San Francisco. And even as he penned the letter he wondered who there might be left to read it, to care. His brothers had no doubt enlisted; he knew several in the village who would unquestionably have, and once they did, well, then the whole crowd would follow. So he wondered. Had his brothers come home? Was his father still alive?

Ah, he thought. It's a whole new life. Years of it now. Look away and look ahead.

CHAPTER 14

MAJOR JOSEPHSON

"I've been told I must talk to you and answer your questions," Major Josephson said. "I'll comply, of course, though I must say I don't know what good it's going to do. We did run our own inquiry out here, quite thoroughly I felt. Of course, you're probably saying to yourself, 'What kind of inquiry could it have been when one of the committee was quite possibly the guilty party?' Well, my feeling is that that fact only smoked up our determination to be as diligent and impartial as we could."

"No one has commented adversely on your efforts, Major," Maynard said.

"Only on the results, eh?" Josephson said quickly with a sardonic chuckle. "Well, we can't argue with that, can we? We didn't find him, did we? I wanted to, believe me. Find him and clear him out. We don't want that kind in the army. They can contaminate the good ones, and those are the ones most precious, Captain: the good ones. You've been through it, Maynard, and you know the answer to this: What's the backbone of an army? Never mind generals and grand strategy. It's those good soldiers, the ones who make the others around them better simply by unwitting example. Those are the men I care about, and believe me, Maynard, I never spent them foolishly or recklessly."

They were sitting on the porch of Josephson's quarters, in the midst of officers' row, facing the parade ground, which was empty at the moment except for the passing wagons of several merchants and contractors in from outlying settlements to trade at the sutler's. They were sitting on the pair of grained, black-painted Boston rockers that had followed the Josephsons from one posting to the next for the past ten years. The morning sun was on the other side of the parade ground, the porch was in shade, the edge of the flat roof looking as if it was painted across the dust.

Josephson's bald head was covered by a blue slouch hat, which he wore pulled forward, the soft brim hanging low over his pugnacious face with its broken nose (which Maynard heard had been received in a barroom brawl before the war). A smoking cheroot, which he seldom removed, was clenched between his teeth and every so often he would expand his lips and grimace around it. It was evident to Maynard that though Josephson was responsive, part of his mind was elsewhere, his eyes occasionally squinting, as if to better comprehend some private image.

"The problem was," Josephson said, "that the army was moving when it happened. Everything was in motion. Terry and Custer were marching out from Fort Lincoln, Gibbon was coming in from the Montana stations, and Crook was marching north with a large force. We were finally going to settle with Sitting Bull and his colleagues. Then this business happened here. Well, under different circumstances it would have been otherwise handled. So back in Washington, Sherman or Sheridan or somebody said, 'We've got our plates full right now; let the on-site officers handle it.' I didn't want it. I didn't like the idea. None of us did. It was bad enough to have to sit here while a campaign of that magnitude was unfolding up north without then having to sit behind a desk and ask a lot of damn fool questions."

"Were you surprised that you were unable to resolve it?"

"I don't know if I was surprised; I was certainly disappointed. We tried our damndest."

"Do you have any theories about what happened?" Maynard asked.

"I'm not a man who theorizes, Captain," Josephson said. "Theorizing gives you an aura of intelligence that you really haven't earned. I hope you're not out here to collect theories."

"General Englund held a post-dinner meeting in his office that night," Maynard said. "Was that formal or informal?"

"Englund was never informal," Josephson said morosely, staring straight ahead.

"He talked about plans for an upcoming campaign."

"That he did, with great relish. He'd heard about some Sioux being in the area and we were going to go after them as soon as the scout reported."

"Duchard?"

"That's right."

"Did you know him?"

"I knew him as a scout, but that was all."

"You never spoke to him other than in line-of-duty capacities?"

"Why should I? What did I have to say to him? The man was a sullen son of a bitch. Was supposed to have traded guns to the Indians some years ago. But he gave good service for his pay, I'll say that."

"And Englund trusted him."

"He did."

"So the meeting that night," Maynard said, rocking slowly, occasionally glancing across his shoulder at the impassive Josephson, "was to discuss the campaign."

"Which never came off, of course, what with all the confusion that followed. Anyway, that fool Duchard disappeared, so we never knew what report he had come back with. We sent out some troopers to reconnoiter and they rode a fairly wide perimeter and saw nothing; but with the Sioux you never know. They can melt into hills and valleys like snow."

"Do you think a few renegades might have breached fort security that night and committed the murders?"

"I do not," Josephson said bluntly.

"And yet two murders were committed, with one of the victims the commanding officer."

"I'm aware of that. I can only tell you who I think did not do it. Further than that, no."

"What about the rest of the commissioned officers?" Maynard asked.

"What about them?"

"How do you regard them?"

Josephson took a moment, seemed to make a deeper study of whatever it was he was thinking.

"Look, Maynard," he said, "you're a staff officer. If some stranger came around and asked you—no matter on what authority—to dish him some negative opinions on your fellow officers, what would you say to him?"

"Probably what you just did, Major," Maynard said with a smile. "Anyway, I wasn't necessarily looking for the negative."

"Then the question was pointless."

"What did you do after the meeting ended?"

"Came back here and went to sleep."

"Your wife was back East at the time."

"Still is, with Mrs. Fordyce. So you want to know how you can be sure that I did as I said. Well, you can be because I'm telling you. Look, Maynard, I respect you because you were sent out here by General Northwood, for whom I have the highest regard. But if you think you can be keener than the accumulated brain power of the officers who investigated this matter, then sharp disappointment awaits you."

"With respect, Major, your accumulated brain power came up with no answers."

"And you think you can?"

"I can only try," Maynard said mildly.

"And I'll clear your path as best I can. If you think this post has been a pleasant place since the incidents, then you're mistaken. It's become rotten with tension and suspicion and ludicrous speculation. You can imagine what they must be babbling about in the ranks. The whole thing is a goddamned disgrace."

"Were you personally close to General Englund?"

"We went through the war together. We had that. I respected him as an officer. But close? I don't think anybody was, beyond his family of course. He was a very proud and severe man. As I mentioned, very formal. You'd think after so many years . . . but no, he could no more unbend than a telegraph pole. But that was his way and I respected it."

"You liked him?"

"He was a brilliant commanding officer. He had the allegiance of his staff as well as the rank and file. I considered it a privilege to serve under him."

"Why would anybody want to kill him?"

"I don't know, Captain. But if you come to it, I suppose that somewhere there's an assassin for every man."

"What about that story of his sword?" Maynard asked.

"What has that got to do with anything?"

"Do you believe it?"

Josephson puffed meditatively on his cheroot. "I wasn't there," he said, "so I don't know." After some moments of silence, he added, "He could make you believe it though, the way he talked about it."

"I understand, Major, that at the conclusion of the meeting that night the general broke out some brandy and offered a toast."

"To the war dead, yes."

"And you appended, 'At Fredericksburg.' "

"I did."

"Which created some tension in the room."

"Did it?"

"As I understand," Maynard said.

"Perhaps."

"Why did you say that?"

Josephson sat silently for several moments, turning the cheroot slowly between his teeth. "Perhaps," he said, "you should ask Colonel Bruckner that question. It has more to do with him."

"You made the toast on his behalf?"

"Not likely," Josephson said dryly. Then for the first time he turned to Maynard, who found himself being studied by a pair of intensely scrutinizing eyes that under the hat brim seemed deeper than they really were. "Which one do you remember, Maynard? And don't tell me they've all come to swim together in memory."

Maynard was silent.

"For me it's Fredericksburg," Josephson said, eyes hardening defiantly for a moment. "And you? Soldier to soldier."

Maynard felt embarrassed; he didn't know why.

"The Wilderness," he said quietly.

"Yes," Josephson murmured, turning back to what had been his fixed field of vision, across which marched a guard detail. "Look at them," he said with an odd mix of pride and disdain. "Our charges. We're responsible for them, aren't we? They hand over to us their trust and their lives. Good men, most of them. Hard and tough. Give them orders and they'll carry them out. Why? Because they believe in our wisdom. Any officer who spends even one of them unwisely or unnecessarily should be shot. What do you think, Captain?"

"As an enlisted man, I certainly held with that."

Josephson laughed mirthlessly. Then he sighed. "But what is a soldier without a war?" he said. "We sit out here year after year and chase the occasional Sioux or Cheyenne. Even with a large campaign going on up north, what do we do? We sit. I was breveted a brigadier in the war, you know. For a time I commanded a division. Thousands of men, Maynard, with flags flying and drumrolls like thunder. Battles that shook the continent from ocean to ocean. The Army of the Potomac was the most magnificent fighting force the world has ever seen. Caesar, Alexander, Hannibal, Napoleon himself never saw anything like it." Josephson lifted his jaw and puffed clouds of smoke from his cheroot and gazed into them. "Oh God," he said softly.

CHAPTER 15

THE GENERAL'S LADY

Leaving Josephson, Maynard walked across the parade ground to the sutler's store where Barrie was waiting for him. The sutler, a round-bellied middle-aged man, ran a small store in a small post. The shelves and counters of his low-ceilinged place of business contained whisky, tobacco, playing cards, canned fruit, shoelaces, needle and thread, soap, combs, and other items the soldiers bought on credit and paid for on payday. Several ollas of cool water hung from the rafters.

Barrie, with money still fresh in pocket from the recent payday, was completing a transaction for a small sack of tobacco. When he saw Maynard standing in the doorway staring at him with the thin patience that was the prerogative of superior officers, Barrie hurried the transaction along, then left.

The several wagons of the daily water-barrel working party were rumbling by, heading out to a nearby spring to refill. They would be back later in the day with freshly refilled barrels for the cookhouse, officers' quarters, and barracks. It was considered one of the choicer work details, preferable to construction or stable cleaning.

Maynard watched the mule-drawn wagons go off, then said, "I was just speaking with Major Josephson."

"Yes, sir," Barrie said.

"He's an odd one, isn't he?"

"Oh, Joe's all right."

"Joe?"

"Major Josephson, sir."

"You like him?"

"There's no officer I'd rather smell the smoke with."

They began walking toward the western end of the fort, toward Company B barracks, behind which were the corral and laundry.

"About two years ago," Barrie said, "we were out to the Black Hills after a band of hostiles who'd done some particularly nasty things. We'd found a couple of our boys tied up and so badly mutilated it looked like wolves had et at them. That makes you mad all right, but also scared. You can't help but to start thinking. Well, we'd tracked real close to those hostiles and were set to hit them the next morning. We camped down that night and I can tell you, Captain, it was real quiet. We had a lot of fresh recruits with us, on their first campaign, and you could taste the scaredness. I was on picket around midnight, and here's Major Josephson pacing back and forth in front of me. Back and forth, back and forth. Naturally I don't say anything, but I'm watching him. Suddenly he stops and comes up to me and starts talking. The only time he's ever done that. 'Sergeant,' he says, 'are you scared?' 'Yes, sir,' I says. 'Me too,' he says. 'So if a couple of old campaigners like us, who've been through it large and small for years, are scared, can you imagine how the new men must feel? We're going to have to rally them on, aren't we, Sergeant?' That's what he said, Captain. And that

was Old Joe—if you'll pardon it, sir—having his men to
heart. Something like that gets into the air and the men
breathe it. We went in at dawn, scattered the ponies and hit
the lodges, and the boys came through just fine. Because
Major Josephson knew how to lead them."

They passed the barracks and continued walking toward
the laundry.

"Different officers," Barrie said, "different styles. The
men know it, too. You were in the ranks, Captain, you
know that. When Major Josephson takes men in, he's not
just thinking of winning but surviving. Now Major
Fordyce—a very good line officer, mind you—he goes in
smelling death."

"What do you mean?" Maynard asked.

"Oh, not that he's reckless; it's just that he fights crusades
and goes in prepared every time to meet his Maker. He prays
a lot. Nothing wrong in that; we're all God-fearing sinners,
ain't we, Captain? But Major Fordyce prays too much. It's
like he's asking God to accept his soul rather than to preserve his life."

"How do you pick up all this crap, Barrie?"

"Oh, by watching people, and by watching the faces of
people who are watching other people. Faces speak a language, Captain."

"And you believe that?"

"You have to believe what you believe, sir, otherwise
you're just a shadow on the wall."

The door to the laundry was open and they could hear
water being sloshed around and could see the laundresses
inside, bent over tin tubs and washboards, wearing long cal-
ico dresses that covered their shoe tops. Now and then one
emerged, clothes pegs in mouth, arms full of wet clothing
which they hung on ropes that were strung from one
wooden post to another.

"Ugly as sin," Barrie said ruefully. "Every last one of them."

"By design," Maynard said.

"By design?"

"How long have you been on the frontier, Sergeant? What happens to any comely woman who makes an appearance? She's besieged by suitors. The agencies back East have a standing order from the army: send out only the most unattractive and unappealing. They'll last longer and cause less trouble."

"That still doesn't stop some of the boys from marryin' up," Barrie said.

"Well, it can get lonely out here."

"You've still got to bring them back home with you one day," Barrie said with a shake of the head.

They walked on to the corral, where several cavalry horses were standing inside the rail fences, flicking their tails and nuzzling against the ground. High above, the sky was a soaring arch of endless deep blue except off to the west, where a flotilla of white clouds was beginning to appear.

Maynard leaned against the corral fence.

"I want to ask you about the Scheffners, Billy," he said. "Is that by any chance a delicate topic around here?"

With unease evident in his voice, Barrie said, "Yes, sir, it is."

"Well, I'm sorry."

"It doesn't have anything to do with the army, Captain. I mean it doesn't have anything to do with fighting Sioux or teaching men how to drill or how to build a travois. It's just people tangling themselves around and the army has nothing to do with it."

Poor Barrie, Maynard thought with some sympathetic understanding. This sly wise veteran of battles prodigious and modest, this self-anointed appraiser of human nature's everchanging colorations, this canny watchdog and inveterate observer of all acts and scenes, this reader of history on the head of a pin—was embarrassed and maybe even flustered by behavior that Maynard didn't think was that uncommon or that exotic, either.

"I don't think, Captain," the unhappy Barrie said, "that it has any approach to what happened."

"Mrs. Scheffner is a very beautiful woman."

Barrie sighed.

"Would the captain understand," he said, "if we didn't proceed on with this?"

"The captain would understand completely," Maynard said with some light mockery of Barrie's stilted usage. "Nevertheless, the captain intends to proceed on with it." Switching to a cajoling tone, he said, "Look, Billy, either I hear it from you and I hear it correctly, or else someone else tells me and makes it sound worse than it is."

"In spite of what you may think of me, Captain, I don't like to indulge in gossip that can be harmful."

"I think very highly of you, Sergeant. I rate your personal character among the most honorable I've ever met. Believe me, I don't want to hear any harmful gossip; what I do want to hear is useful information."

"I don't like to pass judgment, sir, especially on senior officers; but what was happening was in violation of the army code of honor, in my opinion."

"Which officer was in violation?"

"General Englund," Barrie said glumly.

"I think I know how, but I would prefer not to guess."

"He was conducting an illicit relationship with Mrs. Scheffner."

"How do you know this?" Maynard asked.

Barrie gave him a pained look.

"What I mean is," Maynard said, "do you know it for a fact? Do you know it to be true?"

"Well, sir, I can't say I was ever in the room with them . . . but, yes, Captain, it is true."

Yes, Maynard believed it. It was the reason why Patman was reluctant to discuss Scheffner. Patman's had been the signal, Barrie's the confirmation. And anyway, it hardly seemed so improbable, given the spiritual depletion that seemed to have overtaken Lieutenant Colonel Scheffner, compared to the sensual vitality of his much younger wife. Granted, he was not expert in these matters, Maynard conceded (beyond his man-of-the-world perspective), but how expert did you have to be? Although polite society might have preferred to think otherwise, these were hardly uncommon liaisons. What made this one disturbingly ripe for contemplation was where it had taken place and the identity of one of the principals: Alfred Englund. Maynard didn't know why he supposed Englund should have been exempt from indulging in behavior of this nature; he, Maynard, had certainly seen enough senior officers, not to mention cabinet officers and other stiff-backs of government, stepping in and out of the heavily draperied rooms of Washington's better bordellos; and who didn't know about that pillar of the United States Senate (married, yes) who never missed his Friday night visit to his sultry octoroon; or the frosty-faced minister (yes, married) of one of the city's more eminent churches whose trysts with a certain buxom widow had spawned one of the city's most avidly circulated quips: "He visits her religiously."

It was Englund, that was what made it seem so devoid of plausibility. And the idea of its implausibility made Maynard realize that he, too, was in danger of falling under the man's sorcery and that it had better be dispelled if the truth was to be uncovered, for up until now there had been nothing but fear and awe and veneration, the image of a crimson-shadowed icon, an intimidating specter that stood within a circle of flame. But Englund was human, and what had possessed him was human, and, no matter the vibration, what he had sent forth was human, as fragile and fallible as any humanity.

The look of transgression was plainly in Barrie's face as he stared into the corral.

"How many people knew of the affair?" Maynard asked.

"I'm sure all the commissioned officers knew," Barrie said. He shifted about uncomfortably; he had little enthusiasm for this.

"What about the ranks?"

"I never heard any talk. And they would have prattled about it."

"Where did they meet?"

"In his office, late at night. He'd dismiss his adjutant. A few times I'd been in the guardhouse having a cup of coffee with the OD and the adjutant would come in and say he'd been dismissed and I'd get curious."

Barrie missed Maynard's indulgent smile.

"So I'd watch," Barrie said. "And sure enough, here she'd come. Striding through the night. Always wore this long cape, with the hood thrown back. In she'd go."

"She didn't seem diffident about it?"

"Sir?"

"Shy."

"Not for me to say, Captain."

"How often?"

"Couldn't say, Captain. How often does it take to make it what it is?"

"When did it start?"

"Couldn't say that either. I picked up on it during the winter. December, I'd say."

"His family was still here then."

"Yes, sir."

"Do you think they knew?"

"I should think not."

"Do you think the other wives knew?"

"I don't know, Captain. Maybe Mrs. Bruckner, but she wouldn't tell a soul. Real lady, that one."

"How would she have known?" Maynard asked.

"The colonel would have told her, sir. I don't think the others are the type to have told their wives. But the Bruckners, well, you get the feeling they tell each other everything. I mean no offense, sir."

"Was Mrs. Scheffner the only one the general dallied with?"

"I would suspect so," Barrie said. "He wouldn't go near a laundress—especially the ones we've got here—and as far as the other wives, well, Mrs. Josephson looks like a cannonball and Mrs. Fordyce has the dimensions of a buffalo, if the captain will forgive me."

"Colonel Scheffner obviously knew about it," Maynard said.

A large black stallion wandered toward them, neck bent and face nodding at ground level, then stopped and began cropping some grass.

Barrie sighed. "I should think so."

"What kind of man is he?"

"Good enough to feel sorry for."

"I appreciate your telling me this, Billy."

"It's not the sweetest thing in the world to tell, is it, Captain? I mean, a commanding officer . . . I don't mean to say I'm a babe just out of swaddling; I've overturned a few baskets in my time . . . but for someone like General Englund to go pickin' daisies with one of his staff's wives . . ."

"Yes."

"I don't see where this helps your inquiry, but you asked. I hope it won't stain the general's good name."

"If it doesn't have to," Maynard said, "it won't."

CHAPTER 16

COLONEL BRUCKNER THE DOCTOR

Colonel Bruckner received Maynard in the headquarters office.

"I appreciate your giving me your time, sir," Maynard said after having been asked to sit down.

"Time is the one thing we have plenty of around here just now," Bruckner said, sitting back in his chair, as if making himself comfortable for an interrogation.

"Then you think that skirmish we had out on the prairie was just a twilight gasp?"

"I've had men out riding very wide-ranging patrols. There are no signs of any hostiles, nor word of them. What you came up against was a breakaway fragment. The Sioux are finished as a fighting force in this part of the Territory, and very shortly everywhere else as well."

"What will happen to this place?"

"Fort Larkin? Abandonment, I should think. We'll rejoin the regiment and life will go on."

Maynard looked at the black leather couch against one wall. He had barely taken notice of it before; it now seemed invested with unimaginable qualities.

"How are you coming on with your inquiries?" Bruckner asked, studying Maynard's averted face. "Or is that an improper question?"

Maynard looked back to him, smiling self-consciously for a moment, as though his consideration of the couch had been transparent.

"Well, I haven't made any grand discoveries as yet, Colonel. I've been collecting bits of information that are like fireflies—they light up for a second, but when you try to get close for a second look they extinguish themselves and then reappear elsewhere."

"No pattern," Bruckner said. His patrician's face was without expression.

"Not yet."

"That must be frustrating," Bruckner said, voice as toneless as face was expressionless.

"Yes," Maynard said, not at all surprised by the lack of concern.

"I would imagine," Bruckner said, "that you've been turning up a lot of information that, while interesting, is irrelevant."

"Probably; except I can't be sure as yet what is relevant and what is not."

"Of course."

"And so I must go on with my questions."

"If you'll pardon the analogy, Captain, but you're like one of those prospectors over in the Black Hills, poking about here and there hoping to make a strike."

Maynard laughed. "I hope, Colonel, that I'm being a bit more scientific than they are."

"Are you in here now to do some prospecting?"

"Yes, sir," Maynard said. "I want to ask you about Fredericksburg."

"Ah," Bruckner said, "has that come up?" His self-possession remained total.

"Major Josephson made mention of it, then referred me to you."

"I see."

Maynard thought he detected just the briefest glint of amused curiosity in Bruckner's steady, candidly staring eyes.

"One of my fireflies of information," Maynard said.

"Fredericksburg is," Bruckner said, then paused, and as if in mild self-revelation, said, "fourteen years ago."

"I know that, sir."

"Were you there?"

"We were held in reserve."

"Your good fortune, Captain," Bruckner said, then moved his eyes a fraction, away from Maynard, and gazed into the past, eyes taking on an expression that Maynard understood: re-creating in tranquil meditation the storms of shot and peril, holding oneself in perfectly composed stillness, mesmerized by the awe and incredulity of what was flooding the memory. Yes, Maynard thought. Pious equanimity was the only way in which to make the confrontation.

It wasn't just that the battle was bloody and brutal and the casualties horrifying; it was that the whole plan was wrongheaded and ill-advised, barbarously carried out, and hopeless and wasteful. Wave upon wave of men were dispatched after goals they could not possibly attain, openly exposed to murderous fire as they hurled themselves against positions that were impregnable. For hour after hour the carnage numbed all sense in the Union command post: Ambrose Burnside's stubborn incompetence and the heroics of his men, who kept obeying, and dying, for it.

Englund (colonel then) and Bruckner and Josephson (captains then) had felt uneasy from the moment the army was allowed to cross the Rappahannock unmolested by the Confederate batteries and riflemen entrenched on the hilly elevations that rose like a collar around the small Virginia city that was about to be carved into history like a scar, allowed to tramp across the swaying hollow-sounding pontoon bridges and pour into the streets and then to form at the edge of the long plain that swept up to the rebel positions. The idea of being allowed to occupy and possess what was in the range of commanding enemy firepower in stronghold positions was one that sat uneasily within the columns of Union infantry, wherein the general thinking was, *They're letting us in smart and easy. Let's see how we get out.* The elevations were modest in height—maybe fifty feet above the plain, which was empty and almost featureless in the cold December sunshine—but were a defending commander's dream: high enough to hold but not too high to discourage attack. The Confederates had had several days to prepare their positions to their liking, and with pick and shovel had built the hard Virginia earth into piles, using bayonet tips to fashion embrasures, arranging their batteries of twelve-pound Napoleon smoothbores for greatest coverage. And then they waited, bivouacking behind the hills, the pulsing red glow of their campfires visible in the night sky to the gathering Union soldiers below. Through the night there were the sounds of movement, of columns marching across those bridges in constant, endless murmur, and the sounds of civilians leaving the city by wagon and on horseback.

This has a bad feeling, Josephson said to Englund after the division had crossed the river and were trying to settle down for the night. And the men know it, he added.

They always know it, Englund said. Have you ever seen a

herd of sheep when they know a wolf is near? I'm afraid a lot of *If I should fall* letters are being written tonight.

I expect my men to be afraid before a battle, Josephson said. They should be. But when that apprehension is laced with anxiety about their commander's judgment, I don't like it.

And Englund, whose courage seemed to feed on the misgivings of others, said, But we'll show them a good face tomorrow, won't we, Joe?

On the morning of December 12 heavy fog and mist shrouded the plain between the rise of ground known as Marye's Heights and the river. Just after noon the moist veil melted off, revealing to rebel eyes the blue formations in the sunlight, regimental colors aslant above the shoulders of their bearers, symbols of a resolute ritual. The clear unspoiled sunlight touched each bayonet tip as if in benediction.

Advancing in parade ground columns, the forward ranks began their procession. The fences that marked small fields were soon leveled and trampled flat. From behind, the moving tide of blue seemed irresistible. Then a signal cannon boomed from the heights and a few moments later the symmetry of the advancing ranks was torn asunder by fusillades of bullet and canister delivered by squinting riflemen and recoiling cannons. At the foot of the heights was a sunken road shielded by a four-foot stone wall and from behind this suddenly rose up a firing line of gray-clad infantry, each a grim soloist peering along his aimed rifle, and turned loose a blistering lead storm into the now raggedly advancing formations.

More and more Union troops poured into the open field toward the heights, halted for a few moments to re-form their lines, and then, to the astonishment of their officers, began an impetuous rush forward, shouting and yelling as they stormed the open ground, leaping over the kneeling and prostrate wounded and the outstretched dead, seeing but not registering the dismembered and the headless. Once more the bronze Napoleons aimed their ferocious mouths into the charging columns and once more consumed the attackers with bellowing discharges of canister that exploded and scattered their packages of red-hot cast-iron balls and slugs. Nearing the stone wall, the blue infantry were struck by a blinding roar of rifle fire so concentrated and delivered with such simultaneity it looked like a single sheet of flame leaping out toward them. Now the blue columns—what remained of them—turned their faces toward the river and fled.

Josephson, retreating in full fury with his men, would hear forever the *pang ping pong* sounds tolled with somberly varying sonance by a cast-iron stove abandoned in the field as it was struck at different thicknesses by shot after shot. When he returned he found an incensed, haggard-looking Englund—aged years in moments, it seemed—rushing about on horseback, woolen slouch hat in hand, ordering the men to re-form, shouting streams of orders, galloping furiously back and forth and wheeling around precipitously as if hemmed by invisible barriers.

Urged on by their colonel's imprecations to *Storm that wall! We must storm that wall!* the columns re-formed and attacked once more, buttressed by fresh regiments, the voices of officers alternately stern and soothing rising among the din of shot and shell. And then another wave of canister smashed down from the heights and another seething storm of rifle fire and this time it seemed that more men lay prone on the plain than came reeling back.

At twilight, after several more horrendous repetitions, Englund, dismounted, was once more shouting at his men, at their stunned and raging faces, to regroup and attack. At that moment a mounted courier appeared, shouted something, and without stopping galloped further along the line.

What was that? Englund asked, cupping his ear.

The attack is to cease, Bruckner said.

Now? Englund demanded. One more assault will carry us through.

The position cannot be taken, Colonel, Bruckner said.

Englund, hatless, his face looking gaunt and ancient, glared out toward the heights, at the thick drifting smoke, at the disorder of fallen soldiers piled four and five deep in some places, the piles here and there twitching with helpless, pathetic gestures.

We've softened them, Englund said bitterly, and by God's will we can take them. To stop now is blasphemy. One more time. Once. Tell the men to make ready. We'll break that line and turn the position and sweep along the crest. This time. This time.

But, Colonel—

One more time, Englund shouted. This time.

But the order was explicit—

I never received that communication, Englund said bluntly.

Colonel, my men have taken all they can bear.

Goddamn you, Englund said venomously, shoving Bruckner aside. Forward your columns! he shouted to his officers. Form ranks! Shoulder arms! Trail arms! Bayonets! he shouted as he rushed through the ranks of his amazed and stupefied men. Bayonet charge! Don't stop to fire! A straight charge to the wall and over it and clean the bastards out with steel! Then, drawing his sword, Englund raised it and like an actor in climactic speech, cried out, I'll lead you on!

Bruckner remained rooted, his broken spirit resonating with *Murder. Madness.* Crowds of helplessly obedient men swarmed together and followed their colonel. They marched across the plain into the fog of smoke that soon dropped upon them: heads, shoulders, upper torsos being swallowed by the insidious cloud; then legs, the rest of their bodies; momentarily gone; and then reappearing, the clouds beneath them now, as if they were making their ascent upon thin air, following the raised sword that remained poised. And then once more the guns racketed from behind the wall and the cannon roared from high above. From a distance, and after the events of this endless day, it hardly seemed calamitous or personally agonizing anymore. Simply more men falling to the ground.

"He survived," Bruckner said, eyes returning to Maynard's face, reemerging from that glimpse into a gorge of memory that could never restore itself. "Not many did, but somehow he got back. What he did was an act of magnificent lunacy. When he came back I don't think he had more than three or four inches of sword left. It had been struck three separate times, he said, each shot reducing it further."

"Englund and his magical swords," Maynard said in mild amusement.

Bruckner smiled indulgently.

"But the insubordination," Maynard said. "How did you deal with that?"

"I didn't deal with it, Captain."

"Why?"

"You've been through it; you know how impetuously decisions can be made."

"In the ranks, yes; but you're talking about a commanding officer."

"In a moment of high frustration."

"When he should have been the clearest of mind."

"You would have reported him?"

"I would have shot him," Maynard said.

Bruckner nodded thoughtfully. He did not take Maynard's comment lightly; like many of the army's high-echelon officers, he had heard the story of the young sergeant who had carried General Northwood to safety through the Wilderness fires.

"Well," Bruckner said, "I did neither." His tone was faintly explanatory.

"He would have been court-martialed. Should have been."

"Sins committed, sins unveiled. The two branches of morality. Although you would probably demand a more stringent application of judgment, I feel that in wartime men are sometimes entitled to wider latitudes. I don't condone disobeying orders, but there were instances when one man's initiative did turn the tide."

"And anyway," Maynard said with light sarcasm, "for all anyone knew, the courier might have been killed."

"In that confusion the courier may very well have forgotten what he told to whom. The whole day was a farce. I don't have to tell you about Fredericksburg. Look, Captain, Englund had always been an outstanding officer, and he was again throughout the war. One of the most impressive records of any general. I felt a loyalty to him, though I must admit that after that affair I was always a bit wary of him. He knew what I knew, and I think that's why he always wanted me on his staff. He wanted me near. You see, he built his record and his reputation on courage and brilliance. But I think he came to believe that I felt he had panicked at Fredericksburg, that what had seemed like a madman's courage had not been quite that."

"Did you think that?"

"Not at all. It was leadership *in extremis*. Almost an act of willful martyrdom, a man at a pitch of zealous passion the like of which I had never seen before and never want to again. It was like a rage against the heavens. I think it was a case of the Confederates defying Englund . . ."

"And God spoke to Englund."

"Ergo . . ."

"You're describing madness, Colonel."

"Shall we describe it as sublime inspiration?" Bruckner said without a trace of a smile. "But he was a wily man, too. After a while, I began to realize that he believed he had the upper hand on me, that by my silence I was complicitous; and more than that, that it was a sign of weakness on my part. I accepted my responsibility, in my own conscience. I should have acted; I could have saved the lives of countless good, brave men. But I did nothing. Not then, not later. You see, we never came to peace with it. I never said to him, 'Alfred, what you did was foolhardy, but it was brave and magnificent.' I think he might have wanted that."

"Did he ever reproach you for not joining that charge?"

"He never ordered me to."

"Would you have gone?"

"I have no answer to that question. But up to that time, and for years afterward, I never had a problem following the sword of General Englund."

"Did he ever speak of the affair?"

"Never. We'd sit and reminisce occasionally, in this very room, but Fredericksburg was never mentioned."

"For your sake or his?" Maynard asked with a slight smile.

"His, I'm sure."

"He was embarrassed?"

"Knowing Englund, yes. But not for disobeying an order. Not even for an unnecessary loss of life, though he was a caring officer."

"Then for the appearance of panic?"

"No, not that either," Bruckner said. "If there was any self-reproach it would have been for failing to breach the position. That, for General Englund, was the tragedy of Fredericksburg. And remember, Captain Maynard, he did lead that charge himself."

"A mitigating circumstance at best."

"I never thought I'd see him alive again. You can't imagine what it was like on that field. I've never felt so utterly helpless anywhere. But he came back. The man never lacked for courage, say that for him. He believed that God's hand was always out to protect him. And for a long time it seemed that way."

"Major Josephson knows what happened."

"Yes, I did tell him. I wanted him to know. They were mostly his men who were butchered in that charge."

"When did you tell him?"

"Some years after the war. It was one of those evenings when we were sitting and talking. He said he always suspected it. He was nearby when the courier delivered the message; he knew that something had happened. I think he'd worked it out anyway; I only confirmed it for him."

"What was his feeling?"

"Bitter resentment. Not that he ever voiced it. All I got was a grim smile. Joe went up with them, of course. They were his men. 'My little brothers.' That's how he always referred to them. Still does. He got hit twice in that last charge, took shot in both legs and some of his little brothers carried him off—at high risk to themselves, I might add. But that's how his men felt about him. There's a story that a field surgeon was preparing to amputate one of the legs when Joe sat up on the table and aimed a revolver into the surgeon's face and said, 'If you do, both you and the leg will go straight to hell.' It's a story I choose to believe. It bespeaks Josephson."

"Does he ever talk about Fredericksburg?"

"He'll talk a circle around it. He'll talk about the war and all the good men that were lost, and then he'll mention Fredericksburg and he'll say, 'Never was valor more ill-used or ill-spent.' "

"In front of Englund?"

"No, never in front of the general. The toast that he made that night was strange."

"Then the others didn't understand it?"

"I'm sure not. Joe is too sharp a soldier to tell anyone. He wouldn't want word getting through to the men that their commanding officer once needlessly spent lives. *That* wouldn't do, would it, Captain?"

"No, sir," Maynard said.

"Well," Bruckner said, "shall we shift back to the present? In the name of the fullest possible cooperation, I have to tell you that there are some folders here containing General Englund's personal papers. I haven't read them, of course, but perhaps you should."

"You've never looked at them?" Maynard asked. "Not even during your inquiry?"

"We didn't see the relevance. These seem to be very personal papers. Letters and diaries and such. Reading them would have been an ungentlemanly breach of ethics. But I am offering them to you along with an appeal for discretion."

"I would like to see them, sir, and can assure you their privacy will be respected."

"When you report back to Washington I would like it noted that you received the highest cooperation at Fort Larkin."

"That will be the first sentence of my report, Colonel."

"There's one other artifact I'll be happy to put at your disposal, should you want to inspect it."

"Which is?"

"The uniform the general was wearing that night. We believed it might be of some evidentiary import, so it was impounded. It's with the post surgeon and he has orders to release it for your inspection should you so request."

"I would like to see it," Maynard said.

"I hope it can tell you more than it told us."

Bruckner then opened a desk drawer and removed a large, bulky brown envelope and pushed it across the desk toward Maynard. On the cover, written in ink, it read: GENERAL A. ENGLUND: PERSONAL PAPERS.

"You might take them back East with you," Bruckner said, "and return them to the family. I'm sure you'll be seeing them."

"Yes, sir," Maynard said. "I have every intention of doing so."

"Young Miss Englund must have taken this hard. She and her father were quite close."

"Yes, sir, I know."

"You met her?"

"Briefly."

"A most remarkable young lady. Highly cultured, and at the same time has all the grit of a general's daughter."

"Most remarkable," Maynard said quietly.

Several moments later Colonel Scheffner and Major Fordyce entered to see Bruckner about some bit of post business. Maynard took the opportunity to arrange a meeting with Scheffner later in the day, then gathered up the large envelope and left.

Accompanied by Barrie, who had been waiting outside, Maynard went to his quarters, left the envelope in a cupboard, and then headed for the infirmary.

"Why the infirmary, Captain?" Barrie asked as they crossed the parade ground.

"You'll see," Maynard said.

Thunderheads were beginning to crowd up in the west, moving in from the Montana skies and across the Colorado peaks, throwing shadows deep into Black Hills canyons and east across the prairie.

"We're in for a good one," Barrie said, taking note of the distant clouds. He had seen his share of prairie thunderstorms, replete with winds that seemed bent on returning the land to its primeval state.

"It'll settle the dust," Maynard said.

The post surgeon was Dr. Benjamin Gilbert, a civilian contract doctor putting in his time at Fort Larkin. A man whose degree was just a few years old, his stated purpose was to achieve the enticing blend of practical experience and a bit of adventure. Aided by two stewards, the doctor did the best he could under what he considered primitive conditions.

"They asked me if I wanted to be commissioned as a regular army surgeon," he said to Maynard when the latter had taken a seat in the infirmary office. Barrie remained standing at the door in an at-ease position, silent throughout. "No, thanks, I told them," Gilbert said with a laugh. In his early thirties, he was already carrying too much weight, was a large, soft-looking man with generous reddish muttonchops and a receding hairline. He was wearing a spotless white duster.

"The army treats its men like dogs," Gilbert said. "Total indifference to proper hygiene and responsible diet. These outposts breed health problems like sewers. Scurvy, dysentery, venereal disease, diphtheria, typhoid, cholera, bronchial disorders. I sometimes wonder how you fellows can march and fight as you do, when hostile Indians are the least of your problems. They told us to look out for smallpox and when I checked my cabinets I found I had enough vaccine for about a third of the men. Fortunately there was no outbreak. The army medical corps seems to think that quinine, castor oil, and mustard plasters will cure anything. And as a last resort give them whisky. I asked General Englund if I could post a man to oversee the kitchens, to make sure the places were sanitary and the food properly prepared. If we can't always cure, we can at least try our damndest to prevent."

"What did he say?"

"Absolutely. Thought it was a most intelligent idea."

"You liked him?"

"I liked him because he cared about the welfare of his men. He was open to any idea that might improve their lot. He said to me once, 'Better than a brave soldier, give me a healthy one.' In what little time I've spent with the army, I've learned that the best way to judge a man's character is by how he regards his men. So how can I help you, Captain?"

"I would like to examine the general's uniform."

"Yes, yes, Colonel Bruckner indicated you might. Well, we have it right here."

The doctor rose and went to a large wooden cabinet the size of a clothes closet, opened the door, and from a shelf removed an unevenly folded blue uniform, which he placed on the desk.

"They buried him in a crisp, freshly laundered uniform of course," Dr. Gilbert said. "This one's been sitting here since the night of the tragedy. I suppose the family will finally instruct us about what's to be done with it. I can't imagine them wanting it. A bit macabre. But you can never tell, can you?"

They went to a table in a corner of the room where Maynard pushed aside some packages of epsom salts, a few dubious-looking vials, and some stacks of magazines to make room.

"What you miss out here is a woman," the doctor muttered, separating the articles of clothing. "I wouldn't mind having a lady with a lamp." Then, in a normal voice, "He was wearing a frock coat, shirt, trousers."

He unfolded the coat first and laid it across the table, stretching aside the sleeves so they draped over the sides. Maynard studied the one-star shoulder straps, the paired rows of seven gilt-edged buttons, the sky-blue infantry trimming, the dark blue velvet cuffs and stand-up collar, the black lining.

"If only a frock coat could talk, eh, Captain?" Gilbert said.

Maynard lifted the coat and turned it over.

"There," Gilbert said, tapping the spot with his finger as Maynard spread the coat out on the table. "That's where the knife was thrust in. Just between the shoulder blades."

The gash in the material was several inches across, the rending irregular, surrounded by the dried blotches of what appeared to have been a sumptuous bleeding. Maynard lifted the torn material with his fingertips for a moment, then released it.

"Was death instantaneous, do you think?" he asked.

"I would think so," Gilbert said. "Or nearly so anyway. That knife was driven in almost to the hilt."

"Obviously with great force."

"And fury, I should think."

"Do you think he could have cried out?"

"Impossible to say, Captain. Though in my opinion, if this attack was unexpected, as I believe it was, a person could gag on the shock of it and be unable to cry out. The general could very well have been dead before really knowing what had happened to him. In any event, no outcry was heard, as far as is known."

"Were you able to determine with which hand the blow was delivered?"

"I would suggest the right, but don't ask me to swear to it."

"And the height of the assailant?"

"Approximately that of the general. Which just about covers all of your suspects, doesn't it?"

Maynard smiled wryly. "Try to be more helpful, Doctor," he said lightly.

"The flawless crime," Gilbert said, "is supposed to be the consequence of painstaking design and diligent execution; here, it appears to have occurred by chance."

"I'm afraid I'm just an amateur at this," Maynard said.

"That might be just as well, since amateurs plod along without a compass and have very little sense of failure. It's the experts who give in to despair."

Very thin gruel indeed, Maynard thought unhappily, having as a principal virtue naive earnestness.

"And what about Corporal O'Bannion?" Maynard asked, finished with his examination of the coat and beginning to fold it up.

"Stabbed in the abdomen."

"Same weapon?"

"The wounds had a mutual similarity; beyond that I wouldn't want to say. But remember, the general was stabbed with his own weapon, a Bowie knife he was known to keep in his office."

"Which was found lodged in his back."

"Which means it probably could not have been used to dispatch the corporal, unless it was first removed from the general's office."

"Which is unlikely, since the general was there," Maynard said.

"Which—another 'which' I'm afraid—would lead to a conclusion of two murderers. How does that suit you?"

"Most helpful, Doctor," Maynard said sarcastically.

"Or one murderer with two weapons, if you prefer. Haven't you thought of all this before, Captain?" Gilbert asked with a genial smile.

Maynard scowled at him. "I'm thinking of it now," he said tersely. "If someone came into the general's office and killed him with the general's own knife, then with what did he go outside and kill O'Bannion? Commissioned officers don't go around carrying knives."

"And," the doctor said, "if your man killed O'Bannion first, that means he was armed. So why then go to the trouble of unsheathing the general's knife to kill *him*? You have a conundrum here, Captain."

"I take it you examined O'Bannion's body?"

"Yes."

"There was only the single wound?"

"Correct. He was attacked straight on."

"Which means," Maynard said, "he probably knew his assailant. A man on sentry duty is alert to any sound."

"It gets damned eerie out here at night, I can tell you."

"So," Maynard said, examining General Englund's shirt now, "if he heard any sound he would have been sensitive to it. So if he did challenge someone and then saw who it was, he would have naturally relaxed, letting the person come at him."

"And got the surprise of his young life."

"We know he was still alive when Duchard rode in, but for how much longer after that, we don't know."

"But what we do know is where he was killed—about fifty feet away from the commanding officer's headquarters. We know that because we found some very fresh bloodstains on some small rocks."

"O'Bannion bled a lot?"

"Profusely. In fact it was my opinion at the inquiry that he might have died from loss of blood, although I doubt he could have survived his wound under any circumstances. Whoever drove that knife into him pushed far and then spun it."

"And again," Maynard said, "there was no outcry."

"Well, in this case, if there had been it would probably have been heard by General Englund."

"If he was still alive."

"Yes, assuming that. I believe if he had heard a disturbance he would have come outside."

"No, Doctor," Maynard said, placing the trousers on the table now, the waistline at the table's upper edge, the lower part of the legs hanging over the other side. "Generals don't bestir themselves that easily."

"Of course not," Gilbert said, then joined with Maynard in turning his attention to the trousers. "Nothing extraordinary here either I'm afraid."

"Was he not wearing a belt?" Maynard asked.

"Indeed, a very fine leather one. It was buried with him."

Maynard leaned forward, inspecting one of the empty loopholes at the beltline close to the right hip area.

"What would you say that was, Doctor?" he asked.

Gilbert clasped his hands behind him, bent slightly at the waist, and peered down where Maynard had indicated with a finger.

"Blood," the doctor said, his tone suggesting he was offering a quite unexceptional bit of information.

"Why there?" Maynard asked. He was still leaning forward, peering intently at the approximately five-inch-long, two-inch-wide smear of old dried blood that barely discolored the blue material. The rust-colored stain ran straight from the top of the waistline down.

"Why not?" Gilbert asked, still tipped forward and peering, though beginning to frown now.

"How did it get there?" Maynard asked. Both men straightened up.

Gilbert unclasped his hands and ran one palm along the soft reddish hairs of his muttonchop.

"I take your point," he said. "Blood from the wound would never have splattered there."

"Particularly since the area was covered by a buttoned coat. And another thing, Doctor, if you'll notice, that blood ran in an uninterrupted line. Even if it had by some chance come from the wound, how would it have gotten under the belt, which you say the general was wearing?"

"He was wearing a belt at the time of his death," Gilbert said. "I can attest to that. He was laid out in the infirmary."

"And no one noticed that blood? It would have been fresh then."

"If they had, they would have assumed it derived from his wound. There was chaos here that night, Captain, as you can imagine. And anyway, you're making the assumption that that particular stain originated on that particular night. It could have come from an earlier wound or injury, could it not?"

"I doubt it," Maynard said. "An officer as fastidious as General Englund doesn't walk around with bloodstained trousers."

"Then to answer your question as to how it got there," Gilbert said, "I can be blunt and definitive: I don't know. Perhaps some of the men who handled the body got some blood on their hands and stained him."

"That still wouldn't explain how it got *under* the belt."

"Another conundrum, eh, Captain?"

CHAPTER 17

COLONEL SCHEFFNER

Colonel Scheffner had requested their meeting be held in Maynard's quarters. As he sat in a curved-back wooden chair in his small living room awaiting his visitor, Maynard stared out at the darkening afternoon, trying to anticipate the uncomfortable ground he might have to cross with Scheffner and where the pits and bogs might lie. Knowing what he did about the colonel's wife, Maynard decided, was not necessarily an advantage. The cuckold could be unsparing in self-laceration and lack of self-esteem, as well as helplessly sensitive. Maynard would have to guard himself against ambiguities, inadvertent indiscretions, and the merest appearance of judgment. He assumed that Scheffner would believe that by now Maynard had been informed of Mrs. Scheffner's lapses and that it would pile resentment upon resentment in the colonel's mind: toward himself for allowing it, toward Maynard for knowing, himself for being the known cuckold, Maynard again for thinking whatever it was Scheffner supposed he might be thinking.

There was thunder out over the prairie now, the afternoon beginning to darken rapidly. The dust was blowing up in brief swirls around the parade ground, a few grains ticking at his window. He listened attentively, momentarily carried back. He supposed if you had been in the war old artillery battles would always reecho in thunder. But no thunderstorm, no cloudburst, no cavalcade of cloudbursts could ever match the barrage at Gettysburg, when it sounded as if every field piece in both armies had torn away at every other for what seemed an hour. Man had roared to the heavens that afternoon, and forever after God's thunder would sound puny in comparison. Maynard smiled self-consciously: even the guns at Gettysburg were a better thought at the moment than the "conundrum."

Maynard got to his feet when he saw Scheffner coming up the steps. The colonel was moving slowly, as if preoccupied. Maynard opened the door just as Scheffner's hand had risen to knock.

"Please come in, sir," Maynard said, stepping aside.

Entering, Scheffner passed him a dubious look, as though detecting a hint of mockery in the observance of etiquette.

"Thank you for coming, Colonel," Maynard said, indicating the chair he had just vacated, the only comfortable one in the room. When Scheffner was seated he himself took another chair, this one of slightly irregular leg length, which made it wobble whenever he moved to one side or another.

"Don't thank me," Scheffner said, removing his forage cap and placing it in his lap. "This is mandatory, isn't it?"

"More of an official request," Maynard said, hoping to put the best possible face on it.

"When an official request is signed by the President of the United States and the Chief of Staff of the United States Army," Scheffner said, "there's only one way of looking at it."

And you had better know that too, Maynard thought, maintaining a pleasant smile.

"I suppose that's quite so," he said, "though I prefer to stress the unconstrained aspect. It makes it more amiable."

"Why shouldn't it be amiable?" Scheffner asked. There was a morbidly resentful expression in his sallow face; what fire there remained in his thin, tubercular-looking body seemed concentrated in his eyes as they fixed their gaze upon Maynard. His black drooping mustache hung down aside the corners of his mouth like a small ragged horseshoe.

"It should be amiable," Maynard said.

"Or maybe not," Scheffner said. His was a slow, laconic, almost calculating manner of speech; it sounded like a voice honed on cordial but keen-edged dispute. "Someone at this post has cast us all in disgrace. Maybe the whole god-damned inquiry was too amiable, since it found no answers."

"General Northwood found the inquiry to be thorough and impartial, but simply unsatisfactory in its conclusions," Maynard said, and Scheffner's tight sardonic smile immediately told him how ludicrous the diplomatic language sounded.

"I agree with General Northwood," Scheffner said. "So tell me what you want to know."

What I want to know, you derisive son of a bitch, Maynard thought, is did you kill your commanding officer because he was rolling your wife on the headquarters couch?

Scheffner's eyes closed for a moment, and when they reopened they were staring at another part of the room, then began moving inquiringly from object to object as if taking some sort of mental inventory. Maynard waited until that bottomless gaze had completed its leisurely circuit of the room and returned to him.

Sitting in a chair that wobbled whenever he shifted his

weight, Maynard realized to his vexation that he was going to have to sit absolutely still if he was to retain an interrogator's command of the situation.

"There was a meeting in General Englund's office that night," he said.

"There was."

"And you all were there; the senior officers, that is."

"Correct. Bruckner, Fordyce, Josephson, that fellow Patman, myself."

Maynard smiled. "You dislike Patman," he said.

"I don't know him well enough to like or dislike."

"He's been here long enough."

"Some people you know in a day, some you'll never know. Haven't you found that to be so, Captain?"

"But generally there was harmony among the seniors?"

"We'd gone through the war together, Captain," Scheffner said, making it sound as succinct as it was meant to be.

"All except Patman."

"He'll always be a shavetail, no matter how long he serves. They talked about a new army after the war. But I tell you, Captain, and I think you know this, there won't be a new army until all those who were in the war are finally mustered out. *Then* you'll have a new army. I'm not making any judgments, just stating a fact. It may be a better army, though I doubt if there will be an opportunity to prove it. From 1861–65, under the direst circumstances imaginable, the Union Army molded itself into a fighting force of unprecedented strength and capability."

"I suppose we have a right to our pride," Maynard said.

"It's just that after you've taken a half million casualties . . ."

"I understand," Maynard said, then cleared his throat. "Getting back to that meeting, sir."

"It was half meeting, half lecture," Scheffner said dryly.

"Englund would do that occasionally. He could be tire-somely verbose, sometimes passionate; but he was usually direct. I never found him a subtle man. That night we received a disquisition cold with venom on why the Indians must perish from this earth and then advising us we would be undertaking a campaign pursuant to that end. The way it sounded, we were all to be players in a drama about history and Alfred Englund versus the doomed savages of the Northern Plains. And because we knew the man, we understood the underrunning theme to be Alfred Englund executing the will of God. The Creator could sometimes be remiss in executing the will of Alfred Englund," Scheffner added with a malign smile, "but in this instance we were led to believe they were one and the same. I had no objection to killing Indians; I've killed many men, but I never believed it was God's will when I was doing so. No decent man ever should. Unlike some—the late George Custer, for instance—I never relished going into combat and causing death. Do you know how I squared it with myself, Captain?"

"No, sir," Maynard said quietly.

"Whenever I attacked, I always told myself it was in order to defend something, because in a way it always is, be it your men or your ground or your flag, or maybe even an idea."

"When General Englund announced the impending campaign, was there general agreement?"

"Why would there not be?" Scheffner asked with mild contention. "It was a commanding officer telling us what he was going to do, what he wanted us to do. A brief notification, with specifics to come later. You must remember that we'd been stagnating in inactivity for almost a year. The bulk of the regiment were on active duty at Fort Lincoln and other units were constantly in the field. In addition, there was the hue and cry to avenge Custer, which had galvanized the army like nothing had since Fort Sumter. But all we had down here was the occasional renegade band, that and fatigue details and escorting payroll wagons and civilian travelers. Englund had become frustrated. Everyone had, right down to the ranks. We knew that it was not going to be a major campaign, but a necessary one, and to many a welcome one."

The thunder broke closer, louder. Scheffner's eyes shifted to the outside for a moment. The room was quite dark now, dark enough for a candle to be lit, but Maynard did not move; it was as though the gaunt, laconically speaking colonel was best interviewed in the gloom. The rain came suddenly, striking the windows in wind-thrown sheets, splattering on the porch and roof in a thronging multitude of tiny sounds. Maynard could feel wisps of wind slipping through the log chinks. Scheffner sat motionless in the deepening darkness, legs crossed, cap in lap, hands clasped at the point of his raised knee.

All right, Maynard thought, his chair tipping with him as he arranged himself more comfortably. Time to dance across the eggshells.

"Did General Englund have good rapport with his staff?"

He could feel Scheffner's eyes on him in the darkness, fixed with the bruises of wounded pride. *He's wondering*, Maynard thought. *Trying to reckon how much I know, if I know at all, and if I do, what I think about it (and about him as a man) and where I think it might impinge.*

His voice coolly self-possessed, Scheffner said, "He had the loyalty due a commanding officer."

"Affectionate loyalty?"

"I beg your pardon, Captain?"

Maynard felt foolish. *He knows I know.*

"No friction anywhere?" he asked.

"Why should there have been?" The voice was bland.

He wants me to say it, if it's going to be said at all. Maynard felt his own awkwardness: too long a hesitation, an insinuating glide of voice, a too deferent tone—any of it vulnerable to Scheffner's alert sensibilities.

Speaking in a way he hoped was casual, Maynard said, "Sometimes there is."

"We're all professionals," Scheffner said with a touch of pride.

"And men of the world."

Scheffner paused, as if under unexpected provocation. With just enough ambiguity, Maynard felt he had turned it around. *Now he wants to know not what I know—we've passed that now—but what I'm thinking, what judgment.* The impersonal murder inquiry had stalled for a moment; Maynard was talking to a man and a husband.

"And how treacherous a world it is, Captain," Scheffner said. "I wonder if you know that."

"I hope I do, Colonel."

"Most treacherous it is for those who attempt judgment."

"Valid judgments, yes. I'm sorry, sir."

"Men of this world and others."

"What does that mean, Colonel?"

"It means that some people try to transcend their own clay and attempt communion with higher authorities."

"Are you referring to General Englund?"

"I am."

"He had a unique theology?"

"He didn't consider himself in service of the Lord, but rather in partnership."

"He believed that, sir?"

"At times with a terrifying intensity," Scheffner said, still speaking slowly and quietly but now with a moodier, more introspective tone.

"How did this manifest itself?"

"It manifested itself most in you knowing that he believed it. All it takes is for your credulity to be thrown one degree off course, or even the idea that it has been, or is capable of being."

"You mean the idea that your commanding officer might be insane."

"Or worse: not."

"Because of that story about his sword."

"And how it was perceived. What chance, Captain, does truth have against myth?"

"Do you think this was detrimental to the carrying out of his duties?"

"He could be an inspiring leader. He could also demonstrate a very practical turn of mind."

"And he could bend people's wills."

"Yes," Scheffner said tersely.

"Do you think it was a factor in his being murdered?"

"You'll have to ask that of the person who wielded the knife."

"Would you say that you were the least of the mourners, Colonel?"

"I took no satisfaction in the general's death," Scheffner said. "Do you think I should have?"

"With respect, Colonel, I'm not here to dance a quadrille with you."

Maynard sensed an ironic amusement across the darkness. The rain, having achieved a peak in rush and volume, had now subsided to a steady pattering. The thunder was rumbling off, the clouds carrying eastward.

"When the meeting was over," Maynard said, "what did you do?"

"I went to my quarters."

"Directly?"

"Yes."

"Did everyone else go to their quarters?"

"I seem to remember Patman and Colonel Bruckner in conversation. I saw Josephson and Fordyce heading off to quarters."

"You didn't actually see anyone go in?"

"No, but there was nowhere else to go."

"So General Englund remained alone. Did he say why he was remaining?"

"He mentioned something about some work he wanted to clear up."

"There was nothing unusual in that?"

"Oh no," Scheffner said, adding dryly, "General Englund often behaved in a perfectly normal manner."

"Was Mrs. Scheffner awake when you came in?"

"No, she was asleep." And, to Maynard's annoyance, Scheffner added, "What else would she be doing at that hour?"

"And you remained in your quarters?"

"Yes. I went to sleep."

"Colonel, I understand that you and your wife occupy separate bedrooms."

"Does that fact fall under the scope of your inquiry?"

"No, sir. But as you say, it is a fact. And it is also a fact that someone—in all likelihood a senior officer—soon left his quarters and murdered General Englund and Corporal O'Bannion."

Scheffner sat silently for several moments, as if formulating what he would say next. Then, as if offering the most banal of explanations, he said, "I went to sleep, to be awakened a few hours later when the sentry was reported unaccounted for."

"Yes, sir," Maynard said wearily. "I know."

He got up now and lit the kerosene lamp. He found Scheffner watching him with one eyebrow slightly, inquiringly raised, as if to say, *Aren't you going to ask me about it?* Maynard looked away.

"I apologize for the interrogation, sir," he said.

"It isn't the interrogation, it's the implications."

Scheffner sat back, his eyes again making a slow, careful study of the room.

"We've been missing you at the mess table, Captain," he said.

"Under the circumstances," Maynard said, "I thought it might be better if I took my meals with the ranks."

"Quite so."

"Colonel," Maynard said, staring through the window, "I'm going to have to put a few questions to Mrs. Scheffner. Do I have your permission?"

"Of course. Will you be questioning Mrs. Bruckner as well?"

Maynard hesitated, but it was too late; the hook had gone in with the bait.

"Yes, certainly," he said. He turned to find Scheffner smiling wryly at him.

"Well then," the colonel said. "I'll mention it tonight at dinner. To both of them."

CHAPTER 18

MAJOR FORDYCE

Though he had never been to sea, Maynard imagined there must be some affinity within the minds of sailors whose vistas were eternity's unchanging waters and a horizon strung across the compass points like an ever-receding cable and soldiers serving on the frontier who were surrounded by limitless prairie, under skies whose infinite flight left mountain, man, and grain as one. For the sailor the mesmeric entity would be the sea and its ceaseless rolling, for the soldier the sky and its regal stillness. And too much exposure to either, Maynard feared, could make a man fatally a philosopher.

Washington, with its carriages, stately buildings, and crowds of people in their varying costumes, with its noise, shops, promenades, and well-lighted restaurants, had become for him a hard-to-conjure memory, a memory it seemed difficult to sustain on the frontier. So it was with great delight that among the mail carried to Fort Larkin by an arriving train of supply wagons was a letter for him from that city. The moment the letter was placed in his hand, Washington reanimated itself in his mind, like a mural infused with life. He could see John Harrison sitting at the desk downstairs in the parlor of the rooming house, pen moving across paper. He could hear farmers' wagons bumping along the dirt road outside the house, and he could see the park across the road with its luxuriantly leaved shade trees. On the other side of the park he could see and hear the barouches and horse-drawn streetcars moving along the thinly cobbled streets, and beyond that—from Maynard's upstairs window this—the Capitol dome, topped by twenty tall feet of bronze depicting Freedom.

"Hope you are bearing up under the burdens of Dakota social life."

Maynard smiled. He was sitting in a rocker on his porch. Harrison's letter brought with it a sense of detached serenity he hadn't felt since leaving Washington. *The burdens of Dakota social life.* That was John all right, typically; sending a gentle poke in the ribs.

"We have Washington well under control right now," Harrison wrote, "especially since it is currently occupied principally by Americans. The onslaughts of our dread summers do have one salubrious effect—their fearsome reputations are enough to intimidate our foreign visitors and return them to their own more temperate climes.

"I trust you are bearing down upon the solution of the puzzle. I wish you would accomplish it in all decent haste, for your sake and mine. I recently had conversation with a colleague who once passed through Fort Larkin and when I made mention of the fact that a friend of mine was currently installed there the fellow raised his eyes and sighed. Apparently you are at the Van Diemen's Land of United States military outposts. When I told him that you were there in connection with the Englund murders, he said that the probable solution was that both men were asked to be taken out of their boredom-induced misery. If you would enjoy being a corporal once again, you might make that the gist of your report.

"For my part, I want you back because I miss our dinners at Willard's and our billiard games and high-toned conversations later. Our good landlady has asked me to convey her thoughts and to tell you that she misses your good cheer at the breakfast table.

"By the way, there was one pleasant interlude the other evening. I attended a reception for a friend of mine who is soon to be married, and there I had the good fortune to be introduced to someone of your acquaintance. Yes, my dear Thomas, she is indeed the angelic creature you so poetically described. Apparently it was the first social occasion for Miss Englund since the tragedy and she looked positively radiant. I can now understand the sweet agony you are suffering. It would take Byron's pen to give her proper portraiture on the page, but since you already know all that, I shall spare you. But it is more than nature's outer raiment that makes her so singular. She is so poised and direct and well spoken, and I am sure you will agree with the last, given the words she spoke in your behalf.

"When I made mention of the fact that I was the good friend of Captain Thomas Maynard, she immediately asked me to convey her warmest good wishes. 'He is obviously a man of worth and good character,' spaketh she, and went on to say that she every day prays for your well-being and for the success of your enterprise. (If I had such a one praying so fervently for me I think I should have been able to defend the Alamo single-handedly.) She said that General Northwood recently came to tea and that he also reassured her about your tenacity and intelligence. If these accolades of faith and confidence don't bring warmth to your flinty heart and blushes to your manly face, I don't know what will. But how I envy you, old man—working to bring solace to that darling creature. She is Edenic paradise itself (if you will forgive my go at Byron)."

After having read several times again the references to Miss Englund, Maynard refolded the letter and replaced it in its envelope and tapped it thoughtfully against his hand. He had loved once before and had suffered for it; Ad Marston had loved and had died for it. Of all the thousands of gunshots he had heard in his life, the one that reechoed most remorselessly was the one fired in the silent Adirondack forest, the one that had murdered simultaneously his best friend and the sweeter fountains of his desires, leaving him prey to some restless demon that drove him here and there, shorn of root and place. But he supposed it had not been unwise to chance worse, and so he had closed his heart to romantic humors. But now it was evident the closure had not been entire; a passage had been left unguarded (or maybe it was self-forgiveness at last, a hard-won attainment of peace), for he could feel within the healing, murmurous presence of Miss Englund. The chamber of his heart she occupied had been so painfully scraped that he did not wonder at the ache that mere thought provoked. But this was a different love and a different time, and these were the stirrings of the long suppressed, the pangs of renewal. If this be the bliss of a fool, he thought, then so be it. It would be more foolish still to reject the dream with all its aromas and comforts.

At the crisp, almost satirically formal approach of Sergeant Barrie, he slipped the letter into his pocket. Barrie came to attention at the foot of the porch steps and threw off a dress parade salute, which Maynard casually answered.

"Sergeant?"

"Reporting, sir."

"Do you have any information for me?"

"No, sir."

"That's helpful," Maynard said. Then, tongue in cheek, he said, "You know if we don't resolve this matter General Sherman will have your stripes."

"No doubt, Captain. And probably give them to you."

"Levity aside, Barrie, I'd settle for a healthy rumor right now."

"We have plenty of those around here, sir, but they're not worth the empty bottles that spawned them. But don't let him fox you, Captain."

"Who?"

"Whoever's the one."

"I've spoken to damn near all of them," Maynard said. "Fordyce is the last of them, and I'm meeting with him shortly."

"Speak of the devil," Barrie said.

Turning, Maynard saw Major Fordyce coming down the steps of his quarters further along the parade ground.

"Good God," Maynard whispered as Barrie smiled.

Fordyce was wearing a dark blue double-breasted frock coat cinched tightly in the middle by an eagle-embossed belt buckle, with splashes of yellow epaulettes at the shoulders, cuffless sky-blue trousers, and brightly polished black shoes. His black felt hat was trimmed with gold cord, the brim looped up on the right side and fastened with a gold eagle, with three black ostrich feathers on the left side, and on a black velvet ground in front a gold embroidered wreath encircling the letters U.S. in silver Old English characters. At his left side hung a silver-gripped sword in a brass scabbard. He was wearing white gloves.

Barrie looked at Maynard with mischievous innocence.

"Full dress," the sergeant whispered.

"He must think this is a formal inquiry," Maynard said, getting to his feet.

"Will you be needing me, sir?"

"Go away, Barrie," Maynard muttered.

The least he could do, Maynard thought, was button his own coat, which he did as he came down the steps, then ran his hand back through his hair and patted his mustache with his fingertips as he awaited Major Fordyce, who was advancing upon him stride by solemn stride, large eyes fixed sternly on Maynard, who, hatless and casual, was feeling more and more self-conscious. When Fordyce stopped, several yards away, Maynard saluted, Fordyce returning it, slicing the air with the side of his hand. This kind of formal esteem, Maynard thought, was never for your own self or accomplishments but for who or what you represented, in this case President Grant and General Sherman and the Secretary of War and General Northwood. No doubt, Maynard thought sardonically, each would have been pleased. In the distance, walking toward Company B barracks, with his face turned around over his shoulder but too army-wise to allow the merest smile, went Sergeant Barrie.

They walked to the fort's perimeter and then slightly beyond, and then began walking in a long, slow, arcing circle around the assortment of small prairie-bound buildings known as Fort Larkin. It wasn't so much the sight of a major as it was of a major in full dress uniform that startled the sentries from post to post and stiffened their posture as they watched with the puzzled suspicion that had been part of a soldier's facial expression since men had first borne arms, wondering why that captain fellow looked so casual while the major seemed draped out for a Fourth of July parade.

"I applaud what you're doing, Captain," Fordyce said as they walked, white-gloved hands folded behind him. "But it isn't an easy assignment. Trying to see through someone never is, the mask and the face sometimes being identical."

"I'm glad you appreciate that, sir," Maynard said.

"There's no other way to look at it. We couldn't get the

job done. There's no denying that. Fresh brains. Maybe that's what it takes. Fresh brains."

The recent pummeling rain had settled the dust and Maynard noticed that the major's highly buffed black shoes were remaining black as they walked. Fordyce's large, bulbous eyes were studying the ground.

"The Sioux worship this earth," he said. "It sometimes seems strange to us that they should worship anything, but being a man of piety myself I can understand that. I have very little hospitality in my heart for the Sioux, having seen too much of their handiwork, but when I think of them holding in awe something they regard as sacred it gives me pause. It doesn't change my position, only my contemplation of them. The earth represents to them what icons, words, and spirituality do to us. The Indian worships something that is tangible, easily trampled and defiled, and so we tend to look upon his religion as being little more than superstition or paganism."

"Then you have some sympathy for them?" Maynard asked.

"I don't know if sympathy is the word. When you find some of your people—soldier and civilian—lying mutilated to the point of nausea, it's hard to find sympathy for the malefactors. I don't know if I even understand them. The closest one can come, I think, is in *trying* to understand them. You say to yourself, 'Yea, even these are God's creatures,' and with that you make a beginning. But Englund could never do even that much. And here his soul was rent. Here was proof of his blasphemy."

"He hated them, didn't he?" Maynard asked.

"It is a fundamental wrong, Captain, for a soldier to hate his enemies. Tactically it is wrong because it can lead to underestimation, and it is also morally wrong. Plot their destruction, yes; shoot them down by your own hand, yes. But hate them? What of the day when the destruction and the shooting stop, as one day it always does, and the plowshares replace the swords? What of the hatred then? Where does it go? What can it do, but seep back into your heart. The heart has no natural recess for hatred, so when it enters it must displace something else and cause a pollution, and consequently some delicate balance is affected. The heart becomes corrupted and this invites the worst of God's plagues to fall upon us. Because, Captain, as it takes just one man to start a fire, so it needs only one to start a plague."

"And yet General Englund was regarded as a most capable officer," Maynard said.

"He had the gift of leadership," Fordyce said, making a concession. "But he thought he had more, and in so thinking, he had less, critically so. It wasn't just that he never accepted that the Indians were as much God's creatures as any that made him a poor Christian. But Englund went far beyond that. Heavens, but he did," Fordyce said with a mournful shake of his head.

"What was your relationship with him?"

"My relationship with him?" Fordyce asked. He paused and stared at Maynard with round expressionless eyes that for a moment looked as thick as eggs. Sitting above that round beardless face and those bulging eyes, the ornate hat with its looped brim and ostrich feathers and gold trimming and embroidered wreath looked ludicrous, as if wearing it was an act of penance. "I prayed for his soul," Fordyce said darkly, then began walking again, gazing upon the thin alkaline covering, the occasional tufts of hard grass that grew around the fort.

"What about your everyday relationship with him?" Maynard said.

"It was correct. He was my commanding officer." Fordyce raised his head for a moment, the ostrich feathers fluttering. "It seems he was always my commanding officer," he said as if taking a sudden, disbelieving measure of time passed, and then quietly and curiously, as if to himself, "I wonder by what grand design."

"Did you like him?"

"No," Fordyce said simply. "That was not to be."

"I see."

"We were in the war together, of course. And that is when his downfall occurred."

"His downfall, sir?"

"The most shocking act of blasphemy I have ever heard. You have, I trust, heard the story of General Englund and his sword?"

"I have."

"Some people laugh and say it's nonsense. Well, I say it is not nonsense," Fordyce said with momentary vigor. "I say it is a grim and hateful story. Profanation, sir. Naked profanation."

Fordyce stopped, leaned to a side for a moment, and with his right arm hurled an imaginary object up at the high blue sky, his sword and scabbard swinging around him as Maynard stepped back in amazement.

"General Englund," Fordyce said with bellowing theatrics, "hurls his sword at the sky and *God* strikes it with lightning." He put his hands on his hips and arched his back and gazed upward for a moment, studying the bland, cloudless sky. Then he turned to Maynard, eyes filled with an unspeakable question.

"But it did happen, didn't it?" Maynard asked.

"Did it? What are you asking? Are you asking me did he throw the sword, are you asking if lightning struck it, are you asking if the fingers of God were in the lightning consecrating that man?"

After a moodily disapproving glance back to the sky, Fordyce resumed walking.

"Oh," he said dolefully, shaking his head. "Ohhh. I can

tell you what is unforgivably sacrilegious about that story, what is a mortal insult to every pious person on this earth. Englund believed what he wanted to believe, that the striking of the sword was a sign from God of eternal blessing. Of absolution and purification. Englund *believed* that. And instead of being humbled . . . The way he strode about," Fordyce said contemptuously, "so cocksure about everything. I heard him say once, 'The sword was still warm from my hand when it happened.' 'When *what* happened, Alfred?' I wanted to ask. 'When *what* happened?' He was implying that God had reached down and touched him. It was the word and the pose of the antichrist. And what were we to say to him? He was, after all, our commanding officer. Could we engage him in a theological debate that could only end with him being called a blasphemer?"

"Did the others share your view in the matter?" Maynard asked.

"Not as strongly," Fordyce said. "My feelings in the matter run much deeper. True piety equals humility, Captain. As honest men we know that. You don't converse with the Lord, you pray to Him. And if He decides to answer, He will, in time and in a manner befitting. He will not engage in melodrama or theatricals. That is not God's way. To think otherwise is blasphemy or lunacy."

They walked silently for several moments, slowly circling the fort, Fordyce in somber contemplation. And then, quietly perplexed, he said, "And if you come to it, Captain, why would He have chosen Englund? I was by far the more devoted servant. I never despised my enemies, I never betrayed my trusts." Idly, still perplexed, he muttered, "I was much the worthier."

"Do you think Englund was mad?"

Fordyce sighed. "Yes, he was mad."

"Is that why he was killed?"

"It could have been a righteous hand that struck him down. An assassin of the Lord. I don't know. Are you asking me if there's a Brutus among us?"

I don't know what I'm asking, Maynard thought. I'm walking around on the Dakota prairie with a man turned stiff as a corpse with his own piety. What was there to ask that wouldn't sound hopelessly mundane?

"All through the inquiry," Fordyce said, watching several troopers cantering by on routine patrol, "we kept asking, 'Why would anyone want to kill General Englund?' And I kept answering, privately, of course, 'Why would anyone not?' "

"So everyone had his reason?"

Fordyce waved his hand about.

"No, no," he said, "strike that from the record. Let the others speak for themselves. They're all good, God-fearing men; I can see none of them acting so. I understand you're on General Northwood's staff. Fine old campaigner. Fine old fellow. How is he?"

"Very well, sir."

"Give him my compliments. Be sure to tell him that I co-operated fully."

"Tell me, Major, what did you do at the conclusion of that last meeting you all had with General Englund?"

"I returned to my quarters and went to sleep."

"You didn't go out again?"

"There was no reason to, not until the alarm about the sentry. There's a point for you, Captain: why was that fellow killed? Maybe that's what you should be looking into."

"I am, sir. The two murders were obviously connected."

"Correct, correct. Find the answer to the one and you'll have the answer to the other, not that I'm telling you how to go about your business."

"I appreciate that, Major."

"And how is the President?"

"Well . . ."

"I knew Sam Grant at the Point, you know. Cadets together. He wasn't the cleverest, but a world of determination,
which he later proved. You'll give him my compliments.
He'll remember Fordyce."

"I'm sure he will, sir. Major, after you returned to your
quarters that night, did you hear anything untoward?"

"No, Captain. My habit is to offer a few prayers and then
I fall to sleep immediately and rest very peacefully."

"I understand, sir."

"If I happen to pass over during my sleep, I'm fully prepared. It's a very serene feeling."

"I can imagine," Maynard said as they began heading
back in toward the fort.

"Are you a religious man, Captain?"

"That question, sir, is more complicated than it sounds."

"It shouldn't be," Fordyce said reprovingly. "A little
prayer might be of some assistance to your investigations."

"Prayer, Major?"

"Prayer is the toil of the soul and it has been known to
provide respondent solutions."

"Yes, sir," Maynard said deferentially.

"The answers are there, waiting to be properly summoned. They come where they will be warmly received,
treated with respect, and where they know sacrifices will be
made on their behalf."

"I'll bear it in mind, sir," Maynard said.

"Whisky, Sergeant," Maynard said irritably as he returned to his quarters, followed by Barrie, who had been
waiting for him on the porch. "A stiff one."

"He can have that effect on you, sir," Barrie said, reaching for the bottle Maynard had bought from the sutler the

day he arrived at Fort Larkin and which until now had remained unopened.

"Who?"

"Major Fordyce."

"I felt like I was being scourged, that every sin I ever committed was sticking out of me like a broken bone."

"But a very fine officer, sir," Barrie said, handing Maynard a tin cup with three fingers of whisky in it.

"Have one yourself," Maynard said, sitting down. He took several sips, closed his eyes for a moment, and exhaled pleasurably. "Relax, Barrie," he said. Barrie sat down on the irregularly legged chair, tipped its short leg to the floor, and sat still, holding his cup of whisky in both hands. "Yes," Maynard said, "they're all fine officers, and each one of them would have enjoyed sending his commanding officer from this world to the next."

"Well, sir," Barrie said after having a discreet sip from his cup, "now that you've had your finger up the backsides of them all, what do you think?"

Maynard shook his head. "I don't know what to think. They all have the same story: the meeting broke up and they each went to their quarters, where they stayed until the ruckus started. Nobody heard anything. But one of them came out again, Barrie; we have two dead bodies to prove it."

"You still can't know for sure it was a commissioned officer."

"I'm pretty damned sure. You didn't hear those men talking about Englund. They'd been with him a long time, and I tell you, Barrie, the sores and the hurts and the resentments had been festering. Jesus good Christ—if Major Fordyce will forgive me—but you never stop to consider what builds up during a relationship, any relationship, over a number of years. It all goes into the same pot and because of obligations and appearances you have to keep the lid on; but once you take it off . . ."

"An explosion."

"Worse: deadly fumes."

"Yes, sir, Captain," Barrie said, sipping some more whisky, wiping his lips with his tongue, staring at Maynard, who was sitting back, legs crossed, face a complication of bafflement and irritation.

"General Northwood said that when they first heard of the crimes they felt that resolution of the matter would be simple and fairly quick and that the on-site officers would see to it. So they decided not to send out anyone from the Judge Adjutant General's office, which they should have done."

"They still could have done it," Barrie said.

"Doing it two months after the fact would have made them look remiss or casual. Also, I think their first impression was that some renegade Sioux had slipped into the fort and done it. I don't think they ever dreamed it was going to be this kind of situation."

"So they bollixed it."

Maynard grunted.

"And stuck you with it," Barrie said.

"Hoping I could get it done quietly, without fanfare."

"You will, Captain," Barrie said with an encouraging wink of the eye.

"What are they saying in the barracks?"

"They want to know who killed Corporal O'Bannion."

Maynard took a swallow of whisky. "When you die in the shadow of a general," he said, "you tend to become overlooked."

"If you knew in what order they died, you'd have a first step."

"We don't even know that."

"Maybe you can work it out," Barrie said. "If somebody killed the general first and then Obie, why drag Obie's body all the way to the stables? That wouldn't make sense. You'd want to be off as fast as you could."

"And if O'Bannion was killed first, and the intention was then to go inside and kill the general, why take the time to drag the body so far? That doesn't make any sense either."

"It made sense to somebody," Barrie said. "Very good sense, whichever way it was done, because he's gotten by with it."

"I think the surgeon was right. What he said in effect was it makes sense only because it was successful, not because it was especially planned that way."

"You mean it wasn't planned?"

"The thing is, Barrie," Maynard said thoughtfully, "somebody has probably already told me something that's got the answer in it, and I don't know who it was or what it is. It's maddening, but I have the feeling that I *know* something. All of those officers with their stories and their histories and their resentments and their creeds. It's in there somewhere. I know it. For one of them it all became too much. The lid came off the pot. Somebody did it and then got lucky. Got away in the darkness. But somewhere, somewhere a tiny gleam of light is shining." Maynard, who had been speaking primarily for his own benefit, smiled self-consciously. "So you can tell the boys in the barracks why O'Bannion died: he was standing in the wrong place at the wrong time."

Barrie sipped some whisky.

"Captain," he said quietly, "that just about explains every soldier's death, doesn't it?"

CHAPTER 19

COLONEL AND MRS. BRUCKNER

The drums and bugles had sounded the half-hour signal for dress parade, and now Maynard was sitting on his porch watching the officers marching their companies to the parade ground. After the units had lined up he watched the assembly ordered through portions of the manual of arms, the old familiar orders issued crisply, sounding fresh and sharp on the quiet twilight air. They always sounded that way to Maynard, no matter how many times he heard them. It was army, the same things over and over again: boredom and routine to some, structure and reassurance to Maynard, a perpetuation of what he had come to love and feel secure with.

The first sergeant then began roll call and Maynard listened to the peculiar statical music of the responses, some indifferent, some with mischievous spirit, some sullen, some with soldierly decorum.

As the following day's orders and assignments were being issued, an orderly appeared at the foot of the porch steps.

"Colonel Bruckner requests your presence, sir," the soldier said, following his salute.

"Where is the colonel?" Maynard asked, rising.

"At his quarters, sir."

Maynard went inside, pulled on his jacket, adjusted his forage cap at not too rakish an angle, examined himself in the oval wall mirror, having to flex his knees slightly to allow for the mirror's forward tip, and then left.

Maynard found a very stern Colonel and Mrs. Bruckner awaiting him in their sitting room. Compared to his own spartan quarters, the room seemed luxurious. It was carpeted, the chairs sturdy, the settee tastefully upholstered, the windows curtained, the kerosene lamps bearing floral designs, the walls covered with framed Currier and Ives depictions of the changing seasons in a small country village. Two cages of canaries and mockingbirds hung from the ceiling.

Maynard was asked to be seated in a high, spoked-back polished wooden chair, where he sat facing the Bruckners, who were aligned side by side on the settee.

"Captain," the colonel began, as always dignified of tone and posture, "I must lodge a vigorous protest."

"Sir?" Maynard asked politely. An appraisal of the expressions on the faces of the Bruckners had instilled in him an immediate resolve upon entering: he would not allow himself to be intimidated here.

"It has been brought to my attention," the colonel said, "that you wish to interrogate Mrs. Bruckner."

"Merely a formality, Colonel," Maynard said, crossing his legs, sitting comfortably, cap in lap.

"Why is such a formality necessary?"

Because I was snared into it by your son of a bitch lieutenant colonel, Maynard thought, even as he sat perfectly poised. But it was a bit of deviousness he had no intention of sharing.

"In the name of thoroughness, sir," he said.

"I find it highly objectionable," Bruckner said.

"I'm sorry, sir."

"I fully understand, Captain, that you come here under the highest authority, but I must protest that there are limits to the scope of your inquiry."

"I was advised of no such limits, Colonel."

"Then you are acting by your own discretion."

"Without implication, I assure you, sir."

"Nevertheless, I find it intolerable," Bruckner said.

"Frankly, sir, such interrogation as I may conduct of Mrs. Bruckner is in name only and made solely as a matter of equity."

"Equity?" Bruckner asked, frowning with puzzlement.

"Since I feel obliged to put questions to Mrs. Scheffner . . ."

"You *should* put questions to that woman," Mrs. Bruckner, who had been sitting like a client at an attorney's elbow, said. If there was to be any intimidation in the room, Maynard knew he would feel it from the colonel's wife. Gathered in all of her aristocratic bearing—and it seemed so naturally borne—she was staring at him as if from some regal aerie. She was wearing a maroon dress, a loop of small white pearls resting on her high, firm bosom. Above her proudly set jawline her clear, unlined, imposingly handsome face was raised, her graying hair combed up from a high, schoolmistress forehead. They might have been brother and sister, these two, Maynard thought, sprung from the same set of loins, watered at the same statued fountain, and sent forth under the same steadfast injunctions of self-command.

"I intend to, Mrs. Bruckner," Maynard said. "But 'should'?"

"Ever since her arrival at this post," Mrs. Bruckner said,

"that woman has been a demoralizing and disruptive presence. How so admirable a gentleman as Colonel Scheffner could have allowed himself to be beguiled by a woman so obviously wanting of genteel qualities is beyond comprehension. In the name of good taste I shall not go into specifics concerning her derelictions; they are for you to discover, and if you overturn the correct rocks there is no doubt you will bring them to light."

As his wife spoke in her direct, full-throated tones, Colonel Bruckner stared uncompromisingly at Maynard, as if to say, *You will never in your life hear truer words spoken.*

"So," Mrs. Bruckner went on, "when you make an equation that includes that woman and myself, I feel I have been gravely traduced."

"I can assure you, Mrs. Bruckner," Maynard said, "that I implied no such thing and most sincerely apologize for any distress which I may have caused. The fact of the matter is I barely know Mrs. Scheffner, so any equations that may have been implied were accidental and without foundation." *And*, Maynard added to himself, *if that doesn't placate you, go sit on a mule.*

"Are you familiar with Mrs. Scheffner's history?" the colonel's wife asked.

"You mean since her arrival at Fort Larkin?"

"That is precisely what I mean."

"I have heard certain commentary, yes, though I don't know how much credence to accord it."

"You may accord credence to anything you hear about Mrs. Scheffner."

"Are you referring to her relationship with General Englund?"

Colonel Bruckner seemed embarrassed by the reference; Mrs. Bruckner remained impassive, sitting before Maynard as if carven into immovability.

"I said, Captain Maynard," she said tersely, sounding as
if she was nipping off each word with the edges of her teeth,
"that I would not enter into specifics regarding Mrs.
Scheffner."

"If my search for truthful answers has perturbed you,
ma'am," Maynard said with a sense of rapidly depleting patience, "then I'm sorry."

"I understand why you're here, Captain," Mrs. Bruckner
said, "and I empathize. But in the search for the single pertinent thing there is always the danger of turning up the irrelevant many that can only cause harm. And even if you do
find your answer, what might be the consequence of it?
What might you be in danger of defaming and destroying?"

"I don't know, Mrs. Bruckner," Maynard said, returning
her gaze with the same level intensity with which he was receiving it. "But I have a commission to fulfill and I intend to
comply with it. And if somewhere along the way I happen to
unwittingly tip over some barrels of stagnant water, so be it.
Let the good earth soak it up."

"That's impertinent, Captain," Bruckner said.

"My apologies," Maynard said, and then, with some
heat, went on: "And it seems to me, sir, that I've delivered
enough apologies for one sitting"—implicitly reminding
them (Bruckner anyway) of the letter he had brought with
him and what it said and who had signed it. Mrs. Bruckner,
her frozen hauteur unmoved, said nothing. Colonel Bruckner, acting commanding officer of Fort Larkin, shifted his
gaze for a moment, seemed to ponder something, then
looked back to Maynard.

"Captain," Bruckner said, his voice lowering to as concil-
iatory a modulation as was possible for him, "you understand that the objection to interrogating Mrs. Bruckner is
not a formal one."

"So noted," Maynard said. "And that concludes the interrogation." He could not tell whether Mrs. Bruckner's thin, icy smile was of vindication or understanding.

With some mumbled courtesies, Maynard took his leave.

On his way out of the Bruckner quarters a thoroughly irritated Maynard encountered Major Patman crossing the parade ground from the guardhouse.

"Good evening, Captain," Patman said with a genial smile. "I see we still have the pleasure of your company."

"I'm glad someone still finds it pleasurable," Maynard said sourly.

Patman sized him up amusedly. "Charming couple, the Bruckners," he said.

Maynard scowled at the levity. They began walking toward officers' row. The triangles were being struck for evening mess.

"Are you still dining with the enlisted men?" Patman asked.

"I am."

"I would imagine the conversation is lighter."

"Extremely so." Maynard stopped abruptly, Patman with him. "Major," Maynard said, "as a student of Sioux culture, have you ever discussed their mode of worship with Major Fordyce?"

Patman considered the question, whether the substance of it or the asking, Maynard wasn't sure.

"Captain," Patman said, "the subject of theology, whether his, mine, or that of the Sioux is not one you raise with Major Fordyce. Why do you ask?"

"He's a strange man, isn't he?"

"Really a very simple soul. Religious zealotry makes people appear more complicated than they really are. May I ask how you're coming along with your inquiries?"

"You may ask, Major," Maynard said, moving on. "You may certainly ask."

CHAPTER 20

MRS. SCHEFFNER

The daguerreotype taken of Colonel and Mrs. Scheffner on their wedding day showed a rather dour-looking groom. The colonel's hair was neatly combed and parted across his somewhat narrow head and his drooping mustache was carefully trimmed. He was wearing a frock coat. His sword hung at his right side in an iron scabbard. Maynard understood that marriage and its formal observances made for a solemn occasion, but the colonel's face wasn't quite expressing solemnity; the closest that Maynard could come to forming an opinion of the colonel's resolutely cheerless gaze into the camera and its moment of eternity was to think, *Dispiritedness*.

If there was an expression to be found in the brand-new Mrs. Scheffner's posed, camera-stilled face it was a kind of defiance, of whom or what Maynard couldn't say, though it might have been a determination to be happy, which could be a depressing determination to have to consciously make on one's wedding day, though there was unquestionably strength of character in those sensual eyes and proudly set mouth. Her hands were raised and clasped just under her womanly bosom. She was wearing a white gown with lace cuffs and collar.

Behind this couple, who looked like strangers who had been asked to come together for a moment and pose, was a studio mural of cupids flying this way and that amid a sky of painted clouds.

The picture, in a gold-leaf frame, stood atop a four-drawer bureau that, like the rest of the furniture in the Scheffner living room, looked well traveled. The sofa was mahogany-veneered with scroll supports, covered with crushed maroon velvet, no doubt a fine-looking piece of furniture in its day, but like the bureau and the two balloon-backed chairs had been hoisted on and off too many wagons too many times. A pair of ormolu candelabra stood on the bureau on either side of the daguerreotype, but the room was lighted by a kerosene lamp that hung from the ceiling. The floor was covered by a thin carpet.

Maynard, who had been across the room staring at the wedding picture, now resumed his seat on one of the chairs. Mrs. Scheffner was sitting opposite him, in the center of the sofa, watching him with a curiosity that he felt was almost sympathetic. She was wearing a high-collared black dress and around her shoulders was the red shawl she had worn the first night he met her in the officers' mess.

"When the colonel first brought me out here," she said, "I was made to feel welcome, particularly by Mrs. Bruckner. I know what she thinks of me now, but in the beginning she was very kind to me. 'We'll see you become an officer's wife, my dear,' she said. 'A fine officer's wife.' And I thought to myself, 'I'm already an officer's wife, aren't I?' But no. You have to *become* one. Marriage is only the first step. The enlistment, so to speak. The other women have to commission you. You want to be an officer's wife you have to sit with them and make quilts or whatever, or bake little surprises, help plan minstrel shows and tea parties and whatever else stops you from losing your wits in the winter, and make a brave face whenever they ride out on campaign, and know exactly how to comfort a brand-new widow whose husband doesn't come back."

"You objected to the regimen?" Maynard asked.

"Not really. It wasn't that awful. But I started to see something that scared me. Each one of those women had become just like their husbands. Mrs. Josephson never said anything. Mrs. Fordyce talked all the time about God. Mrs. Bruckner is as stuffy as he is. Mrs. Englund was just like the general—or the way I first thought he was—with crazy little eyes that looked at you like your nose was green. I remember eyes like that on a rat I'd cornered in the barn one day, just before I caved it in with the scoop of a shovel. She's a dead soul, is Mrs. Englund."

"Is she?" Maynard asked.

"Do you know why they went back East? To install her in an asylum."

"I didn't know that," Maynard said.

"Poor man. But he bore it well."

"And Miss Englund?"

"I think she was my only friend, but she wasn't given much rein by them. We hardly had any time to sit together."

"I'm acquainted with Miss Englund," Maynard said.

"I liked her," Annabelle Scheffner said. "But Lord knows what she'd ever think of me if she knew the little story. I suppose you know the story by now, Captain?"

"Yes."

"I'm not proud of it."

"Did you feel you were helpless to do anything about it?"

"I'm not a helpless woman, Captain," she said. "Joshua—Colonel Scheffner—didn't find me arranging bowls of flowers in church. My mother died when I was twelve years old and I found myself woman to a farm kitchen and a father and to four older brothers who couldn't keep their hands to themselves. My father would sit in the living room after dinner drinking whisky and when the bottle was empty he'd start talking to my mother and I had those boys—young men—to contend with. When I was sixteen I'd had enough and was old enough to do something about it. I moved into town with an elderly couple and became their servant. My two oldest brothers would come now and then to try and get me back, and one day the old man—bless him, he was the first one to ever take my side—came at them with a rifle and warned them off. From that time on I was a woman on my own and had to look out for myself. Do you want this whole story, Captain?"

Maynard, who had been listening intently, smiled sheepishly.

"No, ma'am."

"I wanted to give you some understanding of who I am."

"You have."

"And who I am not. I think the one is as important as the other."

From outside they could hear the indistinguishable, rote-like sounds of the 9 P.M. roll call being conducted in front of company quarters.

"Colonel Scheffner had family near where I was living, not far from Valley Forge," she said. "He came East for a short time, and we met. He is a very plain and shy man and I could see he didn't know how to say what he most wanted to. So courageous on the battlefield, so shy . . . elsewhere. Are all brave soldiers like that, Captain?" she asked with a teasing smile.

"Not all," he said, with perhaps more emphasis than he intended.

"Anyway, there wasn't much time. Finally I said to him,

'If we're going to be married, then let us be married. We'll have the courtship later.' I knew what would have happened if I hadn't said that. He would have come back here and started writing letters of the heart and I would have answered and finally he would have proposed on the page and I would have accepted and then had to make that trip out here by myself. So we got married back in Pennsylvania. It's almost two years now."

"And you've spent your married life, so far, at Fort Larkin."

"I suppose things have to get better. Joshua says we won't be here much longer, the way things are going. He says this will be one of the first they shut down."

"Most likely."

"Have you ever been married, Captain?"

He shook his head.

"Then you can hardly be a judge," she said.

"I hope I wasn't giving the impression that I was trying to be. But are you saying that only married people can judge other married people?"

"If it's going to be a full and fair judgment, yes."

"I'm not going to judge you, Mrs. Scheffner, please believe it."

"No, I guess not; you look like a man who's too good a judge of himself to want to do that."

That was odd, he thought; was he wearing Ad Marston on his brow? He smiled uneasily, and said, "But I *am* going to have to ask you some questions, and even those will be in the impersonal voice of the United States Army."

"All right," she said, sitting erect, folding her hands in her lap.

"Your relationship with General Englund started when?"

"Sometime in the autumn."

"Did you see one another with frequency?"

"There was no pattern. It could be several times a week, or two weeks could go by without a meeting."

"Do you think Mrs. Englund knew about the relationship?"

"No."

"What about Miss Englund?"

"I doubt very much that she knew. She remained most cordial to me to the day she left."

"But others did find out, didn't they?"

"It wasn't going to remain a secret in a place like this for very long."

"Would you say that all of the senior staff officers knew?"

"And their wives," she said coolly. "I always knew exactly when they found out. They suddenly became so sickeningly sweet to me. I suppose it was the proper way to respond. I don't know what they would have said if it had been someone less than the general."

"How were the meetings arranged?" Maynard asked.

"An orderly would bring a note in a sealed envelope. And I would reply the same way."

"Where did you meet?"

"In the headquarters office."

"Always?"

"Yes."

"Even after his family had left?"

"I was never in his quarters. Men can be rigid that way. It's as if to say that if you don't break the code in your own home, then it isn't broken. The general wasn't the first man I'd known who was like that."

Initially uncomfortable with these questions, Maynard was now, with Mrs. Scheffner's easy candor and poise in responding, beginning to feel more relaxed.

"I take it," he said, "the meetings were always conducted rather late at night."

"Usually well after dinner. Eleven o'clock. Twelve o'clock. He would have dismissed his adjutant. There was little chance of being seen."

Except of course, Maynard couldn't help thinking, by the ever-vigilant Sergeant Barrie.

"There were sentries," he said.

"Sentry efficiency is not one of the glories of Fort Larkin, Captain. They're not always where they're supposed to be."

"When did Colonel Scheffner learn what was going on?"

"Almost from the beginning, I should think."

"How could he permit it?" Maynard asked.

"Well, Captain, you might say he was a defeated man."

"Defeated?"

"A man who was always victorious on the battlefield was defeated in the bedroom."

Maynard was embarrassed. "I realize this is a delicate area," he said.

"This entire conversation, Captain, has been 'delicate.' "

"I do appreciate that, Mrs. Scheffner. Please note that I'm trying to be tactful."

"I know exactly where we are in the conversation, Captain," she said. She seemed slightly amused by his discomfort. "Let me say that my marriage is companionable."

"Companionable?"

"And has been since the first. Colonel Scheffner is a good man. He's kind and patient and understanding. But he's nearly thirty years my senior."

"And you are a young woman of some spirit."

"Well, yes, I suppose I might be described so. Who found herself in a lonely, rather disagreeable place."

"And Colonel Scheffner was unable . . ."

"Quite."

"I'm afraid I don't know much about these things," Maynard said.

"Of course not. You're a young man. But, Captain, I must stress that I'm not a lewd woman. I'm not wanton. I simply led a very free and independent life for years. And then suddenly I became frightened, at being my age and alone, living in a small town, without prospects. When I realized Colonel Scheffner wanted me to marry him, well, I was flattered."

"You didn't anticipate the problem?"

"No, I did not."

"Nevertheless, I don't see how Colonel Scheffner was able to tolerate such an arrangement."

"I suppose such a problem saddens a man and makes assertion difficult. And let me say again, Captain, I am not wanton. I maintained my respectability for a long time, under what for me were not easy circumstances. I ignored the men in the ranks, even though I knew how they were looking at me. And none of the other officers would have dared, though I say that Patman is a bit more man than he looks. But I couldn't have imagined any of the others, from my side or theirs. Josephson? Fordyce? *Bruckner?*"

Maynard allowed an involuntary smile. "Never Bruckner," he said.

"So it became the general," she said. "And I daresay I was flattered. On the journey out here from the East, all I heard from Joshua was what a formidable man his commanding officer was. Finest fighting general in the Union Army. A man of tremendous courage and vision. It was as if he was saying, 'We don't have much at Fort Larkin, but we do have General Englund.' Even before I ever set eyes on him, I was in awe of the general. I had never met any great men. I had always thought of a vicar or a country doctor as being a great man. And now here I was to be meeting and dining with Alfred Englund, a man who had commanded legions. A hero of the republic. Englund spoke to God and God spoke to Englund."

"You believed that?"

She shrugged. "I was told the story of the sword."

"And believed it?"

She shrugged again. "Who is to say it might not have been so? It's a grand tale, and it happened, didn't it?"

"I don't know," Maynard said. "Did it?"

"Men say it did. It's not for me to say it didn't. They all must have believed it, otherwise why were they so afraid of him? Joshua half believes it; he was afraid not to. You're a professional soldier, Captain. Aren't you all taught to believe and obey, obey and believe?"

"Obey, yes; but believe—well, within reason. Did Englund himself ever tell you about the sword?"

She laughed. "Of course he did. More than twice. He'd make a fist with one hand and say, 'God pounced on me. He chose me. Out of the full thronging multitude, I was chosen.' Oh, he'd go on. He was a queer old boy."

"Were you afraid of him?"

"Not after a while."

"Did you like him?"

Annabelle smiled at him, as if knowing that she was about to give a curious and unexpected reply.

"Yes," she said. "I did. I liked him. Because he was—in his daft old way—trying to make me like him. He was a very interesting man, he knew everything, from stories about Julius Caesar to the names of the flowers on the prairie; and even though he was the same age as Joshua he was a man of remarkable vigor. He was courteous to me. Gallant. A gentleman."

"He never showed any remorse for breaking the army code of honor?"

"For taking a fellow officer's wife to the couch? No. He was slightly mad of course, in his way. God had touched his sword, you see, and that cleared the way for him to do anything he wanted."

"He felt he had forgiveness."

"Permission."

"So you liked him?" Maynard said, taken with the declaration.

"He was a fascinating, moonstruck old chap. I don't think I'll ever forget him."

"What did he like to talk about?"

"Nothing small. The war, the battles he'd seen. About God, how so few men truly understood how the Lord worked. And about the Sioux. He had them on the brain. He'd rid the ground of them, he'd say. He said it was his righteous labor."

"So ordered by the Almighty."

"That was the impression he gave."

"Did he think you believed it all?"

"Well, I don't know whether I believed it or not. I listened to it, but I never thought about it later. But he believed it. It was fascinating to listen to. I'd never heard anyone talk that way. And the fact that he had already accomplished so much in his life—well, he wasn't just *anybody*."

"What you're saying, Mrs. Scheffner, is that he was a good show."

She laughed. "You got your penny's worth."

"Now, Mrs. Scheffner, I would like to ask you about the night of the murders. Were you awake when Colonel Scheffner returned after the staff meeting?"

"Yes."

"You were?"

"I was sitting right here."

"What was his mood?"

"Concern. He told me they would be going on campaign soon, that the general had told them. They would all be going, except Colonel Bruckner."

"Why was he left out?"

"Oh, the general occasionally liked to tweak him. I suppose he had his reasons."

"He never told you those reasons?"

"He seldom made reference to his staff."

"How long did you and Colonel Scheffner talk that night?"

"Not very long. He just told me about the meeting and the campaign."

"Did the colonel seem out of sorts in any particular way?"

"You couldn't tell with him, Captain. He has the one quiet mood. When he was born they gave him just the one."

"Could he have gone out again without you knowing it?"

"He could have."

"What did he do? Did he go to his room?"

"Yes."

"And you?"

"I sat for a while. Gave it a little time."

"Gave what a little time?" Maynard asked.

She smiled. Maynard pondered it for several moments.

"Mrs. Scheffner," he said, "were you meeting the general that night?"

"Yes, I was."

"So you went out?"

"You didn't know that?"

"No. When did you leave?"

"In time."

"How much time?"

"Oh, maybe twenty minutes, maybe more. Just to make sure they'd all gone to quarters."

"And the colonel was in his room. Did he know you had gone out?"

"I don't know. He could have."

"And could have followed you."

"Why would he do that? Anyway, I didn't get very far."

"Why was that?"

She didn't answer.

"Whom did you see?" Maynard asked. What had been a casual, rather conversational tone had hardened.

"I simply turned around and came back," she said, her voice drawing its own inflexible line through the air.

"You saw someone, Mrs. Scheffner," Maynard said. "Who was it?"

"I simply turned around and came back."

"Why? Why did you turn around and come back?"

Her eyes told him he was wasting his time. He was the pathfinder who had come to water's edge. Nevertheless, feeling a fierce union of anger and despair, he went at it one more time.

"What made you turn back, Mrs. Scheffner?" he asked, and to her continued silence said, "Two men were murdered that night. Haven't you any feelings about that?"

"Captain Maynard," she said, "I've been very frank with you. I've told you more than you expected to hear. And that is all I'm going to tell you."

"You have a strange code of honor, madam."

"So it may seem," she said. "From a distance."

CHAPTER 21

AN INTRUDER

As frustrating as his interview with Mrs. Scheffner had been, Maynard felt himself coming away from it with at least one curious bit of satisfaction: she had confirmed for him that there had indeed been a murderer. All that he had had up to now were two dead long-buried soldiers and a group of distinguished United States Army officers melting silently off into the night having neither seen nor heard a thing, who had given him accounts of what seemed like a vacuum in time; and one United States Army scout who had vanished altogether. It had almost come to seem as if the murders were the consequence of an invocation gone wrong, Englund miscalculating or misspeaking beyond redemption, his exhortations or entreaties filling the wrong ear or offending a virtuous one. But the person was real, not wraith or specter, real of breath and footprint, real enough to have warned or frightened Mrs. Scheffner away.

The night was very dark as he came down the steps of the Scheffner quarters, the moon a misty patch of illumination behind a heavy cloud cover. As he walked toward his own quarters he could hear the men in Company B barracks quietly singing, accompanied by the thin melancholia of a lone harmonica. He paused to listen. In the endless prairie stillness "Lorena" and "Camping Tonight" sounded so wistful. He supposed that in the barracks darkness they were thinking of home, childhood, sweethearts; a gathering of gentle, disparate memories, in unison tenderly reopening. He recalled the old ghosts that had always returned to him when songs were crooned after lights-out. Remembering was the soldier's secular prayer.

When he stepped into his quarters he felt an instinct plucked like a harp string: something was amiss here. He stood stock-still in the center of the small living room, narrowing his eyes, trying to adjust his vision to this deeper darkness as quickly as possible, at the same time cocking his head slightly to pick up the sound or hint of whatever uninvited presence might be here. And then he remembered that Englund had taken that Bowie knife in the back and he turned quickly around, raising a clenched fist, and stood that way for several moments, half-turned at the waist, fist poised in midair.

The sound came from behind him and he whirled back around, fist ready to drive into the darkness.

"Who's there?" he demanded.

Something moved against a far wall and he went toward it, toward the sound. Then it was coming straight at him, crashing into him and knocking him backward. He felt hands driving against him as he struggled to hold his balance, but then he upended a chair and a moment later got tangled with it and began falling, tumbling back awkwardly, hitting the floor with a gasp and a curse as his assailant came down on top of him. Maynard felt hair in his face, heard determinedly angry breathing as he tried to turn and twist himself away. Then he swung his fist, achieving little leverage or power, but landing it on the side of his assailant's head hard enough to knock him aside.

Maynard spun himself free and rolled across the floor. He sprang to his feet just as the other was rising like a shadow in the dark. This time Maynard set himself and delivered a blow with the full power of his back and shoulders behind it, catching the other in half rise from the floor, upending him with a noise that sounded like the sharp cracking of a strong branch. It was followed by a soft thud on the floor.

Maynard drew back and waited for a moment. He heard a soft groan, followed by several deep, rueful breaths. Flexing his fingers as he moved, Maynard crossed the room and lit a candle. The flickering yellowish light opened up upon the overturned chair and the prone, facedown figure of Joshua Scheffner, whose palms were flattened on the floor at shoulder level as though he was contemplating pushing himself back up.

Good God, Maynard thought. I've smashed a colonel.

Scheffner remained motionless for several moments, restoring himself. Then he slowly drew his legs up under him until he was resting on hands and knees. Awkwardly, he twisted his face around and gazed up at Maynard.

"Colonel?" Maynard said.

"Captain," Scheffner said tonelessly. He got slowly to his feet, pushing his hair back out of his eyes. Standing erect, he pulled down on his jacket and puffed up his chest a bit. Then he stood in the gloomy light, staring expectantly at Maynard.

"I'm sorry about your chair," Scheffner said.

Maynard glanced down; the chair with the already shorter leg now had only two legs.

"May I ask, sir," Maynard said, "what the hell you were doing?"

Scheffner glanced over his shoulder to where the doors of a corner cupboard stood open. Near it, the drawer of a small writing table was pulled out.

THE SWORD OF GENERAL ENGLUND   241

"What were you looking for, Colonel?" Maynard asked.

"I take it you have completed your interrogation of Mrs. Scheffner."

"I have."

"And?"

"I'm sure she'll tell you about it."

"Are you?" Scheffner asked with a hint of mockery.

"I apologize for striking you, sir," Maynard said, having decided it might be politic to say so.

"Not at all, Captain, given the circumstances."

"Colonel, what were you doing here?" Maynard asked impatiently, then found himself suddenly enlightened. "Yes. The general's personal papers. I take it you didn't find them."

"Have you examined them?" Scheffner asked.

"What concerns you so deeply about them?" Maynard asked. "What do you think might be in there? Notes to and from General Englund and your wife?"

"She's my wife, Captain, and her reputation is of meaning to me."

"Pardon me, Colonel—and your reputation?"

"Perhaps."

"Why didn't you tell me, Colonel, that on that now-famous night, when you returned to your quarters, your wife was not only awake but preparing to go out?"

"The answer should be obvious," Scheffner said wearily. "How would you have answered it, Captain, in my place?"

In your place? Maynard thought. If I was in your place I wouldn't have a wife who was squeezing the couch with another man.

"Colonel," Maynard said with evident forbearance, "this inquiry transcends the personal concerns of the people involved. Forgive me for pointing that out."

"I forgive you," Scheffner said with an ironic smile. "But when one man is concerned with justice for the dead and another is striving to protect the good name of the living, it, I'm afraid, causes a mutual transcendence."

"And what interpretation do you think General Northwood would place upon that?"

"Damn Northwood," Scheffner said irritably.

"You said to me the other day, Colonel, that you always attacked in order to defend. What are you trying to defend now?"

"Have you gone through those papers?"

"Why, Colonel? It's common knowledge—at least among the commissioned officers and their wives—about General Englund and Mrs. Scheffner. Are you really that concerned about notes that passed between them? Or is it one note in particular?"

"Is it there?" Scheffner asked.

Her husband had been born with the one mood, Annabelle Scheffner said. The one quiet mood. But that was not to say there weren't variants of it; and here was one—a tension that seemed to run taut every nerve and muscle.

"She has already confided that she was going to see him that night," Maynard said.

"But she didn't see him. She returned after a few moments."

"So she said."

"You believe her, don't you?"

"I don't know, Colonel. Would she have reason to put a knife into General Englund?"

"No, none at all. But there are those around here who would like to think she did."

"And no doubt those who think you had just cause."

"Captain, have you read those papers?"

"Colonel, after returning to your quarters that night, did you then go out again?"

"I had no reason to," Scheffner said.

"Your wife encountered someone when she went out."

Scheffner frowned. "She told you that?"

"You didn't know?"

"Who was it?"

"She mentioned no name."

Scheffner turned his head aside, gazing off into the semi-darkness. "She is a woman of curious loyalties," he said wonderingly.

"Extended to whom, I wonder," Maynard said.

Scheffner looked back to him and smiled wanly.

When Scheffner had gone, Maynard took the envelope from under his mattress and brought it to the writing table. There, by the light of a tall white candle in a brass holder, he sifted once more through the papers. The colonel had worried needlessly and had searched these quarters needlessly (and no doubt it had been Scheffner who had broken into Englund's quarters months ago looking for the incriminating page among these sheets, as reported in Colonel Bruckner's report). But Englund, that supreme tactician of the battlefield, had not been so careless or indiscreet as to leave behind any such page. Scheffner should have known that; but the colonel, Maynard supposed, once cuckolded, had suffered under the anxieties and assumptions, the doubts and fears, that raced without restraint once the keystone arch had collapsed.

What engaged Maynard's interest as he turned the papers in front of him were those letters of affection and concern written to her father in Miss Englund's elegantly composed hand. Maynard shook his head as shamelessly he read the letters over again, enchanted by the well-turned phrases whose strength of character and liquidity of thought were given deeper feeling by the calligraphy that flowed immaculately across the pages in blue ink. How, he asked himself, did that lunatic, libertine old son of a bitch manage to be blessed with so flawless a jewel?

CHAPTER 22

UNEXPECTED INFORMATION

When the wild and raucous yips were first heard from out on the prairie the galloping horsemen were barely visible, little more than spurts of rising dust. A few hundred yards from the fort's outer perimeter, the daily water barrel detail stopped their inward progression and the wagon driver rose from his high bench seat and turned around, a smile broadening across his face. The escort troopers were smiling and so were the sentries, who were advancing out onto the prairie, their shadows stretched behind them in the late afternoon sunshine.

The horsemen—clearly two of them now—came nearer, still yelling and whooping, close enough for their hearers to realize that these were neither intelligible nor meaningful sounds but simply end-of-the-journey exultations. The rolling rhythmic clop of hoofbeats was so rapid they were virtually a continuous sound, soft and frantic and irresistible. The riders were coming in about one hundred feet apart and now it was apparent they were racing each other. One took the reins with one hand and with the other raised his cavalryman's yellow campaign hat and, holding it by the brim, began whirling it around in the air as he came charging upon the fort with a rush of jubilant shouts. The other trooper—they were clearly cavalry now—likewise swept his hat from his head and seemed to become confused as to whether to wave it or throw it; in any event it soon flew up from his hand, shimmied on the air for several moments as if riding an invisible pendulum, and then sank to the prairie. The first trooper began whipping the side of his horse with his hat as the sentries began waving, removing their forage caps and swinging them through the air.

Maynard and Barrie had just stepped out of the commissary and were watching the spectacle.

"Good God," Barrie said in soft dismay.

"Who are they?" Maynard asked.

"Part of a squad that was seeing some emigrants past the Black Hills. The rest of them came in yesterday. These two probably had a few bottles they decided to empty before getting back." Barrie shook his head. "They're for it now, I can tell you. Better lay out some straw in the guardhouse."

Maynard suppressed a smile as he watched the troopers come galloping in. As they passed the water barrel detail they let loose a joyous stream of profanity and kept coming, fervent and inexhaustible, as if to keep going, right on through the east side of the fort and out the west, shouting with a *joie de vivre* that put Maynard in mind of a squad of Union cavalry speeding through the lines with drawn sabres to do battle at—where was it?

Major Josephson appeared, scuttling along the parade ground. He stopped at Maynard's side.

"Those imbeciles are drunk," he said irascibly.

"And then some," Maynard said.

"I'll have them for dinner," Josephson muttered, going on.

The troopers came swooping into the fort. The first one took an astounding leap over a small handcart parked not far from company quarters, the horse swerving in a flash of graceful arc as it came down and then swerving again and galloping between the headquarters building and officers' row, in the direction of the stables.

The second trooper, attempting the same route, leaped mightily over the cart, but as the horse came down the maniacally grinning trooper lost control of the reins and with one loud final whoop of foolish delight he swung about in the saddle as if performing a stunt and slid off, appeared for a moment through the crisscross of running legs and landed on his haunches, where he sat, one hand coming slowly up to his astonished face and covering his eyes as his horse galloped straight up the parade ground, scattered a detail with shovels on their shoulders, and disappeared behind the Company B barracks.

With smoldering dignity, Major Josephson strode toward the dazed man. Coming up to him, the major pointed a finger at the man's head, turned to several enlisted men, and said, "This man is under arrest. Kindly remove him to the guardhouse." Then, stern-faced and resolute, he headed for the stables, where by now the first trooper had probably more or less arrived.

"Captain," Barrie said, watching two soldiers raise the wobbly trooper to his feet, "only a man soaked through the skin with liquor could take a fall like that and not be busted somewhere."

"What will they get, do you think?" Maynard asked.

"Well, since they don't have any stripes to lose, probably a few dollars' fine and a few days in the guardhouse and maybe some real misery details."

"Pity," Maynard said, moving off. "They're the first people I've seen at Fort Larkin who seemed to be enjoying themselves."

Lying on his bed later, Maynard was contemplating what his next move should be. It had already crossed his mind that his efforts might prove no more fruitful than those of the original investigating committee, that he would have to report to General Northwood (who in turn would have to tell it to President Grant and General Sherman and the Secretary of War) that the murders at Fort Larkin might have to be fed into history unattended by justice. But before he allowed himself to do that he would have another conversation with Mrs. Scheffner, maybe with husband and wife together. And maybe another talk with Major Josephson, whose old unhealed grudges may still have been hot enough for belated retribution; or Major Fordyce, whose offended pieties could have . . .

Barrie was on the porch, knocking on the frame of the screen door.

"Come in, Sergeant," Maynard said, getting up from the bed and walking into the living room.

Barrie entered, removing his forage cap as he did and placing it under his left arm.

"Reporting, sir," he said.

"I didn't send for you."

"No, sir."

"Then what . . . All right, Barrie. You have something to say?"

"Yes, sir."

"Then stop being so goddamned army-assed and say it."

"Concerning those two troopers who ripped in this afternoon."

"What about them?"

"It seems that a couple of days ago they separated themselves from their squad and went off on a little toot at a settlement called Washington Gulch, which is about eighty miles northwest of here. According to Trooper Briscoe, who babbled this out while sitting in his intoxicated condition in the guardhouse, while they were there they saw Duchard."

"Duchard," Maynard said softly, as if pronouncing some verbal alchemy.

"Trooper Briscoe said it to one of the men on duty there, who thought it prudent to tell me."

"Was the trooper certain?"

"Well, he's drunk, but he knows Duchard."

"When was this?"

"Two or three days past."

"He could have moved on by now."

"Could be; but if so, somebody there might know where. If he's still in the Territory three months later it means he wants to stay. Probably planning another go at the gold."

"Washington Gulch? What's there?"

"It's a small settlement, maybe fifty families. A few saloons, a small hotel, a few stores. Some ladies who are partial to entertaining. There's a lot of coming and going because of the gold."

"Would you say it's a two-day ride?"

Barrie allowed a pained look. "It's going to feel like a month, Captain," he said.

CHAPTER 23

DUCHARD

It would take two days, maybe three, Barrie said, to reach Washington Gulch on horseback. They would cross the prairie, then follow trails through the Black Hills, and finally pick up the wagon road to Washington Gulch, that hastily hammered together consequence of gold fever.

The weather was cool as they set out from Fort Larkin in early morning, mounted on a pair of cavalry mares. They had with them gray wool blankets as well as rubber blankets to cover the ground they slept on, five days' rations, and some extra rounds of ammunition for the Springfields tucked into their saddle boots.

They rode on across a golden prairie of buffalo grass that swung languidly in a soft wind, under a sky that flew to astonishing height and dove off in all directions so that the world seemed canopied by a tapestry of bluest blue. Now and then the unbrokenly monotonous prairie suddenly descended by a hundred or more feet into valleys of rock formations. Riding up from the valleys, they passed small herds of buffalo as well as black-tailed deer and pronghorn antelope. They camped that first night near a stand of ponderosa pine, nature's harps to the wind, lulled to sleep by the cool air whirring through the pine needles, hearing the ghostly howl of wolves from somewhere deep in the starlit night.

On the second day the somber ridges of the Black Hills rose before them, creating an elevated horizon of jagged pinnacles. Here and there, worn like vestments, were small, dark grassy terraces. Where other parts of the West that Maynard had seen had looked shaped by harsh or graceful wind or storming river, or sculpted by a mad but inspired hand, here were eroded cliffs and beetling crags and desolate arêtes, a world that looked gnawed upon by cosmic appetite, where the ancient chromatic chemistry had exhausted its scale from eye-burning white to richest black.

They skirted the rugged declivities for a time, then entered a defile and for several hours followed a laboriously rising trail laden with small sharply jutting rocks. The trail led down to a stand of tall brown grass and dense copses fed by a long, winding stream lined with groves of plains cottonwood and ash and box elder whose intricate branches flashed with darting sparrows and goldfinches. Further on was a small forest of dead trees, many of them riven by daggers of long-ago lightning, others flung down by the great storms of the past.

Continuing on amid the dry washes that curved among the broken hills, they came down a steep trail that led to a grassy, walled-around bowl that looked scooped out of the hard, rock-souled hills. Maynard raised his hand and they paused.

Below, in the center of the bowl, stood a small, lone tepee. Its strange, lone, human presence made the silence, to which they had in two days become accustomed, suddenly thicken and turn oppressive. They pulled their rifles up and held them upright in their hands, then continued slowly down the trail.

When they reached flat ground they approached the tepee warily, then reined in and dismounted. With his rifle aimed out from the waist, Barrie went toward the tepee, which was built of grimy, ragged buffalo hides stretched over a frame of poles. Maynard stood behind, turning on his heels as he looked up and scanned the blank, hard-ridged walls around them.

Barrie crouched and peered through the opening in the hides, then turned to Maynard.

"Captain," he said. "Have a look."

Maynard walked across the short, dry grass to the tepee as Barrie stepped aside. Inside, stretched on the ground, covered to the chin by a buffalo robe, lay an Indian.

"Dead a long time, I'd say," Barrie said.

The dead man's eyes were shut, his large, sharply carven nose made the more prominent by the withered and shrunken skin around it. Ragged strands of gray hair lay around his head. Near him lay an otterskin quiver with a single arrow, a leather bullet pouch, and a long brown pipe.

They moved away from the tepee.

"Probably came here to die," Maynard said. "In his sacred ground."

Barrie had a skeptical look around.

"Why do you think they find a place like this so sacred?" he asked.

Maynard raised his eyes and studied the stark, silent walls of towering precipices, a nightmare architecture of rocks that looked hastily and recklessly piled, rocks of every size and shape heaped one upon the other with no sense of balance or symmetry, in places defiant of gravity itself. They were jagged and broken and notched, with shelves and niches, and then mysteriously prismatic and grandly columnar, and finally, somehow, with a solemn accumulated dignity. Here they had come tumbling to thundering stillness. Eerily alien in their own silence and in the passionate sunshine, they created their own iconography of shadow and resonance. Stare long enough, Maynard sensed, and you would begin to see images and gestures and postures and the dark paths that moved with the sun; stare long enough and they became one with the soft sky. He felt he was seeing it all now for the first time, and with it becoming more and more the intruder.

"It's not for us to say," he said.

They reached Washington Gulch at twilight of the second day, having made better time than anticipated. The place was, as Barrie had said, a small settlement, about twenty miles from where the most active diggings now were. There was a main street, its opposing buildings separated by a dirt surface ground into rutted irregularity by wagons and stage-coaches. The scattering of buildings on either side consisted of saloons, stores, a barbershop, a bank, a self-proclaimed "photography emporium," blacksmith and stables, and the hotel, this latter a nondescript building (except at two stories it was Washington Gulch's tallest) that could have been anything, with its painted wooden sign over the doorway announcing the "Gold Rush Hotel." There were no side streets, the shacks and cabins scattered around the town looking arbitrarily placed, some of them built on ridges where the earth began to swell up. It was all boomtown construction, the kind you saw so much of in the West, hammered together and risen in haste, unplanned, fortuitous, standing to be abandoned as speedily as it had been built.

Leaving their horses at the stable, they walked along the elevated wooden sidewalk endemic to these sudden blisters of civilization.

"You'd better let me inquire, Captain," Barrie said as they approached one of the saloons. "If there's any deserters in there they might rear up at the sight of an officer, and that's not what we're about."

So Maynard waited in the night, standing aside just without the fall of light that came through the saloon window. He could hear men talking inside, some occasional laughter. It was dark now, the stars piercing the black skies of the Dakota Territory, and chilly, with an intermittent wind swiveling around the corner of the unconnected building. Standing here alone among this assortment of transient buildings gave him an odd sense of duty, of service, for this had been his course and his obligation since leaving the mountains of upstate New York; for thereafter he had always been somewhere else, during the war years and then through his service in the Southwest, with the uniform his only constant. Even the stability of Washington was like somewhere else, though what and where were antipodal to somewhere else he was never quite sure. Perhaps it didn't exist, or maybe those buildings hadn't been hammered together yet nor those avenues surveyed.

Barrie finally emerged from the saloon.

"I thought it might be wise to buy a drink or two, sir," he said. "It makes getting your questions answered the easier."

"I hope you didn't drink in vain, Sergeant," Maynard said.

"No, sir. He's here all right. Rennay Duchard."

"Where?"

"Living in one of the shacks out there."

"Who did you talk to?"

"The bartender," Barrie said.

"Did he have any idea why you wanted to see Duchard?"

"No, sir. I told him I was from Fort Larkin, in for a good time, and was hoping to run into my old friend."

They were walking away from the main street—the only street in Washington Gulch—toward the small structures behind the buildings.

"The people in a place like this," Barrie said, "are always changing. When I said Fort Larkin the fellow never blinked an eye. He probably never heard of what happened there. If he'd've thought Duchard was a suspect in something he wouldn't have said anything."

"It's your innocent face, Barrie."

"Yes, sir."

"A sergeant with sixteen years' longevity who has an innocent face."

"Remarkable, isn't it, sir?" Barrie said.

They crossed some rough ground in the darkness, then stopped as Barrie pointed to one of the cabins.

"There," he said. "He said it's the one with the blanket over the window."

"How long has he been here?" Maynard asked.

"About a month. Keeps to himself, the fellow said. Captain, the fellow said he's in a bad way."

"How?"

"That's all he said: 'In a bad way.' "

The cabin was built of logs, and like the rest of the structures in Washington Gulch looked thrown up hastily, primarily to provide a roof for someone who probably spent all of daylight trying his luck in the gold fields and most of the night in a saloon. It was about twenty feet across, narrow on the sides, with a slanted roof for the snow to slide down from.

When they got to the front door Maynard pointed to it. Barrie rapped several times with the backs of his knuckles.

"Rennay," he called.

"Who's that?" a voice—a low, mistrustful growl—asked from within.

Barrie looked at Maynard with a wink and a nod.

"It's Billy Barrie," he said, tilting his head close to the door. There was a pause, then, "Barrie?"

"It's me, old boy," Barrie said, smiling as if to add some cheer to his voice.

"What do you want?"

"Just come to talk. No harm in it. We just want to talk."

" 'We'? Who's 'we'?"

"A friend of mine. A captain. A good fellow, Rennay. Not from the fort."

"What the hell does he want?" Duchard asked.

"He'll speak for himself."

After another pause, Duchard muttered something indistinguishable, then said, "Hell, come on through."

The first thing that struck Maynard when they entered was the foul odor; it seemed to fill the place with a rank, sickly inertia. Maynard had smelled it before, a long time ago. The cabin consisted of a single room. There was a table and two chairs, with a tin plate, tin cup, and iron utensils on the table. Above the small, cold fireplace a wall shelf held some tins of food, coffee, a few pots and pans, and several bottles of whisky. Articles of clothing—a rough pair of trousers, buckskin-fringed jacket, and blue felt campaign hat—hung on wall pegs.

Duchard was lying near the fireplace on a narrow makeshift bed that was made of a thin sheetless mattress with piles of straw underneath it. He was propped up against the wall on his pillow—a tightly bound bundle of hay that was covered by a piece of burlap. On the floor next to him a candle burned on a tin plate, and next to that a basin of foul-looking water that was floating strips of red- and brown-stained cloth. Duchard was covered to the chest with a United States Cavalry blanket. A long black beard grew chaotically from his gaunt, unhealthy face. His eyes, under thick black brows, held no expression, merely a listless staring, and when his lids blinked it was slowly, as though they might not rise again. His thick dark hair fell to his shoulders. He was wearing long johns, his arms looking scrawny in the long sleeves.

"Fellow lent me this place," he said. "Said he was going off to dig his fortune. Well, good luck to him."

"You don't look too good, Rennay," Barrie said as he and Maynard stood over the pallet and its sickly occupant.

"You don't look so good yourself, Sergeant Barrie," Duchard said.

"Is there anything we can do for you, Duchard?" Maynard asked.

"Yes," Duchard said. "You can leave me alone, but I don't think you'll go that far."

"This here is Captain Maynard, Rennay," Barrie said. "He's come all the way from Washington."

"I wonder what for," Duchard said with a faint note of mockery.

"Just to talk," Barrie said reassuringly. "Nothing but that. You know me well enough, Rennay. I wouldn't bring trouble."

Duchard regarded Maynard with morbid and cynically amused interest. "All the way from Washington, eh? So they haven't figured it out yet."

"Not yet," Maynard said.

"How's old Fort Larkin, Barrie?"

"We're still drumming away," Barrie said.

"And Bruckner's still commanding officer, right? He doesn't think very much of me, the colonel. Well, we don't think too much of him, do we, Billy?"

"Not a chance," Barrie said.

"Excuse my manners," Duchard said, gesturing lazily toward the chairs.

Barrie drew up the chairs and he and Maynard sat down at the side of the pallet.

"What you smell, Captain," Duchard said, "is gangrene."

"I recognized it," Maynard said.

"I had a short dispute with a fellow over a claim in the hills," Duchard said. "He said we'd settle it man to man, only he had his gun already lifted when he said it. He got me in the leg. Right down there," Duchard said, pointing toward the foot of the pallet. "Wasn't too bad. I could walk on it. I could live with it. The only problem was, I wasn't a doctor. And by the time I brought the stinking thing in to see one he said the leg would have to come off."

"The tissues die," Maynard said.

"So I was given to understand. Well, I told him that I'd come into this world with two legs and that's how I planned to leave it." Duchard looked at Barrie. "What good's a scout with one leg, eh, Billy?"

"So that's how you made up your mind, huh?" Barrie said.

Duchard pointed his finger at Barrie and, in a voice allowing for neither argument nor contradiction, said, "That's just how."

"What happened to the fellow that shot you?" Barrie asked.

"He didn't live long enough to say he was sorry."

"Did you finally strike anything up there?" Barrie asked.

Duchard shook his head. "Nothing," he said. "Nothing." With mild curiosity he was staring at Maynard.

"Rennay," Barrie said, "the captain knows you had nothing to do with those killings. He just wants to ask you a few questions, to see if you can help."

"How does he know I had nothing to do with them?" Duchard asked, staring at Maynard but talking to Barrie.

"He's worked it out," Barrie said. "He used logic. But now he needs your help."

"Why should I help him?"

Maynard pulled his chair closer.

"Duchard," he said, "we're strangers, but I think I know something about you. You're a man who's chosen to go out his own way. Some people will think that's foolish and maybe it is.

But it's your choice. So you're either stubborn or you're proud. I'd like to think it's pride. I don't think I'd choose your way, but I'm not you. And I don't think you'd want to go out and leave your name hanging over this business."

"Nobody cares about my name," Duchard said. "Not a soul."

"But you do. You want to take your two legs with you to the grave. Well, I want to see you take your good name too."

"That's lovely, Captain," Duchard said dryly.

"But it's true," Maynard said. "As I say, I don't know much about you, but I do know what Barrie and others have said—that you were a goddamned good scout, that you were on your lonesome a lot, and that you took all the chances. And you're not afraid of dying."

"Rennay was never afraid of anything," Barrie said.

"Yes he was," Maynard said. "He was afraid of something that night, something that made him light out of the fort like a thunderbolt."

"What makes you think?" Duchard asked, frowning for a moment.

"I know it wasn't guilt."

"How do you know?"

"Because you never killed O'Bannion and as far as you knew Englund was still alive when you left."

"The captain worked it out, Rennay," Barrie said. "He knows you couldn't have killed the general."

Duchard turned away. "When I heard that old man was dead . . . that somebody had killed him . . ."

"You couldn't believe it," Maynard said.

Duchard turned back to him, eyes yellow in the candlelight.

"Somebody raise a hand to General Englund?" he said, voice soft with incredulity. "I never believed it till I'd heard it from ten different people. Then I tried to see it in here," he said, tapping his temple with his finger. "But I never could."

"Why not?" Maynard asked. "Englund was no different from you or me."

"Yes he was, Captain," Duchard said. "He was different."

"How?"

"I know he was. That's all. Ask Billy."

"He was different all right," Barrie said.

"And he was the one man you were afraid of," Maynard said. "You were a man who'd ride all night through a country bristling with Sioux and Cheyenne warriors, and yet you were afraid of one old man."

"One old man?" Duchard said derisively. "You didn't know the one old man, Captain. How long've you been at Larkin?"

"A few weeks."

"I take it you've spoken to some people. What did they think of Englund? Afraid of him?" Duchard asked tauntingly.

"All right," Maynard said, making a concession. "I didn't know him. So I can ask you straight questions, without worrying about the wrath of God striking me down. And because I'm going to ask you clean, honest questions, you can answer them."

Duchard coughed several times, stained, grimacing teeth appearing through his beard. He raised one hand.

"Be a good boy, Billy," he said, "and haul down a little whisky."

Barrie took one of the bottles from the shelf, uncapped it, and handed it to Duchard, who took a long swallow, then shut his eyes and breathed easily for a few moments. When his eyes reopened they fixed upon Maynard, their previous emptiness replaced now by a kind of morbid anticipation.

"Tell me what happened when you rode in that night," Maynard said.

"I rode in, I reported, and I went to sleep."

"We know that," Maynard said with an indulgent smile. "Just slow it down. Give it to us one piece at a time."

"What was the report, Rennay?" Barrie asked.

Duchard smiled wryly, eyes still upon Maynard. "He's a shrewd little bastard, our Billy."

"The report had something to do with it?" Maynard asked.

"The report had everything to do with it," Duchard said.

"All right," Maynard said. "Let's get it all in. Start from the moment you rode into the fort."

Duchard took another swallow of whisky, then adjusted himself more comfortably on the straw-crackling pallet, or as comfortably as one could get on it.

"We'd heard there'd been some Sioux moving about in a valley between the prairie and the mountains," Duchard said, "and the general asked me to have a look. So I did. I'd seen what there was to see and now I was back to give him the report. I don't know what time it was when I rode in—pretty damned late, I'm sure. I gave the password to the outer sentries and came in. I dismounted at company quarters and was tying up my horse when the sentry patrolling the north side of the parade ground came along. He was a lad I knew."

"Corporal O'Bannion," Maynard said.

"That's right. We used to talk gold, about some day going out to the diggings and giving our luck a stretch. He was a good boy. When he saw me he came stepping right up and asked straight out, 'Duchard, what's it going to be? Is it going to be a big one?' That's how he asked, just like that. He wasn't looking forward to a campaign, not at all."

In an oddly flat, suggestive voice, Barrie asked, "Why not, Rennay?"

"He wasn't, that's all," Duchard said, clearly uneasy.

"You were planning on lighting out together for the diggings, weren't you?"

"It was talk," Duchard said. "That's all it was. Talk. But he said he'd never leave if there was a campaign coming up. He'd never have done that, Billy. So that's why I told him."

"Told him what, Duchard?" Maynard asked.

"Not to worry, that there wasn't going to be any campaign, that all that was out there was squaws and children, and a few old men."

"That's all you saw?" Maynard asked.

"Let him talk, Captain," Barrie said, lifting his hand for a moment.

"I hung about those ridges for twenty-four hours," Duchard said, "and never took my eyes off of those lodges. There were about fifty or sixty of them, which meant to me about two hundred or two hundred fifty Indians. And I didn't see anybody who could've scared your aunt Nellie, just the squaws, the children, and the old men."

"How long did you talk to O'Bannion?" Maynard asked.

"Just that long," Duchard said. "I saw the light in the general's headquarters and asked if he was there and O'Bannion said yes. So I went in to report."

"General Englund was alone when you went in?" Maynard asked.

"He was."

"And you didn't see anyone else outside while you were talking to the sentry?"

"Not a soul. So I went in and reported. Told him what I'd seen."

"What did he say?" Maynard asked.

"Not much at first. He just listened. He was walking back and forth, hands clasped behind him, taking it all in. Then he stopped and asked me if I'd told anyone else. I said yes, that I'd mentioned it to the sentry outside. Well, at that his eyes turned to ice and I'll tell you, it made my blood run cold. If he was a fearsome old bastard even when he was relaxed, you can't imagine what he looked like angry. Jesus good God. I thought I was a dead man. I turned away, Captain; I couldn't bear those eyes."

"What did he say?" Maynard asked.

"Never raised his voice," Duchard said. "He didn't have to. The effort he was making to keep it low and even was scarier than any yelling he might have done. And anyway he didn't have to say anything. Not with those eyes. They just rammed into you and you could feel them inside of you, moving around. He said I had no right telling army business to anyone but him. Which he was right enough about; except that I'd reckoned the information being what it was there was no harm. Then he told me that if I told another soul what I'd seen he'd have me shot for revealing military secrets. He said that under other circumstances he'd have me taken right to the guardhouse then and there, except that he needed me to lead them out to the lodges."

"You mean he was going to attack anyway?" Maynard asked.

"Haven't you gotten that impression, Captain?" Duchard asked.

"You would have led them out?" Maynard asked.

"You take army pay, Captain," Duchard said. "What would you have done?"

"But a few hours later you lit out," Maynard said.

"Let him get to it, Captain," Barrie said.

"All right," Duchard said. "I finally got away from the office, feeling like I'd just been scalped and hung upside down. I don't mind telling that he'd scared the bejesus out of me. There was a fire burning inside him; you could feel the heat."

"Did you see O'Bannion when you came out?" Maynard asked.

"No, he wasn't around. And I didn't go look for him. I'd had enough. I didn't want any more of it."

"But you did stop to talk to someone," Maynard said.

Duchard closed his eyes, his soft breathing rippling through a tangle of beard that resembled so many tiny sharply severed wires. Stretched out and propped against the wall as the man was, he reminded Maynard of wounded soldiers he had seen trying to preserve or prolong their lives as they sat against walls or tree trunks or rocks, each expulsion of breath pumping out another draining spurt of blood. The conversation had seemed to dispel the rancid odor; now the sudden silence made Maynard acutely aware of it again. The candle was burning down, lowering the mantle of shadows closer around them. A wandering wind was slipping down from the mountains, creating a wily night-sound at the cabin's single window, over which the nailed-up blanket sagged.

Eyes still closed, Duchard said, "He was sitting there. On the porch. On officers' row. I was heading past, walking my horse to the stable, when I heard him."

"Heard him?" Maynard asked.

Duchard opened his eyes slowly, smiling tiredly at Maynard.

"Captain," he said, "it's been my business to see and hear things that nobody else does."

"Rennay can hear a bird tiptoe on a branch a mile away," Barrie said.

"I'd've been dead long before this if I couldn't," Duchard said. "I heard him sitting there. And I stopped and I started to think. I was thinking of what I'd have to do in a few days and I was thinking I didn't want to have to do it, didn't want to have to watch it."

"So you told this officer," Maynard said.

"I was thinking, somebody has to do something about it. It was going to be an outright slaughter. Butchery. And they all would have been innocent, Captain—on both sides. What the hell does a soldier know? He goes in there expecting to meet warriors, starts shooting, there's yelling and run-

ning and smoke and he's scared and then he gets mad because he's scared and he'll shoot at anything that's there.
You been in it, Captain?"

"He's been in it, Rennay," Barrie said. "Don't worry
about that."

"You told this officer what you had told General Englund," Maynard said.

Duchard nodded.

"What did he say?" Maynard asked.

Duchard moved his head slowly from side to side.

"What did he do?"

"He'd come down the steps to talk to me, then he went
back up and sat back down again."

"How long did you talk?"

"A few minutes."

"And then?" Maynard asked.

"Took my horse to the stable, then went to my shack. I'd
had a long ride, Captain; I was tired. I fell right into sleep.
Then I heard all the yelling and running around, and I went
out to see what the hell it was all about. 'Sentry's dead,' a
fella says to me. 'What sentry?' I asks. 'O'Bannion,' he says.
By the blood of Jesus, when I heard that—"

"You knew who had done it," Maynard said.

"I knew, Captain," Duchard said quietly, with a slight
nod of his head. "That put the fright up my trousers like
nothing ever had before. How should I say it: a madman
had gone crazy."

"He wanted to make sure his men went in with their
blood up," Maynard said.

Barrie got up, walked into the shadows at the far end of
the cabin, stood silently for several moments, then walked
back and stood just within the candlelight, his face fixed
with disbelief.

"Captain," he said, "are you trying to say—"

"It's what seems to have happened," Maynard said.

"But such a thing can't be," Barrie said. He looked at Duchard, whose eyes he found watching him with a sad compassion, as if they were telling him that Yes, it was as the captain had said. Duchard then looked back to Maynard.

"Captain," he said, "mind you, it wasn't dying I was afraid of—it was him. I knew I had my name and face inside his head, and it scared me."

"So you never knew," Maynard said, "when you left the fort, that Englund was already dead."

"Nobody knew. They were all howlin' about the sentry."

"Somebody knew," Maynard said with a cajoling smile. "What did you think when you heard that Englund was dead?"

"Never mind what I thought," Duchard said, suddenly turning sullen, as if setting himself for what he knew Maynard must next ask.

"You must have known you'd be suspected."

"Well, I never went back, did I?"

"All right, Duchard," Maynard said. "Now—"

"I won't answer that question, Captain. You've had your fill. I've been a miserable son of a bitch many times over in my life. And right now I smell like a dead mule. And in a short time I'm going to hell. But I'll not take another man over the edge with me. I'll be damned a thousand times over before I'd do that."

"Rennay—" Barrie said, but Maynard silenced him with a raised hand.

"No, Billy," he said. "We can't ask Mr. Duchard to tell us that."

"It doesn't matter anymore," Duchard said.

Maynard smiled privately. Yes, it did matter, he thought. To some people, very much. But Duchard wouldn't be interested in any of that.

CHAPTER 24

THE STORY

Barrie was uncharacteristically quiet during the ride back to Fort Larkin, and Maynard supposed he knew why, in fact was certain of it. He wanted to say, *We can't be sure, Barrie. We're only guessing at it, trying to put it together.* But he didn't, because he knew that Barrie had already made up his mind, was probably considering the same obvious thing: *That's why there was blood under his beltline, from pushing the knife inside his coat and through his belt where the blood smeared off, while he was dragging away the body.* Barrie was thinking so intensely and so emotionally that by the somber quality of his silence his thoughts were being transmitted, leaving the larger issues for Maynard to contemplate. Two professionals, each in his way bailed and bonded by indivisible loyalty, had been similarly shaken. Maynard, the more philosophical of the two, had the more profound reaction to what had happened; Barrie, the more visceral, his feelings so elemental they were apparent in his eyes and by that silence that seemed to have come upon him as though from a concussion.

He just can't corner it, Maynard thought as they re-crossed the Black Hills and then the prairie. That in the year 1876, in the United States Army, in which a man had served for sixteen years and was looking ahead to another sixteen, that a general could slip out into the darkness and murder an enlisted man. Barrie's bitter disenchantment remained steadfast as he watched Maynard across the low flames of that night's campfire, thinking not that one officer had gone berserk but that they were all, finally, contemptuous of sol-dier lives, that officers possessed terrible rights which, when necessary, they would avail themselves of. A lifetime's griev-ances against officers, which he had always suppressed or dismissed or rationalized, were returned within him in full flight. And Maynard, staring back, understood. So mon-strous an act, so bizarre an aberration, was simply beyond Barrie's comprehension, and because the sergeant had so adamantly seized upon the simple explanation, the one that concurred so readily to the enlisted man's gritty, orthodox interpretations, Maynard tried to deal with it himself. From his senior officers he had from time to time through the years known deceit, foolishness, buffoonery, vainglory, in-ebriation, negligence, and all sorts of delinquency rising from lack of brains or character. But this situation. May-nard would finally accept it as the act of a madman (with the explanation having been given to him piece by piece over the past few weeks), something rooted in its own sinis-terly seeded soil. To the resentful face across the campfire Maynard wanted to say that when generals went mad it seemed as if the planets themselves began to swoop and that all a man could do was continue to hold fast in whatever had always sustained him and wait for the inevitable re-alignment of what had always been. But Barrie was not ready to reconcile himself to any of it, not yet. For Barrie it was an act without possible explanation, something that had shaken virtue and insulted fidelity

When they reached Fort Larkin, early in the morning of the third day of their return journey, Maynard recalled to Barrie the original injunction of secrecy that bound him, and then dismissed him. Then Maynard went to his quarters and sat down. What he wanted now was several hours' quiet, solitary contemplation.

Later in the afternoon Maynard was sitting alone in the officers' mess, leaning on his arms on the long, empty mahogany table. From outside on the parade ground came the sounds of a wagon rolling past, horses cantering by, the marching feet of returning fatigue details. Then he heard footsteps mounting the porch steps and a moment later a knock at the door.

"Come in," he said without moving his gaze from where it had been fixed on the polished surface of the tabletop. Not until he heard the door close did he look up. "Please have a seat," he said.

Major Patman walked across the room and took a chair opposite.

"We heard you'd returned from your mysterious journey," Patman said.

"Mysterious?" Maynard asked.

"Destination unknown, absence indefinite." Patman smiled.

"And speculation unbound."

"In a discreet way."

"The destination was Washington Gulch," Maynard said, "where I interviewed Duchard."

Patman's eyebrows elevated for a moment.

"Finally ran him to ground," he said.

"Talking to him," Maynard said, "was like having an artist with brush and palette paint the picture complete."

"And what did the picture show?" Patman asked with relaxed curiosity, folding his arms.

"It showed Duchard talking to an officer that night."

"Did he paint in the officer's face?" Patman asked.

"No. I'm afraid that final touch was missing."

"That must have been a frustrating oversight."

"More of an exercise of some curious frontier code of honor."

"It's reassuring to know some of that still exists, even if only on the frontier," Patman said with a pleasant smile.

"Oh, it exists, Major; probably more than we imagine. But like wine that is poured into ill-assorted bottles, it assumes some odd shapes."

"It must have been disappointing," Patman said.

"What?"

"Finally getting to Duchard only to find him less than completely forthcoming."

"Most disappointing."

"Is he still under suspicion?"

"For what, Major?"

"Well," Patman said, paused, hoisted his shoulders for a moment, and said, "murder."

"I don't think so."

"So, you've established that much anyway."

"Not an awful lot to show for so much effort, is it?" Maynard said, smiling. Patman smiled back across the table at him. They looked as if they were sharing the lone vein of humor in an otherwise melancholy story.

"Will he be returning to the fort?" Patman asked.

"Who?"

"Duchard."

"No," Maynard said, shaking his head. "He won't be doing that."

"And what about you, Captain?"

"Me, Major?"

"Will you be heading back to your desk at the War Department?"

"Yes. I should think so."

Patman looked around the room.

"Is anyone else joining us?" he asked.

"No," Maynard said amiably, shaking his head.

Patman cleared his throat, then smiled. "Why have you asked me here, Captain?" he asked.

"To discuss a rather delicate matter. Soldier to soldier."

With barely a change of expression, a shade of mistrust had entered Patman's roundish, clean-shaven face.

"Yes," Maynard said quietly, abstractedly, as if to himself, as if bringing to completion some inner dialogue. "Most difficult, Major," he said, smiling regretfully.

"What is?"

"I beg your pardon?"

"What is so difficult?" Patman asked, an edge of exasperation in his voice.

"To discuss with you your behavior during the skirmish we had out on the prairie. You recall that, sir?"

"Distinctly," Patman said irritably.

"Of course; your first experience with hostiles, if I remember correctly."

"Are you saying, Captain, that you found some fault in the performance of my duty?"

"I'm afraid so, Major," Maynard said, an expression of regret in his face.

"Captain Maynard," Patman said, sounding a note of formality, "I thought the reason for your being here was quite a precise one. Are you saying now that it also included staff evaluations?"

"Actually, Major, when I was charged to come out here it was without conditions or restraints."

"I find that deceitful."

"You do? I'm sorry, sir."

"Everyone spoke to you with candor and in confidence."

"Everyone was most cooperative."

"And in payment we're all to be subject to your evaluation."

"I don't think it would be right to overlook certain things, Major."

"Certain things? All right. Will you deign to tell me what was questionable about my actions during that affair? It seems to me that we decisively repelled an attacking force, with minimum casualties to ourselves. I trust you took notice of that."

"The result of the skirmish was very satisfactory."

"Evidently not to you. On what are you basing your criticisms?"

"On a marked reluctance to engage," Maynard said, his voice casual, conversational, without inflection.

"But that's nonsense," Patman said indignantly. "That is a most fallacious reading of my actions. For an experienced officer like yourself to form such a judgment is appalling. I never took you for a fool, Captain Maynard, but pardon me if I reconsider that assessment."

"I understand, Major."

"I don't think you do. I don't think you have any concept of what you're saying. Wasn't it apparent to you that I chose to proceed with prudence? After all, there were human lives assigned to my safekeeping."

"Mine among them," Maynard said.

"Did you feel imperiled by my procedures?"

"I've been in surer hands, sir," Maynard said quietly, as if voicing a lamentation.

"What precisely are you accusing me of, Maynard?" Patman asked, folding his arms across his chest, assuming a demeanor of petulant defiance.

"Frankly, Major, your behavior raised some concerns in

my mind about your willingness to command in battle."

"My *willingness*? This is astounding. Are you accusing me of cowardice?"

"I wouldn't be so bold, sir. I only know what I saw; I have no idea what may have prompted it."

"You are actually going to put this ludicrous conclusion into your report?"

"Well, sir," Maynard said, "I couldn't help thinking that if General Englund hadn't died, you would have been in command of a detachment of men on what promised to be a rather vigorous campaign. I tried to imagine your actions under those circumstances, when you would have been called upon to deploy and attack under fire, perhaps outnumbered, forced to make quick and vital decisions. Maybe it was your good fortune that the general was removed from the scene."

"I can assure you, Captain, I would have acquitted myself well."

"But how well would that have been? From what I understand, General Englund was a most exacting commander in the field."

"He was a fool," Patman said sourly.

"I'm not talking about the Englund who sat behind a desk and pontificated, or who had private conversations with the Almighty. I'm talking about the man whose achievements in battle are already legendary, who was noted for courage, daring, resourcefulness, and especially for taking himself to where the fire was hottest."

"I'm sure that's exactly where he is now," Patman said caustically.

"I'm not talking about his character, sir, but rather about his abilities as a leader in the field, where a soldier is truly made."

"And the man unmade."

"Not necessarily, Major. There's a kind of nobility about leading men into battle."

"The word 'nobility' in connection with General Englund is gross misusage."

"You might have learned something serving under him in an action that was going to be more than a skirmish against a handful of warriors making a suicidal frontal assault, an action where you would have been up against a mass of some of the hardest, most daring fighters ever to take the field anywhere."

"Nonsense," Patman said angrily, bringing the flat of his hand sharply down on the table. "For your information that damned fool was setting out to attack nothing more than a band of harmless, defenseless women and children . . ."

Patman ceased abruptly, glaring at Maynard with wide-eyed astonishment, lips compressing for a moment, face reddening. Then his eyes narrowed at the corners as he gauged Maynard's wry, almost apologetic smile. Maynard sat back in his chair, hands dropping into his lap.

"My regrets, Captain," Patman said quietly. "For calling you a fool." He rubbed his hand around his eyes, then held it in place. "I've just painted in the face for you, haven't I?"

"Yes, sir," Maynard said deferently. "And now just a few more brush strokes, if you will."

"Just a few?" Patman said ironically, hand still covering eyes. "But what a few, eh, Captain? Duchard never mentioned my name, did he?" Patman asked, bringing his hand down.

"No, sir."

"Mrs. Scheffner?"

Maynard said nothing.

"Ah, Mrs. Scheffner," Patman said as if savoring the sound of the name, nodding his head.

"Is that why you were sitting on the porch? Waiting to see her?"

"Well, not see her, exactly."

"Observe then."

"Observe, yes."

"You wanted to know if she was going to the general."

"I was curious," Patman conceded. "The general had said he would be working late in his office. It was none of my business, but as you have seen, Captain, Fort Larkin wants for diversion, no matter how banal."

"And then Duchard came by."

"He noticed me and came over. Said he wanted to talk. And he told me what he had to tell me."

"That Englund was bent on attacking."

"Was bent on a massacre, that's what he was bent on."

"Duchard asked you to intervene."

"He said that coming from one of the officers . . . Well, he put it on my shoulders, yes."

"And what did you think?"

"I was appalled, of course, though not all that surprised. Englund was keen on a campaign and would have it, against whom it didn't matter. Duchard went on his way and I resumed my seat on the porch and tried to reason out what to do. Facing down the general was not a decision I took lightly, I assure you."

"I can appreciate that, Major."

"Frankly, I was hoping that Mrs. Scheffner would come by and thus relieve me of my decision. But there was no sign of her. What are you going to do with all of this, Maynard?"

"Write it down."

"And then?"

"Submit my report."

"And this is going to be read by the President and the Chief of Staff?"

"And the Secretary of War."

"Good God," Patman said softly. "Will they understand

my position, do you think? Will you write it clearly and objectively? They must see it as I did."

"Yes, sir," Maynard said. "So you decided to go and see the general."

"I made up my mind to do that, yes. At first I considered waiting until morning and consulting with the other officers. But then I realized they would do nothing. Bruckner had been excluded from the attack, so I don't think I would have got much support from him. I couldn't imagine Scheffner standing up to Englund, for any number of reasons. I thought Josephson might, but then again he was too much the professional. He would never question an order. Do you agree?"

"And Fordyce?"

"No. Too uncomfortable a man to talk to about anything, much less this."

"So you went in."

"I knew he was there, I knew it had to be done, and I knew I wasn't going to get any sleep if I didn't. So I decided to do it then and there and be done with it."

"That took some sand, Major."

"Will that appear in your report, Captain?" Patman asked acidly.

"I hope you understand my previous remarks, sir."

"I do now. You're a sly bastard, Maynard, I don't mind saying."

"Yes, sir. So you went to the general's office."

"He was just entering the building as I approached."

"Entering? Where had he been?"

"I didn't ask. I told him I wanted to speak with him. He seemed momentarily annoyed, but then invited me in. He asked me to wait in the adjutant's office for a moment."

Yes, Maynard thought, while he removed the knife from his belt and wiped it clean.

"And then he asked me to come in," Patman said.

"What was his mood?"

"Impatient. Generally he spoke civilly to me. He once told me that he admired my abilities and intended to mold me into his kind of officer. When I considered the other members of his staff I didn't find that a very reassuring prospect. But that night he was brusque. I realized that he was waiting for Mrs. Scheffner. So I went directly at it. I told him I had spoken to Duchard and had learned from him the composition of the Indian encampment, that it consisted of women, children, and old men. I told him that I assumed this would vacate any plans for a campaign. He said it would not. He was composed but stern, as though *he* was the one trying to contend with illogic and absence of reason. He said it was of little matter whether they were women, children, or warriors; it only mattered that they were savages, and that it was his mandate to rid the Territory of them. I suggested that that mandate was meant to apply to hostiles only."

"And he said they were all hostile."

"It's as if you were in the room with us, Captain. That's exactly what he said. God, but he hated them, with an intensity that was sickening. He wanted to know what was so sacrosanct about Indian women and children. Wouldn't it have been better, he asked, if the warriors that were today murdering white soldiers and settlers had been suffocated at birth? And the women—he called them 'the breeders of the pestilence.' They must share the guilt of what had sprung from their wombs. Again, his words. It was madness in its purest form, and terrifying because it was uttered with such self-righteousness. The man was a living affront to every human creed and belief."

"Did you try to reason with him?"

"Can the leaf reason with the whirlwind? Of course I

tried. I told him that such a raid would be a stain upon the honor of the army as well as a nightmare for the conscience of every man who participated. His response was that the men were soldiers and would carry out their orders. I agreed they would, saying that was exactly why the campaign must be abandoned. Such a bloodthirsty slaughter would only beget more death, I told him. There would be vengeful assaults and then further retaliation, and on and on, the peaceable and the belligerent, the innocent and the guilty, all going to the single damnation."

"And how did he respond?" Maynard asked.

"Have you ever had a raging general on your hands, Captain, sane or otherwise? I was feeling the deepest fear and anger, while the wrath was beginning to burn in his eyes and change the color of his face. I knew I was in the midst of a debacle. I was standing with countless lives in my hands and with the despairing sense that they were about to fall from my fingers."

"How did he respond?" Maynard asked again.

"With threats, vilification, curses. He told me I was cowardly and insubordinate and disloyal, a disgrace to the uniform. He had never met, he said, so insolent an officer or so craven a human being. I was an insult to the face of the earth. He said he could have me court-martialed and shot, that my soul would burn in hell. Oh, he commanded the full lexicon, Captain, and I suffered the barrage. He was a man in a burning pulpit. He told me that if I so much as uttered a breath of any of this to anyone I would immediately be arrested and taken to the guardhouse. He said I was jeopardizing the lives of his soldiers, though God knows how I was doing that. His fury burned me hollow and left me speechless. I kept feeling the fear and the anger rising in me. Fear and anger to their extremes, Captain. That's a deadly mix. So it was surrender or fight. The mind of the soldier, eh? The

training, the sharpening. You surrender the lost cause, fight
for the noble one. You're a professional, Captain. A head-
to-foot professional. What would you have done?"

Maynard, sitting back, hands in lap, watching Patman,
said nothing.

"Unfair question?" Patman asked, speaking rapidly now,
as if agitated. "Under ordinary circumstances, yes. But these
circumstances were hardly ordinary. Think again of the professional, Captain. Moral responsibility, and *real* responsibility. We hold lives in our hands. The few or the many?
Which is entitled to our deeper considerations? When is the
code to be ignored? Whatever the correct answer—if there is
one—I followed what I believed to be my obligation as a
man *and* a soldier. Let me tell you, Maynard, the sound of
shot and shell and the crying of the wounded would have
made it much easier. But I was standing in a room, alone
with one man. But no battlefield could have been as ugly
and menacing. Finally I told myself he was not a man but a
plague and that it had to be stopped. I suppose it was the
fear that ignited the anger. What would you have done,
Maynard? You need not answer me, but you can't escape
confiding to yourself."

"Come to it, Major," Maynard said quietly.

"The Bowie knife was lying on the desk."

"Sheathed?"

"No."

"Had it been there during the meeting?"

"I don't recall it being there, no. I'm certain it wasn't.
Why?" Reading Maynard's eyes, Patman said, "O'Bannion?
He hadn't used it on O'Bannion, had he?"

"Please carry forward, Major."

"Where was he coming from when I first saw him?" Patman asked, of himself it seemed. "He had been out somewhere. Why?"

"Major—"

"Why would he have done such an act? Did Duchard confide in the sentry?"

"Please, Major," Maynard said. "Come to it."

After some moments of puzzling introspection, Patman said, "He turned around and ordered me to leave. He told me he would speak to me in the morning."

If you saw the morning, Maynard thought.

"I swear, Captain," Patman said, "but that knife shouted up to me. I took it in my hand, raised it, and drove it into him. I think he was dead instantly. He never made a sound. And that frightens me. It's as if he's waiting somewhere to howl and complete his own death, and will have me know about it. He was that kind of a man, Maynard."

"Yes," Maynard said.

"I've suffered every night since." Patman smiled faintly. "No," he said with a shake of his head, "not guilt. It's that face. It comes at me out of every darkness. With hatred in its every crease. With a mouth howling silent maledictions. God help me, I've begun to sound like him."

"And you left the office unseen?"

"Not quite. On my way back to my quarters I encountered Mrs. Scheffner. I told her not to go in there, that something terrible had happened."

"Did she ask you anything?"

"No. A remarkably self-possessed woman that. She simply turned around and went back. I've been relying on her silence from that day to this."

"Which you've had."

"On behalf of my life or her good name, I wonder."

"I wouldn't ask her if I were you."

"And now what?"

"Well, nothing, until my report is sent in and acted upon."

"And until then, what is my status?"

"Colonel Bruckner will be informed that you're not to leave the fort. It will be handled as discreetly as possible, until further word."

"What will the colonel know?"

"Nothing more than that. I'm not responsible for what he may think."

"And if I try to leave?"

"Colonel Bruckner will have the widest latitude in that eventuality."

"It's all so preposterous, isn't it?" Patman muttered with a disbelieving shake of his head. "Captain," he said, "satisfy one curiosity, if you will. What led you to me?"

Maynard shifted uncomfortably in his chair. "Well," he said, "as you yourself said, the other officers would have answered the orders without contention."

"And I?"

"Different instincts. Not better, not worse; not any more scrupulous or less. But enough of a difference."

"Am I to be hanged because I'm a more humane person?" Patman asked with bitter derision.

"No, Major," Maynard said. "It wouldn't be for that."

PART THREE

AFTERMATH

CHAPTER 25

SEPTEMBER 1876
WASHINGTON, D.C.

Two weeks after the submission of his report, Maynard was summoned to General Northwood's office. At Maynard's entrance the general waved him forward almost abstractedly and asked him to sit down. Sitting behind a full but neatly kept desk, Northwood smiled avuncularly. The early September sunshine lay bright upon the floral designs woven into the carpeting. A ticking grandfather clock in the corner made the passage of time sound ponderous.

"How've you been keeping, Tom?" Northwood asked.

"Quite well, thank you, sir," Maynard said. He was sitting erect in an armless straight chair in front of the desk. On the wall behind Northwood was a framed portrait of a somber-looking President Lincoln dating from late in his first presidency. Next to it was a portrait of President Grant, shown from the waist up, sitting with his legs crossed, staring into the camera with the stolid impassivity that seemed his chief facial expression. To Maynard, Grant always seemed incorrect in civilian clothes.

"What is he like, this Patman?" the general asked.

"A good man, in spite of all. And a good soldier, too, under the right circumstances."

"A man has to be a good soldier under *all* circumstances. That's the glory of it, and the damnation."

Northwood picked up a half-smoked cigar from his ashtray and slipped it between his teeth.

"Englund was a good soldier," he said, gazing afar for a moment, as if consulting with memory. "We always knew he was a bit eccentric, but, Lord, that's what it takes sometimes. He was a hellion in war. Do you think it might have been inactivity that baked his brains down to powder?"

"I don't know, sir."

"No. We'll never know that, will we? Anyway, your report has been read, Captain, and everyone agrees that you did an excellent job, as I had assured them you would. But—perhaps too excellent a job."

"Sir?"

"Oh, damn it all, Tom, look at it. A commanding officer is having a liaison with a fellow officer's wife, he's preparing a campaign in which he's going to slaughter women and children, he murders an enlisted man, and then to place the final crown of thorns on it, he himself is murdered by a commissioned officer. The whole thing is soaked in Jacobean horrors."

"Yes, sir," Maynard said.

"Everyone who has read the report is in agreement."

"Agreement on what, General?"

"That a court-martial would produce too lurid a scandal for the army to bear. Considering the stern lecturing we've been getting from the newspapers and certain other agencies concerning the government's management of Indian affairs, the revelation of what one of our generals was planning would be embarrassing."

"Yes, sir," Maynard said.

"Not to mention all the rest of it. It would be a nasty business, Tom, very nasty. The newspapers would fire a blunderbuss that would wound us all."

"That would be unfair, sir."

"It certainly would," Northwood said, biting down on the cold cigar. "Most unfair."

"And what of Major Patman, General?"

"He'll be reassigned and then we'll accept his letter of resignation."

"And the whole affair?"

"Soon forgotten."

"I wonder."

"What do you mean?"

"There's still the ghost of General Englund, sir. He takes all honor and glory to the grave intact with him, and with the affair carrying the permanent imprint of 'Murder Unsolved,' such legend as he has will be perpetuated."

"Yes, I can see that. Well, I don't think there's any great harm in it, and it will be some solace for Miss Englund."

"Miss Englund, General?"

"She's been informed, as a courtesy."

"Of 'Murder Unsolved'?"

"Yes."

"I see," Maynard said.

"You might be interested to know, Tom, that a decision has been taken to shut down a number of posts on the frontier. Fort Larkin is one of them. That part of the Territory is now considered secure. Soon all of it will be."

"And one day it will enter the Union."

"I have no doubt of that."

"Including the Black Hills."

"Of course," Northwood said.

• • •

Late that afternoon, in the softening light, Maynard
opened the front gate of the Englund house, closed it quietly
behind him, and walked up the fieldstone path toward the
front door. Looking across the trimmed hawthorn hedges
that grew on either side of the path he could see the garden
where white Queen Anne's Lace and yellow goldenrod were
still in bloom, and the arbor where he had sat with her on
that hot July afternoon, when she had brushed her hand
against his and risen that pulsation that he had carried with
him across the continent and over the Dakota prairie and
through the Black Hills and now back again, constant and
undiminished.

He approached the broad-fronted, three-storied white
clapboard house with its rows of white-curtained windows,
mounted the three front steps, paused, then took the brass-
handled rapper in his hand and struck it twice.

The door was opened by a young Negro woman in a
maid's costume.

"Captain Maynard," he said. "For Miss Englund."

The maid nodded and closed the door softly. He waited.
A few moments later the door reopened and the maid reap-
peared.

"Miss Englund," she said politely, "says to tell you she is
not at home."

He left without looking back.

Either way, he consoled himself as he lay in bed that
night, it wouldn't have been any good. In fact, if she had
been apprised of the report's contents it would have been
worse. So, Maynard thought ruefully, either way . . . But it
had been a sweet and sustaining dream to take along with
him; it had made the journey tolerable and the hollow
nights less melancholy. He had been as entitled to his dream

as she to hers; his now concluded, hers to go on believing
what was finally to her most important—that it had indeed
been the Lord's hand that reached down from the seething
sky and drew fire from her father's ascending sword.

He thought of Billy Barrie lying in the darkness of Company B barracks. The sergeant had become sullen at Washington Gulch and so remained, with nothing thereafter for
Maynard but curt answers and doubting looks, and at the
last a cool and impersonal good-bye. Maynard understood.
The sergeant was wondering how the world could have mis-
led him so. Here was a man who lived by the simple explanation and the unquestioned wisdom of others, only to have
a lifetime's undoubting and reassuring certainties become
suddenly and bitterly confounded. But Maynard had faith in
his man. Barrie, ever the honest man and above all the good
soldier, would finally absorb the tragedy and accept the
mystery without serious confrontation, and through fidelity
of service and snap of salute would see his way through.

He closed his eyes. It was long past lights-out at Fort
Larkin now and the sentries were reporting and there was a
light burning in the guardhouse. The wind was blowing
September-cool through the buffalo grass and the stars were
set high above the Black Hills. Soon they would strike the
colors for the last time and march away forever from Fort
Larkin, Dakota Territory. Men and horses and mules and
wagons stretched for a moment across the prairie in living
history. And then gone, leaving behind the small log buildings to be tipped over by time and the running wind.
Swirling dust would cover the last footprints and then the
snows would pour endlessly, piling upon the small rooftops,
sifting through porous walls into empty rooms, covering the
parade ground, filling the corral, howling over the post
cemetery, burying the lonely grave of General Englund.